I like the smell of b(
books would be, for

-Charles Van .

MW00878255

PRAISE FOR THE LION OF CORTONA

The Lion of Cortona is a mesmerizing love story, made more compelling with mysterious identities, knights, kidnapping. Tensions and conflicts are heightened by crisp dialogue. Surrender to this sweeping panorama of romance and betrayal.

● **Davyne Verstandig**, Lecturer in English, University of Connecticut, Poet, Author, former Director of the Litchfield County Writers Project

Thoroughly familiar with the world of the Middle Ages, Van Doren brings the reader deeply into its arcane world of rites and mores, and a story unfolds with ease and authenticity.

As they move through the thirteenth-century's dangerously stratified world, it is intriguing to watch the book's bold and interesting characters develop, intermingle, and reckon with the consequences of their actions. One wants to read on.

● **Anne Zinsser**, Learning Specialist, Poet, Author

With obvious love for both time and place, Charles Van Doren sweeps us into his richly imagined evocation of life in thirteenth-century Tuscany. And we are truly there, having a grand time following the sometimes rousing, often romantic adventures of his huge and vividly portrayed cast of heroes, heroines, and villains.

● **Joy Gould Boyum**, Professor Emerita and former Director of Arts and Humanities Education, New York University

Philosopher, historian, magician, Charles Van Doren waves his wand to create a picture of Medieval life that, through the strength of his humanity, reveals the fragility of 13th-century society.

● **John Tauranac**, architectural historian, author of *The Empire State Building: The Making of a Landmark.*

SCHOLARLY WORKS BY CHARLES VAN DOREN

How to Read a Book: The Classic Guide to Intelligent Reading, written with Mortimer Adler, shows concretely how the serious work of proper reading may be accomplished and how much it may yield in the way of instruction and delight.

● *The New Yorker*

A History of Knowledge covers not only all the great theories and discoveries of the human race, but also explores the social conditions, political climates, and individual men and women of genius that brought ideas to fruition throughout history.

● **Clifton Fadiman**

[In *A History of Knowledge*] Van Doren has distilled the ideology of scientific progress into a neat, short drink that should win him a place on every library shelf.

● *Library Journal*

The Joy of Reading . . . This engaging love letter to reading follows the great authors and classics that transformed the world: from Aristotle and Herodotus in ancient Greece to Salinger and Heinlein in 20th century America. Like a professor whose enthusiasm enwraps his students, Van Doren explains what's wonderful in the books you've missed and awakens your desire to reopen the books you already know.

Nothing recommends the joy of reading better than the communication of it by a person who has spent a lifetime enriched by the delights of reading. Charles Van Doren is that kind of reader. He has laid a feast before us that is irresistible.

●**Mortimer J. Adler**, author of How to Read a Book

THE LION OF CORTONA

A Novel of the Middle Ages

Volume I: Exiles

Charles Van Doren

R & R Associates • Connecticut

The Lion of Cortona

Volume I: Exiles
Volume II: The Wide World
Volume III: The Return

R & R Associates
Copyright © 2013 Charles Van Doren
All rights reserved.
ISBN: -1484989643
ISBN-13: 978-14849896-4-7

To the memory of Margherita da Cortona
(1247 – 1297)

Contents

Acknowledgments

To the memory of Pericle and Malini Staderini, who helped us learn how to live in Italy. To their children and grandchildren, who became our extended family there.

To the memory of Giandomenico Briganti, who introduced me to Margherita da Cortona.

To the memory of Lucia Steffanelli, who made us a house in Cortona.

To Marisa and Giorgio Postiferi and their family, for their help and guidance.

To Gerald McCauley, my agent, for his loyal support.

To Laurel McKiernan for friendship, comfort, and her skill and help in taming the computer beast.

To T.L. Evans, for his technical expertise and experience.

To Robin O'Connor, my editor and catalyst, without whom the book would not exist.

To friends and family, for loving support and hours of reading.

To Gerry, my wife, for all of it.

Foreword

Cortona, a small city in Tuscany, is surrounded by high stone walls. It sits on the side of a mountain overlooking the large valley of the Chiana River. The valley, once a swamp that has been reclaimed by efforts beginning in the twelfth century and not completed until the nineteenth, is now fertile and farmed. The view from Cortona is stunning. That may be the first thing you learn about Cortona. The second fact would be that it is ancient. When the Etruscans lived there, it was at the intersection of the two main roads in the area. The high walls go back at least to Roman times. The remains of an aqueduct can be traced along the top of one of the walls. But like other walled towns in Italy — Lucca, Montepulciano, San Gimignano, Urbino come to mind – because of the walls and its strategic location, the look, the feel, the spirit of Cortona is medieval.

Our attachment to the city is deep and abiding. It was our second home; we lived there part of every year for more than twenty-five years. In the summer it was full of life with tourists milling about in the center of the town. We lived halfway between the center and the top of the town, often in residence in winter and spring when walking out at night was cold, dark, and silent, more like it might have felt in the thirteenth century. One winter night we knew what Cortona felt like so long ago. We had gone out for a walk after dinner, up to one of the huge gates in the wall. It is called the Porta Montanina. The gigantic doors were open and a light shone at the top of the archway over the opening. The road beyond led to Torreone. We saw and admired in the dim light the walls, the gate, the arch in a way we never had before. Then we took a few steps forward; beyond the gate was total darkness. We knew then the terror of the world that existed beyond the walls of the city in the Middle Ages. It was then, I think, that *The Lion of Cortona* came to life.

My husband needed to know more of the history of the city. He knew of Santa Margherita, who lived and cared for the people of Cortona in the thirteenth century. She appears in his story, but not out of character of who she was, at least from all available accounts. The Casali family lived then too; the Palazzo Casali still stands in one of the two main piazzas of the city. Thomas Aquinas, the philosopher, also has a role in the story, as does the great and powerful Visconti family. Nino, one of the imaginary heroes, meets Aquinas in France. Benno, the main hero, joins the army of the archbishop of Milan, Ottone Visconti. Nina, Nino's sister, loves Benno. But because of his humble origins, Benno must prove himself before he can claim her.

Two of the main events in the novel actually happened. The first is the betrayal and invasion of Cortona by the bishop of Arezzo. A traitor opened the gate at the bottom of the city for his army and the chaos that ensued. Nino, Nina, and Benno were hardly more than children when that happened. The second true event is the Battle of Pizzighettoni, at which Benno distinguished himself as a leader and hero. Between those two events, the story is entirely the creation of a man's imagination, inspired by the city he loved.

Gerry Van Doren

Real (historical) characters

La Comtesse de Chermont
Conte Pietro, ruler of the Torre di Pietro
Santa Margherita da Laviano
Matteo, Ottone's grandnephew
Ottone, Archbishop of Milan
Ranieri Casali, Uguccio Casali's nephew
Saint Thomas Aquinas
Salvato, Santa Margherita's son
Uguccio Casali
Uguccio the Younger, Uguccio Casali's nephew

Fictional characters

Angelica Bordoni
Barone Neroni, successor to Conte Pietro
Beppe, Nino's servant
Benno (Bernardo di Benci)
Bonacossa, Matteo's wife
Capitano Rallentini, follower of Bernardo
Carlo, servant of the Torreoni
Enzo Tornabuoni, friend and follower of Bernardo
Father Rafaelo, Nina's friend
Gian Torreoni, father of Lorenzo, Nino, Nina
Gianna, Giovanni's wife
Gioachino, follower of Bernardo
Giovanni, Benno's father
Lorenzo, Nino's older brother
Mafalda, nurse and servant of the Torreoni
Nina (Mariana) Torreoni, Nino's sister
Nino Torreoni
Robert, Nino's teacher and friend
Ugo Bordoni, Angelica's father

1

Things Will Never Be the Same

Donna Lisabeta was the first to hear the bell that morning. She was already awake, lying with her eyes open in the darkness, worrying about her children, especially her daughter Elena, who wished so much to be married but was still very young. She heard the bell tolling — it must be the great bell of San Francesco — and for a while she paid no attention, for that bell always tolled at dawn to wake the city. She would rise in a few minutes to make sure the fires were started in the kitchen; it was the beginning of February and the weather was brisk. For the moment it was pleasant to lie in bed, warm next to Ser Gian under the feather comforter, and imagine a time when Elena would be married and have children of her own.

As Donna Lisabeta lay there waiting for the courage to swing her bare feet from under the cover and onto the cold stone floor, she began to hear other strange sounds. The bell continued to toll, but now she heard shouting in the streets of the lower town. Why would there be shouting so early in the morning? Wrapping a blanket around her naked shoulders and curling her toes against the cold, she opened the shutter a crack in order to hear better.

She was surprised to see nothing. At first she couldn't understand why. Then, when she looked upward, she saw the stars still brightly shining. It must be long before dawn; but then, why was the bell tolling? Had the monks mistaken the time? But they never did; they were as regular as the sun itself.

Donna Lisabeta shook herself. The shouting was louder now, and suddenly she was afraid.

She returned to the bed, picking her way in the darkness. "Gian!" she whispered, although she disliked waking him. "There's something wrong."

"I'm awake. Why is the bell tolling? It's too early. I can see the Dipper. It's still the middle of the night."

"Can you hear the shouting? It's louder now."

"Yes, I can hear it."

Huddling together, they remained silent for a few moments, trying to make sense of the sounds in the streets and the steady tolling of the bell that should not be tolling at this hour. Her eyes wide, she looked up at her husband as a child would look at its parent.

With sudden resolution Ser Gian sprang to his feet, felt for his clothes, and donned them quickly. "There must be trouble. Why else — " The sentence was aborted by a crash, the sound of screams, and a howling noise. A dog? Someone torturing it? Another crash — this time it sounded closer. There was no doubt, now, that many persons, men and women too, were shouting and screaming. And then, for the first time, he saw yellow flickering reflected off the house across the way.

"Fire!" he shouted. "Fire! Wake the house! Mafalda! Carlo! Wake the children! There's fire in the city!" He ran to the stairs leading down to the floor where the servants and children slept. Carlo was standing on the first step, shoes in his hand. "Master!" he cried. "There's fire in the next street. We can see it from the kitchen."

"Put on your shoes, man," said Ser Gian. "Yes, I saw it. How close is it? Why is the bell tolling — what time is it, Carlo? It's not yet near dawn, is it?"

Carlo shook his head. "The children are awake. Mafalda and Anna are getting them dressed. Master Lorenzo is already dressed. I saw him in the kitchen."

Lorenzo, sixteen and the elder son, came running up the lower stairs. "There's someone at the door," he whispered, out of breath. "What shall I do, Father?"

"Who's at the door?"

"I don't know. It might be Giovanni. I'm afraid to open."

Ser Gian hurried to the door. "Giovanni!" he shouted. "Is that you?" He shot the massive bolts. A tall man, his eyes staring and his white hair tinged by the light of the fires, was on the step. Next to him was his son, Benno.

"The city is betrayed, taken," shouted Giovanni, his voice hoarse. "Cortona is destroyed, and we have no choice but to flee."

The two men were only a few feet from one another, but they had to shout to be heard above the increasing uproar. "Who has taken the city? Who betrayed it?"

"Let me in." Giovanni hurried through the door, his son following. "I heard it — we all did — down in our street. The Becarelli gate — it was opened in the night. The bell was the signal. The lower town is full of soldiers, killing, burning."

"Soldiers? What soldiers?" Ser Gian could not grasp what Giovanni, his swineherd who spent the winters in a hut two streets below, was telling him.

"Aretini," muttered Giovanni. *"Assassini, ladri!* They give people a choice."

"Aretini? Why Aretini?"

"Cortonese Guelphs and Aretini. Together. The Guelphs betrayed the city. So it's said, I don't know. They come to a house and beat down the door. They'll be here soon. They give you a choice. Stay and die, or go, taking whatever you can carry on your back — no more, Master. They don't harm the people who go, but they kill the others. Children, old people, masters, servants, they're streaming down to the gate, even now, struggling under their loads. And where will they go, Master?

It's still the middle of the night. Many will die in this cold, even if the soldiers don't kill them!"

"Where are our soldiers, Giovanni? We have soldiers, too — we pay them enough!" he added bitterly.

Giovanni shook his head. "They light a candle. It flickers and burns in front of the house. As long as the candle is burning, you can gather your possessions. When it burns out, if you're still in the house . . . I saw them kill one old man who couldn't go fast enough. You — we must go, master. Now! You — we must start to gather what we can carry. What will it be, master? You'll have to decide."

Ser Gian leaned against the well, his hand covering his eyes. Then he straightened, looking around the room. His entire family was there now, and all the servants, waiting. The little children, Nino and Nina, were huddled next to Mafalda, their nurse. Lorenzo was trying to be brave. Elena stood next to her mother. Carlo and Anna waited for him to tell them what to do.

"We won't be able to take the horses and the big wagon?"

Giovanni shook his head. "I've seen no horses or wagons, even a wheelbarrow. You have to carry what you want to save."

"So be it. The most valuable thing in this house . . ." Ser Gian began, then paused. "Two valuable things. Perhaps we can carry most of both of them. The gold and the scarlet cloth I was going to sell in Florence. There are — how many? — twenty bolts or so. You know where they are, Carlo. Take Lorenzo and bring them here. We'll see what we can carry. Then, Giovanni, you come with me — we'll see about the gold. We better hide most of it. Even if they promised, they might not let us through."

They hurried up the stairs to the study, a small windowless room at the top of the house. A chest stood against the wall. Candlesticks and salvers and a large bowl gleamed when Ser Gian lifted the lid. "We'll never be able to carry these." His panic had passed; he had always known how to cut his losses. "We'll take the coins and hide them in our clothes. Lisa can carry some, and Mafalda. We can even put some coins in these little purses and let the children carry them." He was working steadily. At last he carried one of the salvers down the stairs, leaving everything in the study behind the secret door, even his account books, all save one, which he held in his hand.

"They're here," said Carlo between his teeth. There were men in the street, around the door, elbowing their way into the kitchen. Suddenly it was full of strangers with swords in their hands. A tall man pushed through the crowd. "Your candle's burning," he grunted, looking around the kitchen with all its treasures in full view.

"We have until it burns out," said Ser Gian coolly. Curiously, he did not feel afraid. "How long will it take?"

The man shrugged. He was already counting the value of the plates and iron fireplace tools and the table and benches and the two fine armchairs. "Half an hour if you're lucky. The wind may blow it out," he added, grinning. "We don't relight candles. When they're out, they're out."

"Leave us alone," Ser Gian said. "We'll be out of this house in fifteen minutes. We've lived here all our lives — give us a quarter of an hour!"

The captain began to usher his men out the door. In a few moments the room seemed empty, although the entire family was still there.

"There are twenty-four bolts of cloth," said Ser Gian, counting rapidly. "We can carry them all, though they're heavy. They're worth more than this house! Here, Giovanni, four for you. Four for you, Carlo. Three for you, Lorenzo — can you lift them? Use your belts to tie them. Two for you, Lisa, and two for Anna. Cover them with your cloaks. Two for Mafalda, one for you, Elena. Wear all the warm clothes you can find quickly — carry nothing else. And you children, take these little purses," he said, tying them around their necks. "There's nothing much in them, but keep them safe. We'll be proud of you."

They ran to their sleeping places and returned quickly. Elena had pocketed her pearls and her gold bracelet, which she showed her father. Lorenzo had his sword, but Ser Gian shook his head. "A dagger if you can hide it, but that's too dangerous. They'd think you were challenging them. None of you do that!" he said, raising his voice. "Don't let them provoke you. They'll try. Elena and Lisa, stay close to me. Mafalda and Anna, hold on to the children. Giovanni — where's Gianna? — ah, there you are," he said, smiling at Giovanni's wife, who had silently entered the room. "Here's a bolt of cloth for you — I can't carry five. Now it's time to go. Be brave and don't look back. Pray to the Virgin to protect us, and then go down the street and through it, God willing, all of us unharmed. Are you ready? Hold up your heads, my family! Andiamo!"

By the time the Torreoni family reached the Becarelli gate — the only one open — their numbers had swelled to more than twenty as other servants, cousins, and an aunt and uncle joined them. A large crowd was pushing and shoving to move through the opening, which had been narrowed by a line of soldiers on each side who were snatching possessions from the unaware, tearing at their clothes, grabbing at young women for a kiss or a feel.

Ser Gian drew his group aside; they huddled around him. "Stay close together," he warned. "Try to stay in the middle of the crowd as you go through. Decide who you're going to hold onto and don't let go. Of course, try to keep your grip on the cloth, but if you can't, don't risk your life for it. Bless you all!" He started toward the gate. "Hold my arms with both hands," he said to his wife and Elena. "Don't let go of me for anything!"

He worked his way to the center of the passage, where the pressure was the greatest as the crowd surged forward. He was nearly through the gate when he tripped over the leg of an old man who had stumbled in front of him; for an instant he held out his hand to keep from falling. And in that instant he felt Elena's hands slip from his arm.

He tried to stop, to stand still, frantically seeking her slim figure in the surging mass of desperate humanity; for a moment he did see her, her face turned toward him, abject terror in her eyes. Then she disappeared, and it was impossible to stand against the weight of hundreds of human beings pushing, shoving, pressing against him from behind. It was all he could do to keep his feet and hold his wife upright; more than once she too was almost torn from his grasp. "Elena," he screamed, "keep going, don't stop, stay with the crowd!" Again he stumbled and was pushed forward. "Oh, God, Madonna, help."

The road outside the gate was narrow, and the crowd surging between the stone walls seemed ever more frantic. Ser Gian and his wife could not pause even to breathe for several hundred yards, when they reached a widening in the road; but here there was another gauntlet of soldiers, falling upon the weakest victims, kicking those who fell, stripping them of what they carried. Grimly he pushed on, looking around to see that Giovanni had gotten through the gate with Mafalda and the little children, and Lorenzo with most of the household servants. Some were ahead, others behind; it was impossible to stop and count survivors for as much as half a mile.

Giovanni, now in the lead, had stopped beneath a tree, Nino and Nina's hands held tight in his rough ones. A trickle of blood ran down beside his ear. "Thank you," Ser Gian said, glancing at the children. "You go on, with the others. I've got to go back to the gate. Elena . . ." His voice broke, and tears wet his cheeks.

Donna Lisabeta had been slumped against him; she started when she heard these words. "My daughter!" she wailed. "Where's my daughter?" She had just realized Elena was not still with them.

"You can't go back," said Giovanni hoarsely. "They'll kill you. She's all right; almost everyone got through, although some were detained for a while. You wait here with Carlo; I'll take the family on — to where?"

"The road to Castiglione. When we find her, Carlo and I will catch up to you."

Donna Lisabeta would not let go, as if releasing him meant she was sure to lose Elena; he had to pry her fingers loose and then hold her up. "Be brave, I'll find her; go to your brother's house in Castiglione. Try to carry the cloth, we'll need it. I'll bring Elena."

Her face was white in the pre-dawn light. "My daughter," she moaned. "My daughter."

"Our daughter." He embraced her, then held her until Giovanni could take her arm. "Go on, all of you, as far as you can. It's cold, but the sky's clear; thank God there's no snow." He looked down at his wife, whose head just reached his shoulder. He kissed her again, mingling their salt tears. "Nothing's to be gained by staying here; besides, it may be dangerous. Carlo and I . . ." There was no way to finish the sentence. He paused. "Giovanni, go no farther tonight than the place where the road branches back to Tecognano. We'll meet you there."

Ser Gian and Carlo began to walk slowly back along the road, picking their way among the throngs of fugitives. Donna Lisabeta watched until they disappeared; then, head bowed, shoulders slumped, she yielded to Giovanni's gentle prodding. He murmured something, but if she heard it she did not reply.

Their progress was slow; it took them two hours to go a mile along the narrow, crowded road. The children were cold and tired, the others near exhaustion from their loads and their grief. Even so, they were better off than many other refugees. Many had come so ill prepared! Wearing their best clothes, not their warmest, including the wrong shoes for a walk of perhaps twenty miles. Bearing preposterous burdens, chairs and huge iron pots and sacks of grain, salt, even firewood. Or just so old or so young they had to be carried, so ill or weak or hopeless they couldn't travel one step farther even though they hadn't yet gone a tenth of the way. As they passed groups of these miserable stragglers, Giovanni and Lorenzo tried to give a word of comfort or advice. A few they persuaded to lay down their heaviest loads and make compromises with the necessity that faced them all. But scores, hundreds of persons were left behind along the road. What would become of them? What terrible story would have to be told about this family or that?

The sun rose but gave little warmth. Behind them they could see, high on its hill, the beautiful city that had been theirs. Trails of smoke drifted lazily across the clear sky. Most did not turn to look again. The family reached the Tecognano road before noon. They sank to the ground, huddling together for warmth, sharing the single loaf Mafaldo had secreted in her clothes. She also had a cup; they drank together from a nearby stream.

Donna Lisabeta lay with her head in Anna's lap, her face turned toward the ground. She responded to no inquiries or words of comfort. Lorenzo knelt beside her and stroked her shoulder, but she shrugged him off and paid no attention to Nino and Nina when they spoke to her. Giovanni beckoned and they returned to his strong arms. "Wait, little master, little mistress, till your father returns. Then we'll know what to do." Soon they were asleep, lying in one another's arms and covered by Giovanni's heavy cloak.

Quietly, Giovanni knelt beside Donna Lisabeta — he knew she was aware of his presence. "I have a plan, mistress," he murmured. "Benno and I will walk back to your farm at Tecognano and see if there are provisions. I've seen no sign of soldiers in that direction. You should continue on to Castiglione, otherwise you may die here of cold and hunger. Master Lorenzo will lead if you tell him the way."

 She began to protest, but he interrupted: "This is what Signore would have me do; I'm certain of it. We must have food and other things. Lorenzo is brave; follow him."

She closed her eyes.

Lorenzo was eager to accept this responsibility. "I should keep going, Giovanni, even though my mother is so tired, isn't that right?" Together they raised her to her feet; she found the strength to walk. Giovanni and Benno stood holding hands until the Torreoni group was out of sight.

The Tecognano farm had not been ransacked. Together with Alfiero, the farmer, and his wife, man and boy harnessed a team of oxen to a large wagon and mules to a smaller one, and loaded them with sacks of grain, flasks of wine and oil, barrels of olives, apples, and dried fruit.

Alfiero watched, his long face woeful, as they climbed into their seats. "The master . . ." he hesitated.

"Do not fear, friend," said Giovanni. "He will repay you for everything, and more."

"Saluti al mi Signore," Alfiero called out as they turned into the winding road. *"E a Madonna."*

Benno drove the oxen, his father the mules, which were refractory. They moved quickly, despite the throngs of pedestrians on the main road, and caught up with the family before dark.

"Let's wait here," Giovanni said, and everyone obeyed him without a word of protest. It was strange how he had almost replaced their master. He distributed food and blankets and they made themselves as comfortable as possible around a fire built by the women. They were beset by hungry people; Giovanni saw to it that everyone received some little thing, a piece of bread, a sip of wine, half an apple. A tent was erected for Anna and her mistress, who continued to refuse to speak to anyone.

Ser Gian and Carlo found them before midnight. Only Lorenzo was awake, standing guard. Startled by the look on his father's face, he knew immediately what it meant. "Mafalda has food," he said. "Giovanni thought we should rest here tonight, then go on in the morning. I'm sorry, Father . . ." His voice trembled.

The man, his face drawn with exhaustion and grief, nodded without speaking. "Where . . . ?" was all he could manage. Lorenzo pointed to the tent, and Ser Gian crept inside to replace Anna. During the night low voices could be heard from time to time, and strangled sobs.

In the morning Giovanni had another plan. He and Carlo would return to the farm and load one of the wagons again, leave the big wagon and the oxen for Alfiero, and drive some of the farm's pigs down the hill. "Benno, come with us," he said.

Carlo sat beside Giovanni while he wrestled with the mules, Benno following with the patient oxen. "Tell me," said Giovanni when they were out of sight.

Carlo was silent for a while. He drew his breath. "There wasn't any news of her. We stood by the road, me on one side and him on the other, asking everybody who went by. He'd say it over and over. 'Have you seen my daughter? She's young, dressed in a black dress and cape. Do you know her? Her name is Elena.'" He swallowed. "Over and over. 'Elena Torreoni. Do you know our family? I lost her as we were going through the gate. Have you seen her?'

"Of course many knew him," Carlo went on. "They're a great family. Yes, they knew her, some of them said, but the soldiers had snatched some girls and women and taken them away.

"'Where did they take them, those girls?' he cried out. It broke my heart to hear. No one knew. Others had lost family in that terrible press at the gate — you remember! Then he began to count the people; he stopped when he reached a thousand. How many is a thousand, Giovanni? I tried to lead him away, but he wouldn't go. 'Elena, *piccola figlia mia,* may the Blessed Virgin stand with you and protect you.' That's what he said. It broke my heart."

Giovanni said nothing.

"Finally the sun came up. For a while there were crowds, then fewer people. Some had been beaten. They recognized him, but they shook their heads. Nobody knew anything. Then the road was nearly empty, except for the people who were hurt too bad to move, or the dead. The dead lay here and there, Giovanni, their clothes messed; of course the corpses had been robbed. He started back up the hill. I tried to stop him, but he just said, 'We'll go together.'

"We came to that place where the other soldiers attacked us. There was no one there, so we kept on going. We got to the gate. Of course it was closed. There were no sounds from inside the city — it was as if everybody was dead. We went closer. I was holding his arm, to prevent him from doing anything . . . Then a man's head appeared above the gate — you know, on the walkway. 'Who goes there?' he shouted — a guard, I guess.

"I tried to hold the master back, but he shook me off and took a few steps forward. 'I am one man, unarmed, a Cortonese who has lost his home and his livelihood,' he said. Those were his words. 'I have also lost my daughter. Can you give me any information?'

"The guard shouted to us to go back. We have orders, he said. He said if we came closer he'd kill us.

"And then, Giovanni, then" — Carlo's voice broke — "then he said, 'Can you at least tell me where they have taken the girls? Where they have taken my daughter?' He knelt down in the road, Giovanni, our master, and held up his hands. 'I'll give you anything you want.' That's what he said, Giovanni, kneeling on the bloody stones in front of his own city."

Giovanni was silent for a long time while he struggled to control the mules, who had little desire to pull the wagon up the hill. He turned to look at Carlo, who was staring straight ahead. "What did the soldier say?"

"I don't know. He seemed to me to have been touched by our master's sorrow. 'You can't come in,' he said. 'Go away, I don't want to kill you,' he said."

Again Giovanni looked at his friend.

"He stood up, and I helped him, he was so weak. He's a strong man, but he was weak. I remember the last thing he said to the soldier, who maybe didn't even hear it. 'Her name is Elena,' he said. 'She's only fourteen. Please help her if you can.' He was crying, Giovanni. I remember because I was too. He didn't even notice. He held my arm. It's strange, but then I felt as if we were just two men, not master and servant."

"Yes," said Giovanni. He reached to touch Carlo's arm.

"We walked back down the hill and found you here. My master stopped and tried to help many who were lying by the side of the road. There wasn't much we could do, but he tried. What you've done here, Giovanni, is a miracle."

Carlo touched the other's arm in return. "What do you think?" he asked.

"Think?"

"Will happen. To Mistress Elena."

Giovanni said nothing. He stared straight at the mules as they strained to pull the heavy wagon upward.

"Will he find her?"

Giovanni shook his head. "You know as well as I do, Carlo, women are booty in war. Especially young girls as pretty . . . They, the soldiers, they can do what they want, and you know what they want."

"Master's rich. He could pay."

"If they haven't already assaulted her, they may think of that. In war there's no time to think."

"Well, and then what?" Carlo hoped he didn't know.

"Why, they'll cut her throat and throw her into some unmarked grave. With the others, so they can't identify the people who assaulted her. That's the way of the world, Carlo. We know it, and Master Gian does, too." He paused. "The family will never be the same."

"No," said Carlo, "it'll never be the same."

They continued in silence until they reached the farm, where they worked together with Benno to prepare for the return trip. They told Alfiero about Elena and tears came into his eyes. He was grateful to have the oxen back and said they could keep the mules and the wagon as long as it was needed. He helped them choose ten pigs, and they left shortly after midnight in the hope of avoiding detection. Benno herded the pigs down the mountain and along the road to Castiglione. He was only eight years old; when they arrived he was welcomed as a hero.

2

Messer Uguccio Casali

"I've heard you suffered heavy losses. I'm sorry. I hope there's something I can do to help. If there is, you've only to ask and I'll do it."

The speaker was a tall man with prematurely graying hair, dressed in armor covered by a tunic and cloak of fine wool. He wore a sword and carried a helmet under his arm with the easy grace of one who was accustomed to doing so.

"None so heavy as the loss of my daughter," replied Ser Gian. He and Messer Uguccio Casali were friends, despite the differences between them. Uguccio was obviously a soldier, a man of the sword; Gian a merchant, a man of affairs. Uguccio was of noble birth whereas Gian was a relative newcomer to the ranks of the *grandi*, as the rich and powerful were called. They admired one another for qualities they shared, even though they didn't always agree. But they could talk to one another and, more important, listen. They had been doing that for a long time, although this was their first meeting since the terrible night that had changed the Torreoni family, and Cortona itself, forever.

"Tell me what you've done," said Casali. "Have you sent a message to the Bishop?"

Ser Gian was astonished. "To *him*? To that monster who is my enemy?"

"I don't deny he's monstrous, but he also needs money. He promised the Aretines a large sum, and he can't pay it. An army, even if it's your own, is dangerous if you break your promises, especially when they've done what you wanted. He hasn't forgotten what happened to his predecessor."

Gian waited for another of his friend's history lessons.

"Bishop Marcellino dipped his fingers into politics, but he ended up on the wrong side. The Imperial party decided he was a traitor; condemned, he was dragged behind a horse all the way to Castiglione, where he was hanged by Frederic's Saracens." Uguccio looked around. "Not this Castiglione; the other one, between Cortona and Arezzo."

Gian ignored this. "Do you mean I ought to approach the Bishop with an offer?"

"Exactly. I don't know what's happened to your dear Elena. Perhaps it's too late; perhaps . . ." His voice trailed off. They looked at one another.

"I have no idea how to do it." Gian sat with his head bowed, his elbows on his knees.

"Perhaps I could. I'm not sure I can reach him, nor am I sure I can persuade him in . . ." Again the slightness of hope was left unspoken.

"Do you know where he is?"

"He's in Cortona, boasting of his triumph. He's issued contracts — which our Podestà, himself one of the conspirators, has signed — declaring the justice of his punishment of our pride and wickedness, and promising the Aretines rewards. He's also offered them plenary absolution for anything they may have done — the last because he prefers soldiers under his command to have clear consciences."

"God have mercy on us!"

Uguccio crossed himself. "Truly," he breathed. "It's also true that God is more inclined to help those who help themselves."

"Oh my friend, my heart is heavy. I've lost my dear girl. My house has been ransacked, my valuables have been stolen, my affairs are in disarray — because we lost some of the cloth I was holding for delivery in Florence next month. I may now owe more than I can pay — and, to top all this, my wife is dying of grief. I too would find death not unwelcome." Gian covered his eyes and began to sob.

Hesitantly — it was not like clapping a fellow soldier on the back — Uguccio rested his hand on his friend's shoulder. He was silent for a while; then, clearing his throat: "My losses are nothing like yours — money and property, that's all. I wasn't in Cortona that night, a fact of which they were probably aware. I've had more time than you to reflect on what's happened and what may happen now. Cortona has lost its independence; it may never regain it. But the city itself remains, even with scores of ruined houses. Most of its people survive, and the skill and quick wit that made us dangerous in the eyes of that monster have not been lost. We live in a time of ferment, of rapid ups and downs of fortune. The Imperial party remains strong in Tuscany; despite the death of our great Frederic. It may even prevail."

He drew his breath. Gian stared at him with a look somewhere between disgust and admiration.

Messer Uguccio looked into his eyes. "We need you, my friend. Cortona needs you. Your family needs you, all the more because they have suffered greatly. Only the fearful are ever really vanquished. We must raise our heads and stand firm. You and I alone are more than a match for Guglielmino Ubertini; we have many allies." He paused. "Today is not the time to begin planning our future. I'll see what can be done to ransom your daughter — if it's possible at all. You must care for Madonna Lisa, Lorenzo, the little ones. I've heard they came through well enough, including the boy Benno — isn't that his name? — the son of your strange swineherd. We'll talk again soon. The Lord bless you and keep you, Gian Torreoni! Without you my task would be much harder — perhaps impossible."

The Bishop of Arezzo may not have been in Cortona during the earliest hours of the assault, but he was not far away. The next day he met his partner in the affair at the small village of Mezzavia, just four miles north of Cortona on the main road to Arezzo. The pre-arranged place was an abandoned farmhouse surrounded by cypresses and evergreen oaks; it was almost invisible from the road. Each was accompanied by a small bodyguard, its numbers also pre-arranged. They were not friends; the word could not be used of any associate of the Bishop, who, if he had ever possessed friends, had long since betrayed them.

His colleague, a man very like him, went by the name of Conte Pietro di Pierle. Of an old but perhaps not noble Cortona family, the Conte was the current possessor of the Rocca di Pierle, one of the most impregnable fortresses in the region. Situated close to the border between Tuscany and Umbria, it had served for centuries as protection against one or the other. At the moment the Rocca was ostensibly protecting Cortona, hence Arezzo, hence Tuscany against enemies in the Papal Territories, a task, again for the moment, not difficult, since the nearest Umbrian city was Perugia, a friend of Cortona for the last twenty years.

"Complimenti!" exclaimed the Bishop when the Conte entered the room. "Your Guelf contingent . . . your arrangements . . . of course necessarily behind the scenes . . ." They did not shake hands. The Bishop looked around. They were alone in the house and could therefore talk without being overheard — they assumed. But walls, as the Bishop well knew, have ears; the Conte was not unacquainted with this fact.

"I believe it went well," he said. "Of course I had nothing to do with it and was not there myself; I've only heard what happened from others, who told me your Aretini were" — he searched for the right word — "thorough in their devastation of the lower town. They even carried away the great bell of the Pieve. Perhaps . . ." He paused.

"The great bell is in Arezzo where it belongs," the Bishop replied firmly. "It was cast with funds rightfully the property of my diocese. As to their 'thoroughness,' we both knew the hatred of the men of Arezzo for the men of Cortona could be counted on. Hatred is a more effective weapon than any other."

They stared at one another. Neither wished to be seen to smile; in the circumstances it was hard to frown.

"One thing concerns me," the Bishop said after a while. "It appears that the daughter of one of your noted fellow-citizens" — he sought for the right word — "disappeared in the melee. She hasn't been found. Do you have any information . . . ?"

"I assume you're speaking of the Torreoni girl. For myself, I know nothing; I assume you'll hear nothing further. As to your use of the expression 'fellow-citizen,' I'm offended. If that man is a citizen of Cortona, I am not; if I am, he is not."

Ubertini, desirous of knowing more than he already did, waited a moment before saying, in all innocence: "I wasn't aware of any bad feeling . . ."

Conte Pietro's eyes narrowed. "I hate the man," he said between his teeth, "not because he's Ghibelline, nor because he's rich, nor because he's an intimate of Casali. He humiliated me. A newcomer, he has no respect for the traditions of our country. He was a leader, behind the scenes, in the movement to deprive us old families of the right to live within the walls. As a result I was forced to sell my house, I believe to one of his 'new' friends." He paused. "I wonder why you're concerned about that man's daughter."

"I assume he would pay a considerable sum to have her back. I wouldn't mind sharing it with you, Count. Beyond that, we may have mortally wounded him. In these days enemies can become allies in the blink of an eye, enemies again before you know it. There are no fixed relations that can be depended on, apart from interest. Torreoni is rich and well-connected; perhaps we've made him an enemy for life. Then again perhaps not; as the saying goes, men forgive more easily the loss of their father than the loss of their patrimony."

Conte Pietro had turned to look out the window. "That man and I can never have the same interest," he said grimly. "You and I, however . . . I'll see if the girl can be found, alive and sufficiently well. If so, will you conduct the negotiations?"

The Bishop, who regretted his remarks about shifting alliances, was relieved to see that the fish had taken the hook. "You can depend on me, Count. And now, I'm as busy as you are . . . Before we part, there's something I want to tell you. I think it will please you. As you can imagine, my expenses in this affair have been great, and my resources are far from being able to cover them." The Conte raised his eyebrows. "I have therefore offered to 'sell' certain properties in Cortona to the Aretines in lieu of payments it would be difficult for me to make. One of them is the Poggio del Gerfalco, at the top of the city; the other is the ruined Castellino in Torreone, which you know used to command access to the high mountain pastures. They say a new castle will be built there; it will be of strategic value." He smiled coldly. "Of course you yourself, Count, will never be impeded from passing there if you wish."

"Those lands are owned by Torreoni," said Conte Pietro.

"Exactly. That's why I thought you would be pleased."

They stood, measuring one another. Each wore armor, as was customary for them both; they were bare-headed, as befitted their present relationship. *"Tante cose,* your Excellency," murmured the Conte as he turned to go. *"Tante belle cose"* was the reply. These conventional parting words were not meant any more sincerely than was usual.

Castiglione Chiusino had sometimes been a part of the contado of Cortona, though often not. At the present time it was pretty much independent, although owing its relative freedom more to the carelessness of its neighbor Perugia than to any strength of its own. Because it was partly Cortonese, relatives of some of the refugees lived there and could provide temporary shelter. This was the case with the Torreoni. Brother Ranieri was far from having room for twenty persons, but room was found nevertheless, and the exhausted travelers, arriving late in the second day of their desperate journey, were too tired to care about comfort. Most threw themselves on the floors of barns and stables and slept for twelve hours. The problem was, when they awoke they were ravenous. Food and drink from the Torreoni farm tided them over for a few weeks. But what then?

Cortona and Perugia had warred for a century over hegemony in their small area of central Italy, but for a generation they had been at peace, and when Messer Uguccio proposed that the exiles should ask Perugia for help, it was forthcoming. More than twenty-five hundred newcomers couldn't long remain in little Castiglione; they needed land on which they could grow their own food and sleep in their own dwellings. After a month of difficult negotiations, conducted by Casali with Ser Gian by his side, the Perugini agreed to lease an area extending along the shore of Lake Trasimeno. The terms were neither cruel nor particularly generous, which meant, in the circumstances, they really were generous, a fact the Cortonese didn't forget. The deal was concluded in March, giving time to sow a crop of winter wheat that carried them over the next winter.

Uguccio didn't tell Gian until after the talks ended why Perugia had been so openhearted. "They want revenge," he said. "Not only for what happened to Cortona, which is more important to us than it is to them. But both Siena and Perugia have been offended, as well as materially damaged, by Florence and its nagging ally, Arezzo. War may be in the offing, and they need soldiers — good ones, not mercenaries. They asked our help."

"What did you say?"

"Well," said Uguccio, a little embarrassed, "I agreed to seven hundred."

"Seven hundred! Are there that many able-bodied men among us, to say nothing of soldiers?"

"Perhaps not from among us exiles, but there are men who could be recruited from the *contado,* the outlying districts where Arezzo has little or no control. I think we could muster some three hundred mounted, with another four hundred foot from the region. The question is, who will pay? I mean, besides myself?"

"You know you can count on me, as much as possible. I suppose you think of this as an investment for the future? As a way to get our city back?"

"I'm not even sure this will do it, Gian. You understand that? We're in a hard place. There aren't many patriots left inside the walls. The . . . patriots are here in Castiglione, and how long do you think their fervor will last? The longer we remain outside the walls, the harder it will be to get back in. Our only hope, it seems to me — of course I may be wrong," he added, darting a sidelong glance at his companion — "our only hope is to do something quick and dramatic, and helpful to our friends. To that end, I've agreed to lead a contingent of Cortonese troops — as many mounted as I can muster — south into Puglia, where King Manfred has great need. I —"

"You've already agreed to this!" Gian interrupted.

"You may think me rash. But without such an offer . . ." He paused. "I don't expect you to accompany me. You stay here, with your feet on solid ground." He smiled; it was an old joke that Gian was no horseman. "But I hoped that your Lorenzo . . ."

"Lorenzo!"

"If you say no, of course I won't ask him. I hope you don't. His presence would be a comfort, and it would add to the reputation of your family."

"May I think about it?" Ser Gian was shocked and, he realized, more than a little frightened. The wound of Elena's loss — no word, from the Bishop or anyone else, had ever been heard about her fate — was still so fresh. It had never occurred to him that his son, born as he supposed to follow in his footsteps as a merchant, might undertake a military career. Service in the present case need not be a career, he thought. The city needed every man; Uguccio needed him and was placing his own life and fortune on the line. "Or rather," he continued a little lamely, "let me speak to Lorenzo. Perhaps —

probably — he will want to follow your banner, my valiant friend. It's only that . . . it surprised me a little."

"I understand. I won't think any the less of you if he . . . can't come with us." It was a gracious way to put it.

But Lorenzo wanted to go. Again his father was surprised.

The Puglia expedition came to nothing; by the time it had been outfitted and trained, and had made the long and difficult journey, the newly crowned king of Sicily and the protector of the Ghibellines in Italy had left to spend the winter in his new country. Uguccio returned to discover there was need of him and his men nearer home. The conflict between the Florentine Guelfs and the Sienese Ghibellines was coming to a head. Finally it erupted on the famous fourth of September in the year 1260, at the place called Monteaperti.

It was a crucial battle in Tuscan history and one of the most ferocious, though its aftermath was a source of heartbreak for all who loved Siena. The Florentines threw down the gauntlet on the first day of the month, arrogantly demanding the immediate surrender of the city, including the demolition by the Sienese themselves of their famous walls. The response of the Sienese was not an arrogant refusal but instead a total submission to the will of their patron, the Blessed Virgin, for whose aid the entire city, man, woman, and child, prayed one whole long day. The Virgin having inspired them to resist, a peoples' army issued from the gates on the third and reached the Florentine camp that evening. The battle was joined early the next morning.

It was a total victory for Siena, the only one it ever enjoyed over Florence. Thousands of Florentine and Aretine Guelfs were killed, wounded, or taken prisoner, and the Florentine *carroccio,* or battle wagon, was captured together with enormous amounts of booty. Aretine losses were especially grave; of the five thousand engaged, about one thousand were killed, including the Podestà who had helped to arrange the betrayal of Cortona. The Bishop survived the battle, but his losses in treasure and followers were great.

Messer Uguccio Casali led his seven hundred Cortonese at the battle and acquitted himself valiantly, being the first of his city to be wounded, yet refusing aid until he knew all his men were safe. Lorenzo Torreoni was there also. By an accident of war he did not actually fight, but his presence on the field was enough to inspire his fellow citizens with respect for his dedication to duty. Uguccio did not forget that his friend had offered him as a possible, though unnecessary, sacrifice.

After its humiliating defeat, Florence lay helpless before its enemies, but Siena, which could have destroyed its tormentor, did not do so; in fact it gained nothing from its great victory. The Cortonese exiles, however, benefited greatly. Having none of the hesitation of the Sienese, they pressed firmly, as always under the leadership of Uguccio Casali, for help from their allies to regain their city. They did regain most of it, returning in triumph on April 25, 1261, St. Mark's Day. The terms, some of which remained secret for years, were not as honorable as they had wished, for they had to agree to share the city with the returned Guelf exiles, and Bishop Guglielmino was not punished, instead being left with much of the power he had usurped. Just to be home again was, for many of the exiles, a sufficient prize, and they accepted it with gratitude not only to their leader but also to the Evangelist, who from then on was worshipped as the city's patron.

Indeed, the first act of the Nuovo Consiglio was to redesign the city's arms, on which it was natural, since a lion is the symbol of San Marco, to feature a lion rampant, holding a book in its paws, on a field of gold, red, or black depending on the whim of those in power. From that time on, the leader of the city was often referred to as the Lion of Cortona, Messer Uguccio being the first to enjoy that title.

The years of exile were bitter for most of those who had survived the march and borne the brunt of the desecration of their city. But for Nino and Nina Torreoni, the years passed quickly. They did not forget their sister, but they had not known her very well, and they soon found new friends in

Castiglione. Their mother, as Ser Gian feared, had died of grief a few weeks after realizing her daughter would never be found. But the two children had not known their mother very well, either; Mafalda had nursed them and brought them up; her loss would have broken their hearts. Their father did not understand, at first, how they could continue to laugh and play, but he forgave them for it, and then learned from them.

For Benno, son of Giovanni, these were wonderful years, the best of his life so far. At home his position as the son of the swineherd, and his need to work many hours a day with his father, had imposed strict limitations on his life. Here, where all were leveled, if only temporarily, by circumstances, and especially after his exploits in helping to provide the family's first supplies of food, he blossomed in the frank admiration shown by all for his intelligence, competence, and courage. It's a wonder, his father thought, it doesn't go to his head. He has my admiration because it doesn't!

Giovanni and his family returned to their small stone house a few steps down from Casa Torreoni to find the door smashed and the contents ransacked. But not much had been lost, Giovanni said; here was one time when it paid to be poor. The table had been broken, but they propped it up and shared a simple meal prepared by Gianna, who as usual said nothing.

"Well, Benno," said Giovanni, "we're home at last."

"Ay."

"You're not happy, then?"

"I'm happy, babbo, and I'm not."

Giovanni glanced at him. He took another piece of bread, tore off a portion, and chewed it thoroughly, washing it down with a draught of thin wine. "You've tasted liberty," he said.

"I don't know, babbo. But for those years I could feel what life could be. Now I feel it no longer."

"Beh!" grunted Giovanni, lowering his eyes. He was silent for a long time, while Benno went on eating.

"I'm the problem, Benno." Giovanni had been staring into the small, smoky fire. "If your father weren't a swineherd . . ."

"Don't say those things, babbo!" cried Benno. There were tears in his eyes.

"Aren't they true? Even so, do they treat you differently because of me?"

"Who? Ser Gian? He doesn't. Nina? She doesn't. Nino? Maybe. Not at Castiglione."

"You think things will change now, Benno? Why do you think so? I've seen them treat you almost as a member of the family. Was I wrong?"

Benno shook his head. "It was something Nino said when we parted, just an hour ago. 'Farewell, Benno,' he said, and he held out his hand. He seemed so strange, so . . . he's only nine years old. 'We'll have few chances to see one another now that we've returned to Cortona,' he said. 'I'll be busy, and so will you.'"

"There's truth in that," Giovanni said.

"I know, and that's why I'm not happy."

"Because your two lives, yours and Nino's, must follow different paths? You've always known that. I've never let you forget it."

"For a little while I did forget it, babbo, in spite of your reminders, and now I've been reminded again, not by you but by him, and . . ." He paused. "Let's not talk about this any more tonight," he went on somewhat more cheerfully. "It really is good to be home, for we've missed Cortona a lot, as much as anyone even if our possessions are very few. Tomorrow we'll go up to the high pastures, now it's April, and walk the hedgerows to see they're still secure. That'll please me very much, babbo, and I'll forget all these unhappy thoughts."

They said no more, but Giovanni did not stop thinking. From time to time he glanced at his son. *He's only eleven years old himself, which isn't so much older than nine, but he's much older than that other, nevertheless. He's tall for his age and strong, but best of all he knows who he is, what he can do. God, let him do it! Please help him find a way!*

Benno's thoughts were elsewhere. He was remembering the joy he had felt because of his prowess as a swimmer.

It had begun by accident. He had come upon some boys playing on the lake shore, below the castle, and one of them had pushed him into the water. He had emerged sputtering and complaining, but another boy, more sympathetic than the first, had dived in and swum close to him. "Here, move your arms this way and your legs that way. You see, you can swim! Hot days, we swim every afternoon. Come and join us, Cortonese. The water belongs to everybody!"

It had taken him a week or two, but then, suddenly, he was good at swimming and enjoying it immensely. In his age group no one could beat him in the casual races that took place every afternoon, and it wasn't long before he could beat many of the older boys. One challenged him to swim with him all the way to Isola Maggiore, and he accepted although the distance seemed daunting. It took them nearly an hour to reach the small wooded island, and more than an hour to return against the wind. That day, Benno was exhausted, but he swam to the island again a few days later and then at least once a week as long as they remained in the city. By the time of his departure from Castiglione, he was accepted as easily the first among the younger swimmers, and one of the best of all.

In part this was because he loved being in water, the smooth feeling along his sides as he moved, the sensation of being held up by forces absent from the land. And he loved the way the fishes swam, so much better even than he. His only fear was of water snakes, for the boys said they were poisonous and of course they too could swim better and faster than a man. But there weren't many of them, and he learned where to swim in order to avoid them. Most of all he liked to lie in the water, his arms and legs outstretched, and watch the white clouds drift by and the birds swoop down for their catch. He could spend hours in the water and regretted leaving it when the sun sank behind the castle and he knew his father could be worried, since he, like most grown men, didn't know how to swim and believed all swimmers eventually came to grief.

Now, back in Cortona, landlocked as it was on its mountain, where would he find a place to swim? The big lake was a day's journey away, and the pond at Soho dried up in the spring. Well, he thought, at least I'll always remember the way it was.

The Torreoni family waited for a month before returning to Cortona. Ser Gian sent the servants ahead to do what they could to make Casa Torreoni livable again. He was encouraged by the first reports. The building had been ransacked and a fire had been started against one wall, but it had gone out without causing much damage. Most of the furniture was gone but the Aretines hadn't discovered the deep cellar, hollowed out of the rock, where some chairs and stools, a table, and a bed had been stored. The most needed repairs were rapidly completed. Of course the horses and most of the tack were gone, but in their haste the looters had failed to find the door to Gian's secret windowless room; as a result the gold left behind survived, though what the family had taken with them in their flight was mostly lost. And the account books were still where they had been hidden beneath a pile of debris.

Giovanni returned twice to describe the progress being made; the third time he said the family ought to go back although they shouldn't expect their home to look as it had when they left it.

"The persons who would have cared the most won't be going with us," said Gian. "I don't suppose the children will even notice. Lorenzo and I . . ."

"It may be better than you think."

"I would give all the gold and the account books and everything else to be able to take those two with me to Cortona. Without them it won't seem the same even if . . ." Giovanni was loading the wagon. "Let me help you," said Ser Gian.

Ordinarily Giovanni would have refused such an offer. Now he didn't. Silently, they worked together. When the mules were harnessed, Mafalda, Nino, and Nina climbed to the back of the load, the children's feet almost touching the ground, while the two men settled onto the driver's seat.

Giovanni handed over the reins, but his master shook his head. "You can deal with those mules better than I could," he muttered. "To tell the truth, I'll be glad to return them to Alfiero as soon as we can."

"They've been useful even so, and they've gotten a bit more civilized. We might even keep them, at least until you find some new horses." Realizing he might have misspoken, Giovanni glanced at the man at his side.

"We'll get horses and everything else we need. There's the irony of it, Giovanni, maybe you haven't noticed, but despite our losses, other men have lost more, and the value of what we saved that night more than doubled, maybe even tripled. Then, with Florence floundering after Monteaperti, we had even greater opportunities. I . . ."

Giovanni glanced at him again.

"I was about to say I feel guilty about benefiting from the misery of others, but I've suffered, too." He was silent for several minutes. "I owe you a great deal, my friend."

Giovanni shrugged; the mules were pulling so hard he didn't have to respond.

"Have you ever thought you might change your mind?" Ser Gian looked back.

"They can't hear us," said Giovanni. He bit his lip, his face turned away. "But no, I never have."

"And you never will."

"I never will."

"You know I'll always respect that. Even so, I'd like to give you something."

Giovanni shook his head, his face still averted.

"At least you know I'll always care for Gianna if something should happen. And Benno, what about Benno?"

"What about Benno?" Giovanni swung to face the other man, his eyes flashing, his mouth twisted. "What about Benno, Gian Torreoni?"

Ser Gian reached for the reins. "Let me drive awhile, and you rest. As usual, you've worked harder and longer than a man should."

"How hard should a man work?" Giovanni looked down at his empty hands. "And do you talk to me about hard work? You, who spend whole nights at your desk, planning, judging, supporting all of us!" He waved aside the protests. "As for Benno, the boy's who he is. He'll make his way."

"I hardly think of him as a boy any longer. He's shot up these years of exile. And from what I've heard, he's popular among the other youths."

Giovanni mumbled something.

"You can be proud, although I know you'll never . . ."

"Never's a long time."

"Even so, if you ever want me to help, aside from paying a customary wage . . ."

"Please, master, let us not talk of these things!" Giovanni said quietly.

"What should we talk about then?" Ser Gian smiled.

"Well, about going home! About how beautiful the city is, even with those ragged gaps in her walls! About how happy many people will be to see you, Ser Gian! Friend or foe, they'll welcome you. That's the custom of the times."

Gian's face darkened, his eyes narrowed. Again he looked back; Mafalda and the children all seemed to be asleep. "I hate them," he said quietly. "Do you know how much I hate them, Giovanni? Those devils . . . I wake in the night thinking of her — she was still just a girl. And my wife, weak and thoughtless as she often was . . . God, Giovanni, I hate them. I haven't even tried to forgive them, though I know my Christian duty."

He glanced at Giovanni, who was looking away across the plain at the city, now visible on the mountain where she lay. *"Che bello!"* he murmured, out of long habit. Then he asked:

"Have you forgiven . . . ?"

"No," said Giovanni in a low voice. The flesh of his face seemed made of stone. "No. I'm a man, not a saint. I don't ask you to be one either." He paused. "Truly," he said after a moment, "let us talk of other things."

The Becarelli gate had been closed by a double-thick wall of stones cemented in place, never to be opened again to friend or foe, and so it remained for seven hundred years. Giovanni had to enter by the other gate and climb the long hill to the piazza, from which it was only a few paces to Casa Torreoni. Gian was saddened by the signs of devastation all around them as they picked their way through the crowds — it was market day — and around piles of rubble that had not yet been removed.

"Whoof!" he said suddenly. "It stinks!"

"More than it always did?"

"Oh yes, or so it seems."

"A section of the sewer was destroyed in the fighting and it hasn't been fixed yet. You get used to it."

Every house had been damaged, some seriously, by fire or looting or both. Only one house, wide and tall with a high portal and frescoed decorations between the window openings, seemed to be untouched. Gian pointed it out.

"I noticed it too. Everybody did."

"Do you know who owns that house?"

Giovanni shook his head.

"Conte Pietro, lord of Pierle. When the constitution was changed to ban the rural nobles from living within the walls, he tried to sell the house to me. He asked too much, and I refused. But I arranged a lease with the Gandolfi, and they lived there but they didn't own the building."

Giovanni nodded. "I know of them. I believe they are planning to return."

"They're good people — and neutral in our interparty strife. Which can't be said of Conte Pietro."

Giovanni seemed puzzled.

"There is no more passionate partisan, but he doesn't declare his Guelf sympathies publicly. To hear him you would think he is neutral too. And he puts it about that I forced him to sell the house to a friend." He paused. "It's strange, isn't it?"

"Strange?"

"Some one of us must have organized the treachery. And his house is the only one to survive untouched. You don't suppose . . ."

"He wasn't here that night."

"You know that?"

"So they say. Conte Pietro was safe in his tower at Pierle. It's common knowledge."

"Ah," said Ser Gian. They had arrived at the door and the street was crowded with welcoming figures.

3

Nino and Nina

The younger son of Ser Gian lay in the afternoon sun on the grass outside the Montanina gate, watching a score of men rebuild a portion of the city wall. Scaffolding had been set up inside; from outside, where he lay, the men were visible only from the waist up. They shouted to one another as they laid the new stones, aligning them by a string stretched tight between iron pins, and their trowels made a steady tapping as they eased the stones into place. It was a song Nino loved.

From time to time young men would appear, rising as if by a theatrical device with baskets on their backs; they would have climbed up the long ladders, balancing their loads. Stones and mortar were transported upward by block and tackle, but there were many other things that had to be carried, and the young men ran up and down the ladders in the certain knowledge that only the swiftest would be promoted out of the apprenticeship they served. After five or ten years, if they hadn't been crippled in a fall, they would be appointed one of the city's masons — its *muratori*. Nino wanted to be one when he grew up.

The new walls of Cortona rose forty feet or more from the ground because of the rebuilding that had been proceeding furiously since the return from exile. They sloped steeply to a crenellated parapet running between towers that rose every hundred yards or so, and along which lookouts walked, back and forth, night and day, even here in the afternoon, on the part of the wall being repaired. Nino didn't know how long the wall was, circling the city; all he knew was that it took an hour to run all the way around, as he had done more than once, the watchmen raising their weapons in mock threat as he passed, for he knew them all.

He turned his head, attracted by the gentle sound of the bells worn by the swine on leather thongs around their necks. Two sows were grazing, their bells tinkling as they moved slowly across the hillside. They were his father's; this land was his father's, above and below the mountain road that led from the gate to Torreone, where, in the distance, the little castle lay. It had only recently been recaptured and returned to the family. Badly damaged in the siege, it might, Ser Gian said, be repaired one day.

A small dog came bounding through the grass and squirmed into the boy's arms. "Canino!" he cried, hugging the dog and burying his nose in its sweet-smelling fur. Giovanni must be near, Nino thought. There he was, down the slope, his long crook in his hand. The boy lay flat in the grass, hoping Giovanni hadn't seen him.

The swineherd was singing a song about Giovannino, the name given to the young John the Baptist when he was the childhood friend of Jesus.

"Giovannino was a prophet
And he foretold his fate.
He knew his head would one day be
The bitter price of hate."

Giovanni kept on singing, although he was close to Nino now.

"Giovannino was a prophet,
He rode upon his ass.
He saw the baby Jesus,
A - lying in the grass."

He reached out with his crook and caught the boy around the neck.

"Well now!" he exclaimed. "Is this the baby Jesus?"

Nino sat up straight. "You know very well who I am, Giovanni," he said, trying to imitate his father's tone when he talked to his *coloni*. "And you should call me Master, and not make fun of me," he added, blushing because he loved Giovanni and he knew Giovanni loved him and he was ashamed for talking that way.

Giovanni ducked his head. "Ay, Master," he said softly.

"You may call me Nino," the boy replied.

"I'll call you Master," said the man, "and let others call you Nino, because I'm your father's swineherd."

"Master is all right, but I like Nino best." He felt sorry for himself, as he always did when people took him seriously when he hadn't meant them to.

"Ay, Master Nino," said the swineherd. He sat down on the ground, plucked a blade of the thick grass, stripped the leaf from the stem, and placed it between his lips. When he blew he produced a piercing, guttural sound. His dog, who had curled up beside him, pricked up its ears.

They sat for a while, looking down the plunging mountain-side, past the woods and the distant olive groves and vineyards, down to the valley of Sodo far below. The only sounds at this distance were the chirping of birds, the tapping of the trowels, and the tinkling of the bells.

"Your sister is looking for you," said Giovanni.

"I know."

"If you know, why don't you let her find you?"

"She wants me to go meet Brother Clemente. But I don't want to go home and meet Brother Clemente." Nino turned on his stomach, plucked a blade of grass, and blew on it. It squeaked.

Giovanni said nothing. The men shouted on the wall, the trowels tapped on the stones, the chirping of the swallows became insistent. It was getting to be evening. Nino buried his head in his hands, smelling the fragrant grass all around him.

34

Giovanni touched his shoulder.

"I'm going to the monastery," said Nino, "to live with the fat old monks."

The swineherd whistled the tune he had been singing. Then he sang some of the words. "Giovannino was a prophet / And he foretold his fate."

"My father wants me to learn to read and write Latin and keep accounts and play music and . . ." Nino didn't know all the things he was expected to learn.

"Those are good things," said Giovanni. "I don't know how to do any of them."

"I don't want to learn them either!"

"Then, when you grow up, you'll be a swineherd, like me."

"I want to be a swineherd," said Nino earnestly, rising to one knee. He looked at Giovanni. "Or a *muratore,* or a watchman on the wall."

"But you can't be any of those things," Giovanni said, "because one day you'll own land. You'll own men and families, they'll depend on you for their life, and you'll have to see that they have it."

"My father doesn't own you, Giovanni."

"That's true, Master, for I'm a free man. I own myself, and my own family, and my house, which as you know has only one room, and one sow ready to litter, a knife and a bow and six good, sharp-pointed arrows, and a few worthless trifles, like this dog." He stroked its head. "But I belong to your father, nevertheless."

"When I grow up I'll set you free," the boy said in his frank and open way.

"I won't go. I'll fall on my knees and pray to let me stay. Others may leave; Benno may leave, when he's old enough. Many young folk leave their masters now and run away to the city, where they're not known. If they avoid capture for a year and a day, then they become truly free men, and they can travel about the country, work for copper pence, and find women who will follow them wherever they go. I have no desire to do those things, Master Nino. I'm already as free as I want to be."

"And I already know all the things I want to know," said Nino. "I know how to talk to Canino and make him sit and stay and retrieve the birds you've brought down with your arrows." He looked at the dog, sleeping at their feet. "Canino, sit!" he commanded. The dog opened one eye, then struggled to his feet and sat, crookedly, on one haunch. "All right, then, lie down." The dog sighed and went back to sleep.

"You're right," said Giovanni. "Canino obeys you as well as he does me."

"I know how to lay stones on a wall and how to carry the basket up the ladder," continued Nino, paying no attention. "I know how to call the soldiers down below if there's an enemy. And I know other things, Giovanni. I know how to find plants that make hurts feel better — Gianna taught me. I know how to set a snare and lay birdlime, how to kill a squirrel with a stone if it isn't too far away, and how to skin a rabbit. Those things you taught me. What more do I need to know?"

"It's true, Master, you know many useful things. You're quick to learn, and you remember well what I've taught you, and my Gianna, and the old man Barbo, who has shown you how to milk the cows and the ewes, and Carlo, who has tried to teach you about horses, although there, Master, you still have much to learn," he added, smiling. "And the others too. We've all tried to teach you, and you've willingly learned much. But you haven't learned to be a master, not yet, and that's the only thing you really have to learn, because a master of men is what you'll someday need to be."

Nino's narrow shoulders began to sink under the weight of this prophecy, but he soon raised his head. "Conte Pietro doesn't know how to read. Father thinks so. I'll be like him. He's a potent master — the most feared of all the Signori."

"Ay," said Giovanni.

"For all that I wouldn't want to be Conte Pietro," said Nino thoughtfully, "for no one loves him, though all fear him."

"Ay," said Giovanni. He didn't look at the boy, his eyes fixed on the far distance, on the mountains that lined the horizon to the north, between Cortona and Arezzo, on the white line of the valley road that led past Arezzo to Florence. His hair was white, his face darkened by years of wind and weather. He sang the rest of the verse: "He knew his head would one day be / The bitter price of hate."

Conte Pietro di Pierle had worn out two wives through child-bearing, but neither had given him a son. It seemed astonishing that a man of his eminence should have had just two surviving daughters; what's more neither was pretty nor had he been able to marry either well. And so he had decided to take another wife, a young and beautiful one this time. Youth and beauty would be more important than her dowry. Not that he would refuse a fine piece of land if it were offered with the hand of a lovely, healthy girl, with brothers. He liked land, but most of all he wanted a son to carry on his name.

For three generations Conte Pietro's family had lived at Pierle, a tiny hamlet ten miles east of Cortona almost on the border between Tuscany and Umbria, at a place where a narrow valley became a veritable canyon and no one, not even a mouse, could pass without the Conte being aware of him. His watchmen on the mountain looked down at the Rocca whose foundations had been laid by soldiers of the Emperor to keep the Longobards out of Tuscany, centuries before. After the return of the Cortonese exiles, the Rocca was repaired and given over to Conte Pietro to defend the Commune from attacks by enemies in the Papal Dominions in Umbria, to the east.

The Rocca lacked grace. Square, with walls of rough, dark stone rising straight up from the ground for more than eighty feet, it was so high it could be seen for miles on its east side, that is from Umbria. It wasn't visible from the west until the very last moment, when it appeared around the last curve to a traveler from Cortona with awesome and terrifying suddenness, and the dark canyon began.

The inside of the Rocca was hardly more pleasing. A narrow portal, permitting only two horsemen to enter abreast, led to a courtyard surrounded by high walls that blocked out the sun. Against the walls were sheds for animals and hovels for the serfs who cared for them in time of siege. There was a well in the center, but the water was drunk only in emergencies; it stank of horse and cattle urine, which ran down the stones and seeped into the earth. In a siege any water, of course, was better than none.

At one side of the courtyard, narrow steps led upward to a series of apartments, where Conte Pietro and his most trusted servants and guards lived. Although these rooms faced south, they were as cheerless as the rest of the fortress, for there were only a few narrow windows to protect against enemy arrows; what windows there were provided no protection against the winter wind that swept through the valley.

Conte Pietro's wives had brought the Conte land in the southeastern quarter of the Commune, and he had also inherited land from his father and from an uncle who had died childless. Next to Messer Uguccio, he was therefore the wealthiest man in Cortona. And Nino was right: He was the most feared.

He had discovered while still young that few men were totally ruthless, even though the few who were, he believed, were invariably successful. He had therefore taught himself to be merciless in dealing not only with his enemies but also with his friends. As a result he no longer had friends, but he didn't care, for he had what he wanted more than friends, which was loyal and obedient followers. There were many of them, and although they feared the Conte, they also admired him. He was a natural leader with a genius for military organization; he could take a seeming rabble of men and horses and turn it amazingly quickly into a disciplined, potent force. Among the Signori only Messer Uguccio was his equal in this respect, although Casali could call upon greater resources and was therefore currently the more powerful. Acting together, the two men had fought well at Monteaperti. The prospect of their being on opposing sides in civil conflict was fearsome to all those who knew the talents of both. Then, choosing to follow one would mean making an enemy of the other.

The only thing that made the choice a little easier, especially for the rural nobles, was the difference in age between the two leaders. Conte Pietro was now forty-five, Messer Uguccio some fifteen years older. The time might not be far off when the Conte would face no credible opposition. Then, he would have his pick of allies; the sooner one offered oneself, therefore, the better.

The Conte liked hunting the wild boars living in the mountains around the Rocca. He preferred to kill the animals himself after they had been weakened by his dogs and his huntsmen, who beat them with sticks when the dogs had cornered them. When he returned from hunting he was always in a rut and demanded services from his wives or any other women who might be providing them at the moment. The women didn't, or couldn't, object. Even so, he had been unable to father a son. This was the greatest disappointment of his life.

Apart from hunting, his favorite activity was bringing lawsuits. He wasn't a notary — basically illiterate, he employed notaries — but he was ingenious in finding legal ways to harass those of his neighbors he had not already reduced to vassalage. His knowledge of matrimonial law was unsurpassed; he employed a Roman agent who kept him up to date on the twists and turns of Papal pronouncements. Since he was related to many of the minor nobility, devious and circuitous paths of consanguinity had more than once led to successful challenges against the passage of an estate from one of his relatives to another, even from a father to a son, with the result that Conte Pietro had ended up owning property that should, by all rights except those of matrimonial law, have belonged to someone who needed it more.

He was feared as an antagonist in any quarrel involving armed conflict; he was even more feared in courts of law. He came to court not only with knowledge of the latest precedents but also with ample funds to sway a recalcitrant judge. Thus a suit brought by Conte Pietro was almost bound to be a disaster for the defendant who, even if he won, would be exhausted both emotionally and financially because his adversary was indefatiguable. If the Conte didn't win the first time he might bring another suit, basing it on a different and even more abstruse loophole in the law.

Again a widower, he hadn't yet decided which young women of Cortona most pleased him. He believed the current crop of marriageable girls between fifteen and twenty — although twenty might be too old — was not promising. But he could wait. In the meantime there were plenty of older women, including wives of his neighbors, to satisfy his needs.

One neighborhood family interested him. It was headed by Signor Ugo Bordoni, a minor landowner who had once, prior to various counts of ill fortune, owned more land than he did now. Signor Ugo was one of the Conte's followers because he saw no other way to improve his lot. He was about the same age as Pietro, but he had married late in life and fathered three sons, all now dead of various accidents, and a daughter, Angelica.

Angelica Bordoni was still too young even for Conte Pietro. But she was a beautiful girl, with golden hair and blue eyes inherited from her mother, a southerner with Norman blood in her veins. Angelica was worth considering. He therefore had a very tentative discussion with her father, whose eyes shone like stars at the idea — it was merely a suggestion, the Conte said — that his daughter might someday become the next lady of Pierle.

Signor Ugo didn't mention this discussion to his wife for some time. She hated Conte Pietro, who tormented her with his cold-hearted advances which, while posing no real threat, were nevertheless humiliating to resist. Then that winter, when things were especially hard for the Bordoni, her husband broached the subject. "My lord has spoken to me of Angelica," he said one evening when his wife had been complaining that their circumstances seemed to be going from bad to worse.

Her eyes flashed. "What has my lord had to say about Angelica?" He was sorry he had mentioned the subject. He was afraid of his wife although he often struck her or shouted at her.

"He spoke of her beauty. He said the day might come when he would take another wife whose son would be the heir to his farms, his castles, and his handsome house in the city."

"And he asked for her hand? She's only fourteen years old!"

"He didn't ask for her hand outright. He only said she was beautiful and mentioned that his next wife would give him an heir."

"As to being his heir, my lord knows how to catch fish, and if I were you I would feel in my mouth for the hook. As to her being his wife, that is impossible."

Bordoni's voice began to rise. "Why impossible?" he shouted. "He must marry someone in order to have a son, and Angelica has pleased him. We could be rich."

His wife stared at him with her cool blue eyes. "Angelica will never marry that man as long as I live," she said quietly.

Signor Ugo raised his arm but he didn't strike her. This was one time he believed patience might be more effective than blows. He was sure the hook that had caught him would eventually catch her, too. He would wait, and it would happen.

After his conversation with Ugo, Conte Pietro was certain he could have Angelica if he wanted her when the time came. Curiously, her availability (apart from what she or her mother might feel) lessened her in his regard. She was certainly beautiful, but her father had very little to give her as a dowry. Of course this was not of crucial importance if he really wanted the girl.

Unknown to Bordoni, the Conte was considering another possible choice. This was Nina Torreoni. She wasn't as pretty as Angelica Bordoni, but even as a child she already possessed the kind of feminine charm that was likely to increase with time; she had two brothers; and her father was already wealthy and growing more so all the time. Best of all, he was a close friend of Messer Uguccio Casali, the very man the Conte wanted to supplant as the veritable ruler of Cortona. A good first step toward that goal would be to become an apparent Casali ally by marrying the Torreoni girl.

Conte Pietro knew Ser Gian disliked him — at the moment — as much as he disliked Ser Gian. But Bishop Guglielmino was right: In politics, relations either of love or hate were never permanent. Ser Gian had ambitions of his own, which, the Conte had heard, involved the political fortunes of his son Lorenzo who, he had also heard, was not competent to succeed on his own. Modest support for the young man, unknown to everyone except Ser Gian, might turn out to be advantageous; he could always be dispensed with when no longer needed.

Ser Gian, the Conte felt sure, would be unwilling to accept him — a man nearly forty years older than his daughter and moreover a presumed enemy of her family — as a son-in-law. But in the right circumstances . . . Torreoni had married a woman who was distantly related to himself and to Conte Pietro, as most of the Cortona nobility were. It might be possible to discover some ties of blood that would make the marriage illegitimate — that is, incestuous in the eyes of the Church. In effect, it might be possible to prove that he, Conte Pietro di Pierle, was the rightful heir to the properties, now grown substantial, that Donna Lisabeta had brought to her marriage. Ser Gian possessed much; he also owed much. The loss of these properties might break him. Would he be willing to offer his daughter as the price of the Conte's renunciation of the claim?

It was certainly worth considering, perhaps even worth talking to the Bishop about. Then again, perhaps not. Probably the less the Bishop knew, the better.

"I don't know that song," said Nino. He sat on the hillside with Giovanni, waiting for Nina to find him, which he knew she would.

"I made it up this morning," Giovanni said.

"So, you already know one of the things they want to teach me!"

"Ay, Master Nino," said the man, and he grasped another blade of grass, held it to his lips, and blew a great squawk that echoed in the valley. "There she is now, on the road." Nino sprang to his knees and peered through the afternoon haze at his sister's small figure far below them. He sat back. "She hasn't seen us."

"I dare say she has," said the swineherd, "for good as your eyes are, hers are better."

Nina had certainly seen them, for she was running up the hill, waving her arms to tell them to stay where they were. She tumbled in between them, into the warm nest they had made in the grass, trying to catch her breath. She settled herself close to Giovanni and reached up to kiss his rough, brown cheek. "Eh!" she exclaimed. "You smell like a pig." But she didn't move.

"As well I might, Mistress."

Nina glanced at her brother. "I wouldn't kiss you for anything." She ducked as he waved his fist at her.

"Even though he doesn't smell of pigs?" Giovanni smiled.

"He doesn't smell of pigs, but he smells of ink and candle ends and mouse turds." She wrinkled her nose.

"I do not!" said Nino. It wasn't fair to blame him for what he couldn't help.

"Brother Clemente's waiting, and he's impatient. So is Father. He's probably going to beat you for keeping them waiting," said Nina, her black eyes sparkling.

"Well, I'm not going."

"Yes, you are going," cried Nina. "You're going, you're going, you're going!"

She threw herself on her brother, tumbling him backward in the grass, sitting on his chest and pinning his arms. She held him with all her strength.

She released his arms and grasped his ears and pulled. It hurt, and he raised his head. She banged his head down on the ground, over and over. Even though the grass cushioned the blows, he felt a little dazed.

"You're going!" she wailed.

With a convulsive effort he threw her off, being careful not to hurt her because after all he really was going, rolled her on her back, and sat on her chest as she had sat on his. She stuck out her tongue. "Mouse turds."

He felt her slim, wiry body squirming under him. He remembered the games they used to play when they were younger, and the blood came to his cheeks. "Be still, Nina," he said, "or I'll hurt you. Anyway, I'm not going, and that's that."

"You have to go," she said, lying still. "You're a boy, and boys have to learn many things. Father says you'll come home at Easter and for a while each summer. When you're not here, Carlo will teach me to ride better than you."

"Beh," he said. He climbed off and sat looking down at her. She brushed off her tunic — she was dressed like a boy, not like a little woman, as most girls were at her age.

"I'll visit you," she said. "I'll sneak into the monastery after dark and find you in your cell. The monks won't catch me."

"Don't do that. Don't even say things like that." He feared the monastery with its grim Franciscan brothers padding about barefoot with brown cowls over their heads, rope belts around their waists, their eyes glittery and hidden. He also respected the monastery's authority, its dark power. "San Francesco lived there," he said. "It's holy. Women aren't allowed to set foot in it."

"Santa Chiara could have visited him," said Nina. This saint, beloved of San Francesco, had just been canonized.

"You aren't Santa Chiara," said Giovanni gently, "and he isn't San Francesco, and this is foolish talk. If your father wants you home to meet the friar, who is waiting patiently or impatiently for you, then you must go, Master."

Nino stood as tall as he was able. "I wish you hadn't found me," he said.

"If I hadn't found you, I wouldn't have seen you before you left," Nina said. She jumped to her feet. "I'll kiss you after all." Her lips brushed his cheek; then she turned away, because she didn't want her brother to see her cry.

"I'll walk with you to the gate, Master," said the swineherd. "Wait for me here, little mistress." He whistled to the dog, which followed the man and boy down the hill. Nino looked back and waved, seeing that Nina was watching. She raised her hand in a brave salute.

Giovanni stopped when they reached the gate. "I've been thinking you might be lonely."

Nino's heart rose in his throat. "Perhaps," he said.

"I'll give you Canino, as a companion."

"He's your dog!" cried Nino. "You can't do without him!"

"I've been training a puppy. And this dog obeys you as well as me. Take it. If they'll let you. I think they will."

"Thank you," said Nino. "No one is so good to me. Come, Canino." He started off, then turned back and embraced the swineherd. He did smell of pigs, but that didn't matter.

Canino followed the boy through the gate and down the path to the narrow street leading to his home. Once or twice the dog hesitated, but it trotted willingly when he talked to it. Giovanni said the secret of dealing with animals was to talk to them as if they were people, for they understood more than you thought.

Part of Casa Torreoni had been restored, but the work wasn't finished, as it had been delayed by the work on the city walls. The shop facing the piazza had been rebuilt. The kitchen had been cleaned and whitewashed, and a new water system installed; there was now a lead pipe from the well, so water didn't have to be carried; this was an innovation only the better houses enjoyed. The hall, or dining room, had been restored to its former beauty.

The upper floors still needed much work; the family slept in the kitchen, the hall, or the deep cellars hewn in the rock.

When he reached the house Nino found the women waiting for him in the kitchen, the first room one entered from the street. They scolded him, though not angrily, for they were sorry to lose him. He stood straight while they washed him and combed his hair, then dressed him in hose of white wool, soft brown leather boots, and a red tunic of leather and wool, pleated at the waist, which filled the room with radiant color. Around his waist they buckled a wide belt made of the same leather as his boots and then placed on his head a soft cap of blue velvet that fell gracefully on one side of his face. He wanted to wear his hunting knife in a scabbard attached to the belt but they said no.

His father and Brother Clemente were seated on stools placed on a balcony running along the south side of the hall, its floor the ceiling of the shop. The two men sat without speaking, intent on the activity of the piazza. Brother Clemente stood when Nino appeared, which was courteous because he didn't have to do so for a boy. Nino fell on one knee, grasped the monk's hand, and kissed it. He kissed his father's hand as well.

"It took a long time for my sister to find me," he said; it was an explanation that was hardly believable, but perhaps acceptable. The monk continued to stand, his hand on the railing.

"It's agreed that you will come to live with us and study for a certain period?"

Nino nodded.

"And you're ready to come?"

"Now?" Nino realized he hadn't taken seriously what his sister had said, that he would be leaving immediately.

"The few things you'll need have been packed," his father said. "Although you look well in your red tunic, you may not wear it — am I correct, *frate*?"

The monk dipped his head. "Nor should you wear such fine hose or such boots," he said gravely. "We wear no shoes, nor will you. In summer you will need only a few shirts of homespun, wool for the winter, and a robe for cold days with a hood you can draw over your head to keep out the wind."

Nino looked down at his finery. He didn't really mind. He was beginning to be excited. He would miss the women in the kitchen, especially Mafalda, and Carlo and Giovanni, and — terribly — Nina. He would even miss his father and Lorenzo, though he saw little of either of them. He would miss what was warm, familiar, and comfortable, but except for Nina he wouldn't miss it too much. And the thought of the new life ahead of him was thrilling.

"I'm ready," he said simply. He knew one duty still had to be done. He knelt again before the monk, who looked at him curiously. *"Frate,"* he asked, "will you be my confessor?"

The monk glanced at Ser Gian. "Brother Anthony will decide, but I believe so. Yes, I think so."

"Then I must tell you, *frate*, I have no vocation for the monastery. I've searched my soul, but I've found nothing."

"Stand up," said Brother Clemente. "This isn't the time or place for a confession, as I'm sure your father agrees. As for God's forgiveness — well, God can forgive anything to a contrite heart. However, you're not coming to us to enter Holy Orders, you're coming to be taught certain sciences and arts without which your life would be the poorer. We can worry about a vocation at a later time, when you're of an age to receive it from the same God who forgives you now."

Nino had expected this answer; even so he was glad to hear it and glad his father had heard it too. He didn't want to enter the convent at the end of the valley under false pretences. At the same time, he didn't want to insist — it wasn't the time for that, either — on what he considered to be the impossibility of his ever having a vocation.

More than once in recent sleepless nights he had tried to discover in himself any faintest sign of a desire for a career in the Church. His brother would inherit the estate and one day be Ser Lorenzo. A younger son might be a churchman. The prospect didn't attract him.

He didn't really want to be a *muratore* when he grew up. Nino knew he was more ambitious than that. But his ambition was unfocused. He truly didn't know what he wanted to be. If he had been the elder brother, he might have been content. But he didn't envy Lorenzo, whom he didn't really like even though he was his brother. The fact that the next few years would be spent at the monastery learning things he couldn't even guess at was far from unpleasing. There would be time to think, to decide.

Nino returned to the kitchen and changed his clothes. The women clustered around him, petting and kissing him; he was their favorite. He clung to them, but soon, remembering he was now a man, he straightened his face and kissed them cooly on their cheeks.

Mafalda, who had nursed both him and Nina, burst into tears. *"Figlio mio, tesoro!"* she cried. The others comforted her; Nino took the opportunity to go to the door. Canino seemed to know what was expected of him; he waited, tail wagging.

Brother Clemente and his father were standing in the street. At a little distance waited Carlo, holding the bridle of a donkey that would carry the boy's possessions. Carlo would spend the night and return in the morning.

Nino approached Brother Clemente, the dog at his heels.

"May I take him with me? I love him and he loves me. He was a gift from a friend."

His father stared at Canino. "Isn't that Giovanni's dog?"

"He gave him to me, Father."

"Ah!" said the man.

Brother Clemente had said nothing.

"The dog doesn't want to be left behind, as you can see, *frate*," Nino said. Indeed, the dog was sitting, his ears cocked, his tail wagging vigorously.

"Brother Anthony doesn't approve of dogs in the convent," said the monk. "Nevertheless, there are many, and cats and birds and other creatures. We shouldn't forget we are Franciscans, and our Little Brother loved all animals. One more won't hurt."

Nino stroked the dog's head.

"Mind you, he mustn't come into church. Brother Anthony is strict about that."

"I'll be careful, *frate*."

They set out, Nino and the monk leading the way, Carlo and the donkey following. At the turning of the street, Nino looked back and was surprised to see his father standing by the door. He waved, and Nino waved back, his heart full.

They reached the monastery well before midnight. A sleepy monk opened the small door; the donkey was just able to squeeze through. "A place will be found for you in the morning," the monk said. "For tonight, you and your man may sleep in the hall or the courtyard, as you please."

They stood in the court, three sides of which were flanked by the convent's walls. On the fourth side a low wall permitted a view of the stream that ran beneath them and of the valley in the distance. The stars were very bright, the silence absolute. Nino had never heard such silence. Carlo and the boy spread blankets and lay down on stone benches by the wall.

Nino had determined not to sleep, instead to lie awake all night and plan his future. But he was asleep in an instant, Canino curled at his feet.

He woke during the night. It was very dark except for the stars, which blazed like torches in the sky. He didn't know what time it was, but then he heard the tiny silver sound of the monastery bell that marked the half hours. It's two hours before dawn, he said to himself.

He thought of home, of Nina, of Cortona. The city wasn't far away; he could almost see it from where he lay. But he couldn't reach it. It would be months before he could go there even if he wanted to.

I forgot to say good-bye to Benno, he remembered. What will he do while I'm gone? Will he envy me my education with the brothers? Do I envy him his freedom? I'm sure I won't envy him, but I think he may envy me. I don't know what Benno wants. The next time I'm in Cortona, at Easter, I'll tell him I'm sorry I didn't bid him farewell. I may even write him a letter in Latin. But of course he would never be able to read it.

Giovanni saw his young master through the Montanina gate, the dog following obediently at his heels, and then returned to Nina, who had remained in the spot where he had left her. When he sat down, she let her head fall on his shoulder and began to cry.

He hadn't seen her cry so hard for years, since she was a baby. "What is this, little mistress?" he asked, holding her.

She cried for a while and then sniffled and wiped her nose with the back of her hand. "I don't know what it is," she said.

"You don't want him to go."

"You're right, I don't want him to go. Yet I do want him to go. And I don't want to go, yet I do. I'm stupid. I don't know what I want."

"You aren't stupid just because you don't know what you want. Master Nino doesn't know what he wants, either. He'd like to be a *muratore*, but at the same time he knows he can't be."

"I'd like to be a *muratore*," said Nina thoughtfully. "I could lay the stones as straight as a man!"

Giovanni thought this was probably true, but he went on. "Master Nino will become a master and a leader of men, as I have told him, even if he doesn't understand that now. But will you ever accept your fate, little mistress?"

"And what's my fate, Sir Wisdom?" she asked, smiling.

"To be a woman and a wife and mother. That's your fate. And you'll do it very well, too, if you accept what you are."

They sat for a long time while Giovanni sang his songs to her, including the new one he had just made up, and they talked of the past and the future, remembering the long days in Castiglione del Lago where they had lived as exiles, and looking forward to the time, only a few months off, when Nino would return for Easter. It began to grow dark, and the church bells rang in the city.

Suddenly Nina saw the watchers preparing to close the Montanina gate. She stood up, frightened. She had never spent a night alone outside the city. "I have to run," she said, but her legs felt weak.

"Don't worry, little mistress," said the swineherd. "Let us sit here awhile longer, in the beauty of the evening, and I'll sing you another song. And when I'm finished I'll show you a great secret if you promise never to tell anyone what it is, as long as you live. In return, I'll promise to get you inside the walls without your having to plead with the soldiers to open the gates again, which they would be loathe to do even for you, my lady Mariana Torreoni."

Mariana was Nina's real name, though only her mother had called her that, and Benno, and sometimes Giovanni.

He held her in his lap, with her head against his shoulder, and sang her another song and then another and another, old ones that she loved. It grew dark, but in the west the Evening Star shone with a terrible brightness, and she crossed herself for she felt there were spirits all around her. And if there were in fact no spirits, there were several great hulking shapes of swine, attracted by the sound of singing or not, who knows? Their bells tinkled as they grazed.

When he was finished singing, Giovanni stood, told the swine to wait for him, and took the girl's hand and led her silently along the base of the wall. He led her a long way around and up, up to the highest curve of the wall, and then down again partway on the other side. No one lived here, for it was exposed to the cold winter winds that swept down over the mountain. Trees grew close to the wall; Giovanni moved among them, searching.

Nina shivered, for she had never been so far around the wall at night. The swineherd gripped her hand and she saw that he held his finger to his lips. Slowly, silently, he crept into the midst of some bushes that huddled around the trunk of one of the trees.

Here it was almost black dark, and the girl was very frightened. Ahead of her she saw an even darker shape; it seemed to be set against a pile of large stones. Giovanni's face, with his white hair, came close to hers and then, suddenly, disappeared. She caught her breath; but his hands, faintly white, reached for her out of the dark shape in front of her. It was a hole in the pile of stones, she realized, and she climbed through, the man holding her so she didn't stumble. They were in a pitch-black space but, strangely, she could still see his hands and face, like ghostly things. She followed, crawling on hands and knees, while he led her down a long passage that turned more than once. When the passage grew wider, he stopped and raised himself to his knees.

He leaned over her, whispering in her ear. "We're inside the wall. We'll rest, and then we'll crawl again." They waited a minute or two and then she followed through another winding passage, led more by the faint sounds he made as he crawled than by anything she could see of him. Finally she felt cool air on her face, and they were out under the stars once more.

Nina started to speak but he quickly placed his hand over her mouth. She looked back. They were within the walls, but she could see, outlined against the sky, the figure of a watchman staring outward, away from them. She followed Giovanni, slowly, silently, until they were hidden by a grove of small trees. He sat down on a stone.

"One of my pigs found it," he said after a while, when her heart had slowed its beating. "I don't know why it's there, but I suppose it was a tunnel the Old Ones could use to escape or reconnoiter during a siege. I don't think anyone else knows it's there; at least I've never heard tell of it, and as long as that's so, it's no danger to the city." He was silent for a moment. "And now you, too, know the secret, little mistress. Will you keep it safe? If you won't, I'll have to tell the soldiers so they can seal it up."

"I swear by the Mother of God and all her angels that I'll never tell a single living soul even if they should tear me on the rack or torture me on the wheel, as they did the holy St. Catherine," said Nina fiercely, crossing herself over and over.

"I believe you," said the swineherd, smiling. He took her hand and led her through the wasteland here within the upper walls. Once the city had been more populous, when the Romans had ruled it and, before that, the Old Ones, who had left their altars in dark cellars and, it was said, laid the enormous heavy stones at the bottom of the city walls. They climbed over ruins and passed through vineyards and orchards that were no longer tended. Soon they reached the stunted vines that marked the edge of cultivation, high up where the winters were fierce and long, and at last they reached a path leading downward to a street. There wasn't a light to be seen anywhere, and they had to pick their way.

When they reached her house, Giovanni told her to say she had been playing among the ruins and become lost. "They won't blame you if they think you were inside the walls." She nodded and gripped his rough hand in her small one. She climbed on the bench that stood outside the portone — the large front door — of her house and scratched on a wooden shutter. "Mafalda," she whispered. "It's me."

The shutter swung open and a woman's head was silhouetted against the faint light of the fire in the kitchen. "In with you," the woman said curtly. "Quick, before they see you." Nina scrambled through the narrow window, like a monkey, not turning back to see if Giovanni was still visible, for she knew he wouldn't be and she didn't want to betray him.

The shutter closed again. Giovanni sighed and retraced his steps, up the hill to the dark tunnel and out again to his swine, patiently waiting, their little bells tinkling under the stars.

Nina wasn't scolded by Mafalda, or only a little, nor did the nurse bother to inform anyone that she had been out so late. Nina didn't seek out her father, either, but remained in the kitchen. The only light came from the fire that smoldered in the big chimney, big enough for two persons to sit in and warm themselves in winter.

"Are you hungry, Mistress?" asked Mafalda. "Will you eat?"

"No, I'm not hungry," said the girl, but when the nurse handed her a small wooden tray on which was a crust of bread and a piece of sweet cake, and a bowl of cool, frothy ale drawn from a stone tub that stood in the corner, she ate and drank as she did every evening, although rarely so late.

"He's gone?" she asked finally. The nurse nodded.

"And would they let him take the dog?" Nina began to cry, but she soon wiped her eyes. She lay down on a mat on one side of the fireplace, with a warm blanket around her. She wanted to go to sleep so she could wake up early the next morning and see Carlo when he returned, and ask him about the journey and if Nino and Canino had arrived safely, but for a long time she couldn't sleep.

She glanced across at the nurse, whose mat lay on the other side of the fireplace. "Mafalda," she whispered so as not to wake her if she were sleeping.

"Yes, Mistress," came the whispered reply. "Why aren't you asleep?"

"Can I talk to you?"

"Of course. Move over so we won't wake the others." Nina pulled her mat so she could lie close to Mafalda. She reached out her hand, seeking the woman's.

"I was thinking about what Giovanni said."

"Well, Mistress?"

"He said my fate was to be a wife and mother." She hesitated. "I know that's what happens to everybody, but it seems impossible for me."

"Impossible?" Mafalda pressed her hand.

"It's not that I want to marry Nino." She shuddered. "That's a wicked thought, and may the Blessed Virgin forgive me. I don't love Nino . . . that way. But I love him anyway. What can I do?"

"You miss him. It's natural, little mistress. Don't worry. You'll feel different later."

"The trouble is, Mafalda, there aren't any other boys who are interesting. Except for Benno, of course." She was silent for a moment. "Nino and Benno are the only ones I like. But I can't marry either of them."

"You're right, Mistress. You can't marry Master Nino, and you can't marry Benno. Even if you really wanted to, which God forbid, your father would never allow it. Now try to go to sleep. Here, I'll put the blanket around us both. Be patient. Someday, maybe soon, the man you want to marry will come. Suddenly he'll be there. It's what happens." She stroked the girl's face, for she felt her trembling.

"I won't marry anyone, then," said Nina softly. "I'll tell Giovanni tomorrow."

4

Benno, Son of Giovanni

While Nino was at the monastery being educated, Benno and Nina became even better friends than they had been before.

Benno was the only person Nina wanted to talk with about her brother and how much she missed him. Benno could understand this, because in a way he missed Nino, too, despite his occasional distrust of him. But sometimes he was jealous although he tried hard not to reveal it. He didn't want bad feelings to come between them.

He admired Nina very much, almost more than Nino did, and for many of the same reasons. She was a girl unlike most other girls. She liked to do the things he liked to do, such as climbing in the mountains to gather blackberries and porcini mushrooms. He showed her the place where he and his father gathered the mushrooms; he had never showed anyone else. She was a good hunter and sometimes went with him when he hunted in the fall and winter. She could be as quiet as a man, and in some ways she was as skillful as most of the men Benno knew.

He enjoyed doing things he thought would please her. She had a passion for flowers, and he planted her a small garden that he tended zealously, supplying her with fresh flowers from May to November. Giovanni had supplied the Torreoni with flowers in the past, so everyone thought it was natural for Benno to do so. She would have preferred to tend her own garden, but she knew Benno liked to do this for her, so she acted as if gardening itself had little interest for her.

Nina and Benno both liked to fish, although she wasn't especially happy when she caught a fish because she would feel sorry for it. They had a favorite pool in the narrow stream that tumbled down from Torreone, and they would go there and sit on the bank, fishing and saying nothing, on bright spring days. In summer the stream dried up and they were unable to fish again until the rains came.

"Where do the fish go when there's no water, Benno?"

"There's always some water, Mistress." Like his father, he was always very polite to her. She would have preferred to have him call her by her name. "They find it, even if the water is underground."

She thought of the fish living underground, hiding from the cold, and she felt even sorrier for them.

Sometimes Giovanni would go with them on their excursions, for Ser Gian trusted Giovanni to take care of her and had no fear even if they were gone for a night or two. The three would climb high onto the mountain above the city and choose a clearing where they could make a fire, cook their meal, and spread blankets on which to sleep. Nina loved these trips into the high country, especially on moonlit nights when they would stay awake talking. She wouldn't have wanted to go alone, for she had heard there were bears and wild boar and even wild men in the forest. Giovanni said he would keep them safe, and Benno thought he could, too.

Once one of her friends, a girl named Rosanna who was the daughter of a wealthy friend of Ser Gian, asked Nina what she could possibly see in a swineherd and his son. "Of course the son isn't bad-looking, even if he has to dress in rags, but the old man must stink of pigs, and I imagine his son does too. Really, Nina, you're always saying you can't come with us because you have a date to go looking for mushrooms or something. I can't imagine anything more boring than poking around in the dirt looking for porcini. I suppose the pigs help out — they're supposed to." She saw the look in Nina's eye, so she added, "I'm sure it's pleasant sometimes to get away from the city, especially in nice weather. But you might ask me to go with you!"

"Benno doesn't have many clothes, but I don't think they look like rags." Nina was determined to hold her temper.

"Benno! Is that his name? That's a peasant name. Maybe it's short for Bernardo. Why don't you call him Bernardo and see if he answers. I'd like to see the look on his face."

"I've always called him Benno, Rosanna. I've known him since I was a little girl. We're friends. Now, this afternoon, I've promised to help him feed the swine because his father isn't feeling well. Believe it or not, I won't be bored."

Conversations like this one, which occurred from time to time with Rosanna and other friends, only made Nina happier that she had a friend like Benno, who never said cruel things about anyone.

One beautiful spring day when Benno was sixteen and Nina thirteen, as they were walking up the steep path from Torreone that led to a mountain house owned by her father, Nina slipped and started to fall, and Benno caught her in his arms. She blushed, embarrassed to have slipped, and he let her go, her slim figure bravely striding ahead of him up the rocky path. It was at this moment that he first realized he loved her. He also realized his love for her hadn't begun then, but that he had always loved her, since she was a little girl and he had played with her and the other children during their exile.

This recognition changed Benno's attitude toward Nina. From that time on he wasn't as easy with her as he had been. She noticed this and wondered if she had done something to offend him. She asked Giovanni, when they were alone, if there was any reason why Benno should like her less than he used to.

Giovanni stared at her, surprised. "I don't think he likes you any less, little mistress," he assured her in his quiet, courteous way. Then he turned away, for he didn't want her to learn the truth from him. "He's no longer a boy, and young men are often moody, and you don't always know what they're thinking," he added, as though that were any kind of explanation.

Nina thought about the fact that Benno was no longer a boy. Yes, he was a man now, but did that mean they could no longer be friends? She shook her head. If I have to live without both Nino and Benno, I will be very sad, she thought.

Once he became conscious of it, Benno's love grew at a frightening rate. He loved everything about her: her sparkling black eyes, her tight black curls, her face, sun-burned more than was normal or decent, the scrapes on her knees, her small breasts, just beginning to show, her hands, toughened by work in the outdoors, her slender hips, her interest in new things, her impatience, her attention to him. But the more love filled his heart, the unhappier he became. For his love, as he knew, could never be expressed. It was impossible.

Nina was the daughter of his and his father's lord. He was the son of a swineherd. He didn't know how to read or write, he possessed nothing, he couldn't look forward to ever possessing more than a small stone house, a calf, some pigs, and perhaps, if he were very lucky, a horse. Nina would be the wife of a lord, and her brothers would be Signori of the city. The chasm between them was so wide and so deep it could never be bridged. And so Benno decided not to love her, so that he might go on living the life he had to lead.

But no one can choose to love or not to love. Benno continued to love Nina, and his love continued to grow. Soon, others guessed. But not Nina, because when he was with her, he tried his best not to let his love show.

Despite his torment, and his need to be away from her, he was nevertheless happy when she suggested to him, after her brother's second Easter visit, that they should learn Latin together from Father Rafaelo, the priest of the church of San

Cristoforo at the top of the city near the Montanina gate. It was Nina's favorite church because it was small and simple, with bare stone walls and a few rough wooden benches. The priest was old and poor and people said he was stupid and knew nothing, but Nina thought that, since he was a priest, he must know Latin. If he knew it, he could teach them without her learning Latin becoming something for her family and friends to talk about.

"Why do you want to learn Latin?" asked Benno.

"Nino speaks Latin to me and refuses to speak Italian. I can't talk to him. He's a bore and I don't love him, but I don't want him to know Latin when I don't."

"I understand that," said Benno gravely, trying not to smile. "But why do you want me to learn Latin, too?"

"So we can speak to one another, and practice, and then when he comes home, we'll surprise him."

"I have much work to do, Mistress, and very little money, but I'll ask my father if I may take the time to study and learn with you, and if we have enough to pay for the lessons. I'd like to learn Latin."

"Father Rafaelo won't charge anything for the lessons, so you don't have to worry about that," she said. She had already spoken to the priest and told him that she would pay his very modest charges for both of them. She asked him to say nothing about this arrangement.

Benno asked Giovanni that evening, believing he would have to withhold permission. But his father seemed pleased he would have the opportunity. He agreed to keep the project secret.

The lessons began immediately. Father Rafaelo was glad to have pupils, which he hardly ever did because no one thought he knew enough of anything to teach it. In fact he knew Latin well; many years before, at the monastery where he had learned it, he had won a prize. It was not stupidity that had held him back in life, but doubt: doubt about his own vocation, and about the meaning of religion in the lives of his few parishioners. After many years this doubt had made him slow and uncertain in his speech. But he had no doubt he could teach Nina Torreoni and her fellow student, who, he was surprised to learn, was a servant in her family.

The two young people were good students, for they both had a passion to learn and they worked hard, Nina incessantly, Benno whenever he could find time. The need to speak together privately, so no one would overhear them and guess their secret, took them to far places together, into the fields and woods, sometimes for other purposes like tending the swine or gathering food, sometimes just for the sake of speaking Latin. These times with Nina, alone and far from the city's eyes, were both paradise and hell for Benno. He ached to tell his love, in Latin if need be, but he did not because it was impossible, and he was afraid if he ever said anything about it, he would never be allowed to see her again.

Father Rafaelo taught them not only to speak but also to read Latin and write it, too. Nina was more adept at this than Benno, because she already knew how to read and write some Italian. Benno was illiterate, and at his age it was hard to learn the complex skills requiring both physical dexterity as well as mental agility. But he struggled and succeeded to some extent. And once he brought something he had written to his father.

Giovanni held the small piece of parchment in his hand. He stared at the letters. "It's well done, my son," he said. And he began to say the words, softly, under his breath. "Our Father who art in heaven, hallowed be thy name . . ."

"You're reading Latin, babbo!" said Benno, astonished.

"Am I?" asked Giovanni. He smiled. "No, I only guessed, because it started *'Pater noster,'* and I knew that from the priest showing me the words written on a stone. I guessed the rest."

"But you said the rest in Latin!"

"I remembered the words. Now let's go up to the high pasture and see if the big white sow has dropped her litter. She was ready." They walked up the path together. Benno didn't cease being puzzled. His father had always said he couldn't read or write. If he could, why would he deny it?

In time Nina and Benno became almost as comfortable in Latin as in their mother tongue. It was during one of their conversations that Nina learned something about Benno she hadn't known before.

They were seated under a tree in a pasture with the swine. Benno reached and picked a leaf off a tiny plant. "This is for headache," he said in Latin, "if you steep it in hot water and then mix the liquid with ashes and place it on your brow."

Nina had learned the uses of many plants from Gianna, Giovanni's wife. "You are your mother's son," she said.

"Ego non sum."

"You're not what?"

"My mother's son. That is, I'm not the son of my father's wife."

"Then who is your mother?" In her astonishment, Nina forgot to speak Latin.

"I don't know," answered Benno, also in Italian. "She died when I was born, and my father has never told me who she was."

"Have you asked him?"

Benno nodded. "He won't tell me. He'll tell me sometime, when I'm older."

"What does that mean?" Nina was intrigued by this mystery.

"I don't know what it means!" Benno told her about his doubts concerning his father's supposed illiteracy. "It's all very puzzling."

"I'll ask my father," said Nina. "He'll know about it."

"Please don't ask him," said Benno seriously. He looked into her eyes. "If my father doesn't want me to know, Mistress, he has a good reason. I'm willing to wait. Will you wait too?"

"I won't ask." Benno was sure he didn't have to make her promise, because when she said she wouldn't do something, she never did it, and when she said she would do something, she always did it. It was another thing he loved about her: she could be trusted with a secret.

Nina seemed to be deeply religious, but she rarely went to church, did not confess or take communion, or do any of the other things a good Catholic girl who cared for her reputation ought to do. She believed in the Virgin and the saints, especially the female ones, and she prayed fervently each morning and evening. She also spent time doing good works, carrying food to the poor and hungry, tending the sick, comforting peasant mothers who always had more to do than any human could. It was almost as though she had a private religion of her own.

Mafalda knew this, but she believed the Master did not. Because she loved Nina and was afraid, not only for her reputation but also for her soul, she spoke to Ser Gian about it.

He agreed that something should be done. Nina's behavior was not only imprudent, it was also against the law, which required all but Jews to attend church and at least act like Christians. And so he spoke to the old priest of San Cristoforo about his daughter because he wasn't her regular priest (a handsome young man with high ambitions who couldn't be trusted in such a delicate matter) and because he had a reputation for being odd himself. Father Rafaelo, because he had promised, didn't tell Ser Gian he was already teaching the girl Latin, but in truth he had become suspicious. He promised her father he would talk to Nina, although he said nothing about his suspicions.

What he feared was that Nina had been seduced by those who worshipped the Devil. Most of the city folk went to church on Sundays and holy days, although many were only marginally Christian. But in the country, the old priest thought, the majority were not Christians at all. They would cross themselves at the mention of the Devil, but there was always doubt whether this gesture was meant as a sign of fealty or abomination.

At the same time, they were deeply religious in another sense, he believed. They were pious and gentle to one another and God-fearing. And their religion was very old, going back many centuries, perhaps even to the time before Lord Jesus had come to save mankind. Father Rafaelo had read a book, secreted in his little house because he knew he shouldn't possess it, and he knew more about the old religion than he would admit, certainly more than he would ever admit to his Bishop in Arezzo.

Piles of stones looking suspiciously like altars were set up alongside many of the rural paths, but the old man knew these had never been shrived by any Christian priest. They were probably places where the old gods, perhaps even the Devil himself, the chief god of the old religion although the Anti-Christ of the new one, were worshipped. Or perhaps they were just piles of stones.

Father Rafaelo had heard tell of orgies taking place around these altars, if they were altars, but he doubted those stories. In his youth he had traveled much in the region, walking here and there in the countryside, asking questions of all he met. He had found no evidence of orgies, whatever that meant. Yet the old priest suspected the country folk worshipped other gods besides his own, and he had seen clear evidence that their worship was sometimes tinged with a kind of ecstasy he didn't find, nowadays, in Christian churches.

In a long lifetime he had decided there was more than one way to worship God, even for Christians. If this wasn't so, then either he or the Torreonis' regular young priest wasn't a Christian, for surely they differed in many ways. And if one of them wasn't a true Christian, the old priest was not at all certain it wasn't the other, rather than he, who strayed from the true path, despite the younger man's very public piety.

As a consequence of these opinions, which of late had troubled him more than ever, Father Rafaelo had said nothing to Bishop Guglielmino about Nina Torreoni, although she was of an important family and would doubtless be of great interest to that august and fearsome personage. But he did want to examine the girl and discover whether she was one of those who, more or less unwittingly, worshiped the Devil. If so, he would try to save her, because he liked her.

Once, quite casually, he asked her to stay after their lesson. He said little at first, wanting instead to let her talk, waiting to find out what she believed.

She tried to explain why she didn't go to church or take communion. She couldn't do the latter, she said, because she didn't confess to any priest. And the reason for this, she said, was that she sincerely believed she wasn't in a state of sin.

"Not to receive Holy Communion is sinful in itself, child," he said to her. But he wasn't severe. He didn't want to challenge her yet; he knew how stubborn she could be.

"I know that, Father, and I'm sorry. I don't make a point of it, like those who go to church and then leave before communion, and therefore I don't go to church at all. I don't want people to judge me without understanding. I confess to the Blessed Virgin my inability to confess to our own priest — I would also be unable to confess to you — and I feel she forgives me. I'm truly penitent, but I don't want to be told to repent by anyone except the Blessed Virgin." Nina stopped. In fact she was more troubled than she wanted to admit.

"You know, child," said Father Rafaelo gently, "the Blessed Virgin cannot shrive you, unless in a manner that would have to be called miraculous — and I think we are not speaking of miracles. Only an ordained priest of the Holy Catholic Church can do that, for it is his office to hear your confession of sins, to decide whether you are truly sorry for them, and then to bless you, giving you God's, and not Our Lady's, blessing. The Church holds, moreover," he added, "and rightly, I believe, that a priest cannot err in this office. His blessing is that of God. You persist in living without that blessing, which is to live in darkness. Aren't you afraid the Devil will find you there, all unprotected by God's grace?"

Nina crossed herself. "God save me," she whispered, lowering her eyes. The old priest stared at her. He was certain she was honest, that the signing was genuine. But he still feared for her.

"I don't want to frighten you," he said after a few moments. "In fact, many good men and women have gone for long periods without confessing to a priest, when circumstances didn't permit. For example, San Benedetto, when he was living alone in the desert, saw no other living person for three years. His food was brought by a kindly monk, who lowered it to him on a rope. During that long time, San Benedetto could not have confessed to any priest."

"The monk attached a little bell to the rope," said Nina eagerly, because she was anxious to show she knew the story, "so when he lowered the food, the saint would come to eat it. One day a demon broke the bell, and a crow had to fly to tell him his dinner was ready, for he was very forgetful and preoccupied."

Father Rafaelo smiled. "I was about to remark that despite his failure — which was not caused by moral weakness but by physical circumstances — San Benedetto didn't confess his sins. For even he sinned, child. He confessed them to God, and God forgave them."

"To God, not the Virgin, you mean, Father?"

He nodded. "He also prayed to Our Lady, for he was a holy man."

"From now on I shall confess my sins to God, if I have any to confess, and pray that He may bless me," said Nina.

The old priest was silent for a while. He was touched by the girl's sincerety. But her response was not what he had hoped — although, as happened often these days, it interested him deeply, because it wasn't what he expected.

"San Benedetto was forced to make his confession directly to God," he explained. "You are not. I want you to consider these things. I don't believe you are in a state of mortal sin, for in fact you have confessed to me today, whether or not you wanted to do so. But your soul is in some danger. Therefore, pray for guidance, child."

"I will," promised Nina. She glanced around his little stone house, which reminded her of the caves the poorest peasants lived in, dark holes dug out of the mountain. She asked him about Rome, where she assumed he had studied. He had never been to Rome, but he told her stories about it anyway, and she didn't mind that they came from books and not firsthand experience. He also told her about His Holiness Pope Gregory X, whom he had never seen. And they shared their intimate knowledge of the saints, telling one another stories both knew and loved.

In the end, he blessed her, that first time and many subsequent times, even if he wasn't completely certain he was right to do so. But he thought God would forgive both her and also him if he was in error. He believed in Nina's faith, no matter how unorthodox it was now, and thought she would be saved eventually — that is, she would find her way back to the Church, from which, he felt, she had never strayed very far.

He feared some terrible accident might happen and that she would die unshrived. If he could reach her, he would bless her, even if another priest might not. But they wouldn't send for him, an old, odd priest of a parish not her own. This was a chance she, and he, would have to take, for he couldn't force her to do what she deeply believed she could not. That would throw her into the Devil's arms.

And so the old man prayed for her, gave her father good reports, and blessed her when she needed to be blessed, crying out for it in her strange, silent way. He comforted himself with the thought that if the rest of his small flock were like Nina, different as she was, his work would be easier to do.

Certain as he was of the essential rightness of her heart and soul, he was not so sure of Benno's. Could it be, he sometimes wondered, that this friend of hers, with his peasant origins, was the source of her odd opinions and dangerous behavior? If so, he ought to do something about it. But because he liked Benno as a person, he felt it was only fair to ask Nina about him before he spoke to anyone else.

"Benno is very pious. He goes to church often and takes communion. He's not like me," she said fervently in response to his queries.

"You are sure of this? He hasn't led you astray?"

She laughed, as though that wouldn't be possible. "He's very solemn and I tease him about it. He tells me not to."

"He's not involved in any . . . activities of the country people? Revels? Covens?"

She grew serious. "Have no fear, Father. He's honest and good. Better than me."

Father Rafaelo didn't mention his suspicions again, but Nina told Benno what he had said.

"God save me!" he cried, crossing himself. "He suspects me, but what have I done?"

"He thinks you've turned me away from the church. I told him it wasn't true."

Benno crossed himself again. "It's because of . . . because I'm a peasant. You remember Tito di Pietro? The young man from San Martino in Bocere? They said things like that about him, that he had corrupted the son of a lord. He denied it, and others vouched for him, but they were peasants too and they didn't believe them. So they tortured him to make him say things that weren't true and then hanged him and cut him down before he was dead and . . ."

She had reached out and touched his lips with her fingertips. "Tell me no more, dear Benno. I remember it. I don't like to think of it."

"I wake in the night sometimes and hear his screams."

She shook her head. "I told Father Rafaelo how devoted you are, how you take communion. I told him you had done me no harm, that you're better than I am. You are, Benno. It's I who have corrupted you, put doubts in your head. Forgive me, friend."

He swallowed. She looked so serious, so beautiful in her concern. He wanted to tell her she could never corrupt him, whatever she did. Instead he lowered his eyes, murmuring that they suspected him because of his low birth, not for anything he had done or said.

"Your birth isn't low," she said, still serious. "High birth or low, a man is what he does. You do good and generous things, for me and your father and my father and many others. Be proud of yourself, Benno, as I'm proud of you!"

He tried, but it was hard to be proud of his meager home, his worn clothing, his lack of learning. I'm not even honest, he said to himself, despite what she says. I'm afraid to confess that I love her, even to my priest. Truly, she is better than me, for her life is not a lie.

5

A Gift for the Virgin

The memory of Saint Francis still burned bright in the minds of many men and women in the towns of Tuscany during those years only three or four decades after the saint's death in 1226, and nowhere was the image of the tiny man whose great soul had inspired all Europe more vivid than at Le Celle. This small monastery, tucked away in a deep ravine a few miles from Cortona, had been a favorite of San Francis, as Nino Torreoni knew, and he had lived there for several months shortly before his death, at the Porziuncula, near Assisi. The monks of Le Celle treasured their recollections of the Master, and they said his voice still echoed among the rocks, as it had done, miraculously, during the saint's sojourn among them. They kept his cell just as it had been on the day he left it, with a candle burning at the head of the narrow stone shelf that had served him for his bed. There he had lain, reading, always reading, and praying, in terrible pain as everyone knew. No one was allowed to enter the little room except the Abbott, and he did so very infrequently, to replace the candle or to make some other minor adjustment. But there was a narrow passage outside the room in which the monks would kneel and say their prayers. Nino spent much time there,

69

for he was fascinated by the great and wonderful man whose life had approached so closely to his own, and changed it, he was sure.

Nothing about St. Francis was so interesting to Nino as the stigmata that, typically, they said, the saint had always tried to conceal. The boy knew the story well, how in the summer of 1224 Francis had gone up into the mountains above Asssi to celebrate the feast of the Assumption of Our Lady, on August 15. He had remained there to prepare for St. Michael's Day, on September 29, by fasting for forty days. He prayed day and night that he might come to know how best to please God. As he prayed one morning, about the time of the Exaltation of the Cross, on September 14, suddenly he beheld a figure coming to him from heaven, descending on rays of light. What happened then had been described by Bonaventura, general of the order, and Franciscans knew his words almost by heart.

"As it stood above him," Bonaventura had written, "he saw that it was a man and yet a Seraph with six wings; his arms were extended and his feet conjoined, and his body was fixed to a cross. Two wings were raised above his head, two were extended as in flight, and two covered the whole body. The face was beautiful beyond all earthly beauty, and it smiled gently upon Francis. Conflicting emotions filled his heart. For although the vision brought great joy, the sight of the suffering and crucified figure stirred him to deepest sorrow. Pondering what this vision might mean, he finally understood that by God's providence he would be made like to the crucified Christ not by a bodily martyrdom but by conformity in mind and heart. Then as the vision disappeared, it left not only a greater ardor of love in the inner man, but no less marvelously marked him outwardly with the stigmata of the Crucified."

As Nino knelt in the narrow passage outside the saint's cell and whispered these words to himself, staring into the room and imagining that the small figure was still lying on his stony bed, Nino often felt his hands and feet begin to tingle, together with a strange, small pain in his chest. Like the saint, he hid this from everyone, not even telling Fra Clemente in confession, although he feared this was a serious fault. As he walked in the courtyard minutes later, he would notice that his hands were still clenched tight, and he would almost be afraid to open them and look. Never was there the slightest sign upon his palms, or upon his feet, or beneath his heart, where the cruel point of the spear had pierced the body of Our Lord. An hour later he would forget the experience, only to undergo it again the next time he knelt on the step and prayed.

Nino believed fervently in the stigmata of St. Francis. He was aware that some of the monks were a little dubious, although officially, of course, they all accepted the sanctification of the Founder that the stigmata signified. Nino believed that it had happened just the way Bonventura had described it, because one of the men who had been present at the saint's death, Fra Elia, had hailed from Cortona. Nino knew several people who had heard Elia preach, and he believed such a man — had he not been chosen by Francis as his successor? — would never lie. What he said he had seen he must have seen; and he said he had seen the wounds in the hands and feet of Francis and in his side, had seen the red blood flowing from the wounds, and he had understood with a terrible vividness the suffering that Francis had undergone as he imitated in his own body the Passion of Our Lord.

His credulity did not stop Nino from asking questions, although he kept these questions to himself. For example, he wondered about the bleeding. According to the story told by Fra Elia, the wounds had bled copiously. But how could a man bleed profusely for years without losing consciousness? Nino asked himself. He had seen animals bleed; they usually died within minutes. He didn't think men were different. Of course the stigmata had been a miracle, but did that really answer the question? If the bleeding was miraculous, then was it real bleeding?

Nino admired St. Francis for having concealed the marks of God's favor; a lesser man must have been tempted to boast of them, he felt sure. But how had Francis been able to hide his wounds? If his feet bled continuously, why weren't his shoes

CHARLES VAN DOREN

always full of blood? And if he went barefoot, why didn't he leave bloody footprints that would call everyone's attention to his condition? Even if the wound in his side only seeped, eventually it would soak his habit and, once again, betray his secret. But no one knew of it until he had lain on his deathbed and his body had been examined by the doctors from Rieti who had tried to cure him of his final illness.

Nino never discovered satisfactory answers to these and other questions, but, strangely enough, the fact never troubled him or disturbed his belief. While still a boy, he supposed that when he grew up he would understand what everyone else seemed to understand. When he became a man, he didn't cease to believe in the story of St. Francis, although he never understood it, and he supposed that this was because the story, and the experience of the saint, was miraculous. He never thought that because he didn't understand it, the story wasn't true. It was as though there were two universes, existing side by side. In one universe, men bled to death. In the other, they could live for years despite bleeding from grievous wounds. And Nino felt comfortable about living in both universes, not just one.

Another of his favorite stories was told by Bonaventura in his life of the saint. At his death, which occurred in the evening, when the light was failing, all of the larks of Assisi flocked to the house where the body of Francis lay and alighted in a great crowd on the roof. This was surprising, because larks prefer the light of day, and it was already becoming quite dark. After having crowded upon the roof for several minutes, the larks flew off and wheeled around the house for a long time, singing songs that were more than ordinarily beautiful. They didn't leave the place until midnight, when they returned to their nests. This miracle delighted Nino as much as the stigmata, although it was equally hard to understand.

Nino's interest in St. Francis pleased Fra Clemente, who was both his confessor and his sponsor within the monastery. It betokened, the friar believed, a growing movement of the boy's soul toward a life of service to God — and of temporal success in the Church, which, Fra Clemente believed, was what his father desired. And so the monk made efforts not only to teach Nino about the great founder of their own order but also about other great monastic founders, like St. Benedict and St. Bernard of Clairvaux. However, to his distress, it became evident that his pupil had no talent for theology or even for Church history.

Nino liked St. Benedict very much because he was a builder of monasteries and was excellent at laying stones, and at inducing others to lay stones. Nino would lie awake at night imagining the construction of the enormous abbey at Cassino, which Fra Clemente said was very beautiful. He especially liked the stories of how St. Benedict aided the builders. Many times, as St. Gregory told the story, the builders would find that such and such a stone was too large and heavy for them to lift, and they would plan to cut it into smaller pieces. But when St. Benedict would bless the stone, then they could lift it, and they would realize that it was not the stone itself that was heavy, but the Devil who made it heavy.

Fra Clemente would lecture to Nino about the famous Rule of St. Benedict, which still, after seven hundred years, laid down the law to most monks and nuns in most monasteries and convents throughout Europe. But Nino was seldom able to remember the main points of the Rule, although he knew he should do so and prayed for help and guidance.

The details of St. Bernard's battles with Abelard and others during his stormy career were also of little interest to Nino, much to Fra Clemente's disappointment. But the boy nevertheless was fascinated by St. Bernard, which pleased his teacher, even though he wasn't sure the reasons were the right ones. Bernard's asceticism especially intrigued Nino, and he tried to emulate it. The story, for example, of how he slept in a narrow cell hewn out of the rock at Clairvaux in which, in winter, the water rose to a depth of several inches, for the floor of the cell was below the level of the river that flowed past the monastery. Nino brought cups and bowls of water into his own cell, on cold nights in January, and stood barefoot in the water he had spilled on the floor to see how it felt. When his feet were almost frozen, he would jump into his little bed and lie curled up in a knot, although he realized St. Bernard would never have been so weak as to feel the cold. And he would stay awake as long as he could in the hope that the Virgin would appear to him, as she had appeared to St. Bernard.

It was his great love of Our Lady that made Nino feel close to St. Bernard, for he, too, was passionately devoted to the Mother of God, even more, as Fra Clemente sometimes feared, than to Her Son. The name of the Virgin was seldom absent from Nino's lips during his years in the monastery, and he spent at least an hour every day on his knees before the tiny image of Mary in the dark niche at the corner of the small monastic church. He would say ten or twenty Hail Marys — if he had not been very good — but then his mind would wander. He would try to imagine Bethlehem and would wonder if the ox and the ass that had been present at the birth of Jesus had been special beasts that could understand language, or had been brought to the manger by the sheer and miraculous power of God. He supposed that the latter was the case, but he never lost his deep affection for these two famous animals nor did he cease to suspect that they actually knew more than they seemed to. He also liked the donkey that carried Mary and Her Son on the flight into Egypt. How did that donkey feel with God upon its back? Was God heavier or lighter than other burdens? It was a disappointment to the boy that Fra Clemente seemed uninterested in such questions, just as it troubled the monk that his pupil desired answers to them — answers that, after all, could be no more than vain and perhaps even blasphemous speculation.

If he was no theologian, Nino was at least a linguist, as Fra Clemente soon discovered. The boy took to Latin and could soon converse in it almost as well as he did in the local dialect that was his mother tongue.

Nino was less talented when it came to reading and writing. Writing, in particular, in both Latin and Italian, seemed for a long time to be quite beyond his abilities. His fingers, so skillful at notching an arrow or laying a snare or skewering a wriggling worm on a hook, became awkward and stiff when it came time to make letters. During the five years he spent at the monastery, Nino never advanced beyond the first lessons in writing, although when he left he could form letters fairly well and could read his breviary well enough to satisfy the Abbott, who examined him once a year. But he could chatter on in Latin as though it was his own language, and indeed it became the source of much satisfaction for him, because he could speak Latin to all the monks, whereas many of them were unable to speak or understand his native Italian.

Once, when he went home at Easter, he spoke only Latin to Nina, never relenting when she begged him to speak Italian so they could share secrets. He kept his tongue tied even though she beat him with her fists as hard as she could and until it hurt. The next year he was surprised to discover that his sister understood him when he spoke Latin to her, and could speak to him in Latin in return; very well, he had to admit. He asked her who had taught her, but she wouldn't tell him despite threats of dire tortures.

Fra Clemente himself lacked computational skills, and he turned over this branch of Nino's education to Fra Ugo, a small fat monk from the Kingdom of Naples who did not speak any Italian at all that Nino could understand but who was adept at teaching boys how to use their abacus. *Abaco*, in fact, was the name of the upper level of primary school, which boys entered when they were ten or eleven and where they spent two to four years. Nino joined a class that was already in progress, his abacus held awkwardly in his hand. But he soon caught up with his classmates, for he enjoyed solving the intricate, difficult problems posed by the big monk.

Every major city in Europe, as Nino knew from overhearing his father speak of it, not only had its own currency but also its own system of weights and measures, and this made conversion of commercial quantities fiendishly difficult. A barrel of Rhenish wine, for instance, was not the same as a barrel of wine made in Tuscany, and indeed the cubic volume of a barrel varied between one Tuscan city and another. A *braccio,* or "arm," of cloth also varied from one city to another, as did weights of grain and silver and stone. As a result of this enormous and perpetual confusion of units, weights, measures, and equivalents, a successful merchant had to be able to calculate both quickly and accurately the amount of whatever he wanted to buy or sell.

At first the boys were taught to solve such problems using their abacus. Later they learned to solve them, or at least arrive at very close approximations, in their heads, since a merchant could always be taken advantage of if he was too dependent on his calculating machine, for he might not have it with him at the crucial moment.

The boys were also taught various devices for recording sales and purchases and for keeping accounts. This was fiendishly difficult, always remembering that you might be dealing in two or more currencies, the value of each of which might change from day to day. Fra Ugo tested the boys to see if they could solve such problems without revealing any signs of stress, which could be pounced on by an opponent.

Nino became adept at gauging and keeping accounts. As the son of a very successful merchant, he had often heard and seen problems solved that were even harder than Fra Ugo's. He wanted to please his father, who tested him whenever he came home.

Even so, Nino wasn't sure he wanted to follow in his father's footsteps, a fact that troubled him as time went on.

Nino had two good friends who helped him endure the long, cold, and lonely years at the monastery. One was a man, the other a woman.

A young monk, Fra Lorenzo, had been chosen by the brothers to supply meat for the *misericordia.* According to the Rule, the monks could eat no meat, not just during Lent but throughout the year. However, even the strictest monastery had its *misericordia,* a small room next to the larger hall where most of the monks dined in silence. Monks who for one reason or another had a special need for meat dined in the *misericordia,* and since there were many such needs, the *misericordia* was never empty.

Fra Lorenzo worked hard to supply the brothers with meat, but he faced a major obstacle. Again according to the Rule, no monk could practice venery, the signal vice of the nobility — that is, they couldn't hunt. From time to time Fra Lorenzo did hunt rabbits and pheasants in the woods, but he feared that if he were caught, he would be punished. He was therefore happy to find that Nino was a skilled hunter. Nino, not being a monk, could hunt with impunity, and he soon found himself on frequent expeditions on behalf of his friend.

With the help of Canino, Nino caught and killed rabbits, squirrels, ducks, pheasants, and pigeons, and managed to keep the *misericordia* reasonably supplied year-round. He much preferred to hunt his favorite game, deer and wild boar; unfortunately, huntsmen of the local lords, including Conte Pietro, often invaded the monastery's woods, killing most of the deer and making them hard to find. When Nino pointed out that this was illegal, Fra Lorenzo shrugged his shoulders. "What can we do?" he said.

Wild boar was dangerous game. Occasionally Nino would sight one in the woods, rooting up food from the soft turf with its great tusks. For a long time he was afraid to shoot at one of these ferocious beasts, for fear that he would only wound it and then in its fury, it would attack him and perhaps maim or kill him. He practiced with his bow and sharpened his steel-pointed arrows, as Giovanni had taught him, shooting at targets as well as smaller animals. Finally, when he was nearly fifteen, he determined to hunt one of the wild boars that lived in the forest nearby.

"Fra Lorenzo," he said to his friend, "I have great need of your help. I don't ask you to hunt with me; I only ask you go with me to help bear the beast back to the monastery, if I succeed, and to carry me back if I don't. I would not wish to die alone in the forest."

"I may do as you wish," said the monk, "although I think it will be the first thing that I do and not the second." He was confident in Nino's hunting prowess.

They set off before dawn on a cool October morning. Canino seemed aware that something serious was afoot, for he followed them silently, as in fact Nino had spent many weeks training him to do. They arrived at a place where there were many acorns. Soon a boar appeared. It snorted and turned its head back and forth, sniffing, but it apparently did not detect them, for it began to devour the acorns that covered the earth around it. Nino crept into position, only a few yards in front of the beast. He notched his longest, heaviest arrow and drew the bow as far as it would go. The arrow sang across the clearing and pierced the animal just behind its left foreleg, as Giovanni had taught him. The beast staggered, then raised its great head and screamed. Nino's blood ran cold. The boar lowered its head and began to charge toward him, its heavy shoulders humping as it quickened its pace.

Nino notched another arrow. He had imagined this and had determined that he would not turn and run, whatever happened. He waited until the boar was within ten feet of him and then let fly once more. The arrow thudded into the animal's chest, stopping it dead. It stood still, then moved slowly forward. Nino shot another arrow, which pierced the beast's eye, entering its brain. The animal fell forward, gasping out its life.

Nino let out a great cry. He threw his arms into the air and rushed forward, drawing his knife as he ran. He knelt by the big animal and sank his knife to the hilt in its neck. Blood spurted upward, spraying the boy with its hot stickiness. The dog howled in triumph.

"Frate!" shouted Nino. "I've done it!"

The monk answered him, his voice filtering down through the branches of a tree. Evidently he had not been totally confident in Nino's abilities. He slithered down the trunk. "I was seeking acorns," he said. "Just in case we might not be eating meat tonight."

"I killed it!" said Nino. "It charged and I stood my ground." The monk nodded. Nino felt a wild joy. "Did you see how it slavered at the mouth, how it grunted as it charged? It would have killed me if I ran!"

"Yes, you were very brave, my young friend. I will never forget it, and I'll tell the other monks."

"No," said Nino, "don't tell them. They won't understand it." And he set to work to dismember the beast, which was too heavy for them to carry all in one piece. He slit the animal's stomach from its penis to its throat, cleaned it, cut off the head and feet, and finally severed the large sac of testicle that hung slackly, now, between the hind legs.

"These are for me!" He tied the sac at the end, his hands slippery with blood, and swung it around his head. "Beware, O boars of the forest, I will kill you all," he shouted. He was astonished at the blood lust that surged within him.

He buried the offal and feet of the boar, and then, in a final act of defiant boastfulness, thrust a stick up through the neck of the animal and fixed the other end of the stick in the ground. The one remaining fierce eye of the beast stared out at him, and its tusks glistened. Nino dipped his finger in a pool of blood that lay near the carcass and wrote an inscription on a piece of bark. "Ser Cinghiale," it said. He helped Fra Lorenzo shoulder his heavy load, then shouldered his own.

They reached the monastery before dark, and that evening the *misericordia* rang with praises of the young boar-slayer — every monk, as it turned out, needed meat that day. They even toasted Canino in the fresh new wine, although the Abbott looked uncomfortable.

Maria, Nino's woman friend, worked in the monastery kitchen. She taught him another kind of blood lust.

He had at first been surprised to find, after all, that there were women in the monastery. In fact, there were many. Quite a few more or less lived with their monk, as if they were wives. Only recently had celibacy become the Church's rule, and it still wasn't observed everywhere.

Maria was a large, cheerful woman who had had at least one husband and several children — more, she said, than she remembered the names of. She was in charge of the enormous soup pot, and Nino liked to sit by the fire (which as a lay member of the community he was allowed to do) and watch her stir it. At first she treated him like a child but then, as he grew tall and strong, she began to tease him. She was well aware of the effect her teasing had on him.

Servant women wore long skirts of heavy homespun, homespun shifts, and a kerchief around their necks that covered their bosom. When the fire was hot, Maria would remove her kerchief and wipe her brow with it; when she did so, her large, heavy breasts would almost spill out of her dress. Nino would stare, transfixed. At these times Maria would approach him and lean down to whisper something in his ear, whereupon he would smell her strong womanly scent.

And she would smile at him, revealing her crooked teeth, and then slap his face. "*Ragazzacio!*" she would say. "Look how this big boy stares at me," she would shout to the other women. "As if I were made different from other females." Nino would blush and, to comfort him, she would seize his face and press it against her bosom.

In summer Maria would sit with her thick legs apart, a bowl of vegetables in her lap, her heavy skirt creeping up her thighs. "Sit!" she would say to Nino, and he would sit near her, trying not to stare at her. But she was clever and would manage to arrange herself so he could see between her legs and no one else could. He was fascinated by the dark shadow that lay at the juncture of her thighs, and again he would be stirred. Maria, noticing, would lean forward, her hand on his thigh, close enough to torture him.

"*Ti piace Maria, magari?*" she would ask, her breath smelling of onions and wine, her teeth gaping. He would nod, unable to speak.

Not long after his triumphal conquest of the boar, which everyone said was one of the largest that had been seen in the region, in the fall of the year, after the harvest and the making of the new wine, when the days were growing shorter and the nights colder, he found himself in the kitchen at a later hour than usual. And Maria was there. He sat by her as she knelt to tend the fire, which blazed then soon died down again. She turned toward him, and he became suddenly aware that she wore no kerchief, and that her breasts were bare. He reached to embrace her, and she melted into his arms. *"Ragazzacio,"* she whispered, as her hand found its way into his clothing. Dizzy with desire, he was unaware of how she undressed him and herself, but he knew he was marvelously housed. Afterward they lay by the fire for a long time, relishing one another's warmth.

It wasn't long before everyone knew what was happening in the kitchen on cold winter nights, and Nino was called to the Abbot's cell.

Brother Anthony was a tall man, miraculously thin, with a cragged, severe face. Nino was afraid of him.

"You wanted to see me, my lord?" he said, trembling because he was suddenly aware why he was there.

"I wanted to see you, yes, and to talk to you, Nino Torreoni. You are making a fool of yourself, and your father would not be pleased if he knew."

Nino hung his head.

"You have been devoted to Our Lady, the brothers tell me," said the Abbot. "But recently you have not been spending your daily vigil in Her company. Why is that?"

Nino continued to look down. He couldn't speak.

"Is it because you believe She would disapprove of your actions? I think that is so; that is, I believe you think so, and also that She would disapprove. Or does. So what shall we do?"

"I have indeed been a fool," whispered Nino. "I have given up Our Lady for another woman, who is not Her equal."

"I should say not." The Abbot was more than a little shocked by the implied comparison, but then he realized that this big boy, now almost a man, loved Maria, the lusty keeper of the soup pot. And his voice grew gentler.

"Maria is a fine woman who has been with us for years. She likes young men and has seduced others before you. Do not be angry; she would tell you if you asked. But I still want to know what we should do."

Nino thought hard. Finally he said, "I must leave the monastery."

"Yes," the Abbot replied, "you must leave. I am glad you have come to see this yourself, without my having to tell you. For one thing, you have learned most of what we can teach you. For another, Maria, they say, is hard to resist." And he smiled a tight little smile that showed strangely on his thin face.

"But before you leave," he continued, "you must make your peace with the Mother of God, who will doubtless wish to punish you, although she will also doubtless forgive you if you are truly penitent and contrite. I sentence you, Nino Torreoni, to a week of solitary confinement in the crypt below the church. You will be given food and a candle, for the darkness there is total when the doors are all shut. There is a small shrine of the Virgin; you will talk to it, and discuss the state of your soul, and the degree of your penitence. And when you come forth from that place, you will go home."

"Yes, my lord," said Nino, kneeling.

"And with our blessing," said the Abbot.

It was the longest week of Nino's life, so far. The crypt was never silent, for he could hear the shuffling of the bare feet of the monks as they walked in the choir above his head, and at night there was the constant rustling of the rats within the walls. He kept the candle burning and knelt for hours at a time before the tiny shrine. And in the end the Virgin, in Her infinite pity and patience with human weakness, forgave him.

Before he left he wished to give her a present. But what should it be? He searched through the sack in which he had brought his few possessions. His fingers fell on the small bag containing the boar's scrotum. He had wanted to take it home to show it to Nina, for was it not his proudest possession? And because it was, he gave it to Our Lady, placing it carefully before the shrine, covering it with stones so the rats wouldn't disturb it. "Hail Mary, full of grace," he whispered. "Accept this gift, small and poor as it is, for I would give You all that I have, or the best of it, if it would please You."

He didn't tell anyone he had done this for many years, and even then he only told the Countess. When he did so, she looked at him strangely for a long time, and then she grasped his hand and kissed it passionately.

"Mauvais garcon!" she whispered.

6

Robert and Caterina

Carlo was there with his donkey on the morning when Nino was to return home, so he knew word of his disgrace had preceded him. Fra Clemente wanted to accompany him on the homeward journey.

They walked in silence for a long time, Carlo leading the way with the laden donkey while Nino and the friar fell behind. Then the friar said, "The Abbot asked me about your vocation. I told him you had none."

"I'm sorry. I said many prayers and asked God to help me."

"That is not true," said Fra Clemente. But he didn't sound severe.

"Perhaps not," Nino conceded. "I still don't know what I want to be, but I do know I can't be a monk."

"Because of Maria?"

Nino colored. He turned to face his companion. "No," he said finally. "Not Maria. It's because of the wild boar, and the birds, and all the servants, men and women. I have to take care of them. I can't explain it."

"Perhaps you were born to be a master of men. Perhaps the estate should be shared between you and your brother."

"The estate is my brother's," said Nino simply. "Father wants it to be so, and I don't think he's wrong. My brother enjoys working with my father, but I don't. If I'm ever to have an estate, I'll have to find it for myself."

"Men don't just find estates," said the monk, in Latin for emphasis.

"I hunted the boar," replied Nino, also in Latin, "and killed it and dressed it, and carried it to the monastery, by myself."

"With the help of Fra Lorenzo and the dog." This in the vernacular.

"Yes. But no man can accomplish anything entirely by himself." He whistled, because Canino had lagged behind, investigating a hole. The dog ran up, his tail wagging.

"Despite everything," said the monk after a while, "you'll be missed. It's apparent that you don't belong in a monastery, but I'll be sorry to return without you."

Nino was touched as well as surprised. "I'll come visit, and bring something for the *misericordia,*" he said, laughing at the thought of the freedom he would enjoy for the rest of his life.

If Nino expected to have little to do now he was back home, his father quickly disabused him. On a warm day in May when they were at Torreone reviewing the ongoing work on the castellino, Ser Gian told him he had asked a relative of his mother's, a Frenchman, to come and teach Nino how to be a gentleman.

"I'm making this arrangement for your sake. You need a challenge." Ser Gian hesitated before using the word, almost as though, Nino thought, someone else had suggested it. "Squire Robert will take of that . . ."

"Squire Robert? I don't know him."

"You do not. He was your mother's cousin, but you've never met him. He is expert in the arts of attack and defense, and he'll also teach you French, for you'll need to know it when we go together to the fairs at Troyes. All the languages are spoken there; the more you know, the better."

Nino looked forward to these studies, especially those having to do with the practice of arms.

"You don't ask, so I'll tell you. We'll leave quite soon for Troyes, where Robert will meet us. You'll be ready?" He paused. "I have something else to tell you."

His tone was serious, and Nino glanced at him apprehensively. "Don't be concerned." Ser Gian smiled. "I think you'll consider it good news. I'm giving you the castellino."

Nino was astonished.

"You don't want it?" His father continued to smile.

"Oh, I do! But I always thought Lorenzo would have it."

"He'll inherit the major portion, part when he marries, the rest when I die. But you must have something. I thought . . ."

"Thank you, Father," Nino said. His heart was singing.

"You don't have to thank me." Ser Gian stood, then walked across the courtyard, his back to his son. "We can think of all kinds of things to make your castle better, more livable," he said after a moment. But Nino had seen tears in his eyes.

When Benno returned that evening, he told his father about the gift. "Nino told Nina, and she told me. She was very excited for him."

"It's small as castles go," said Giovanni after a long pause.

"Yet it's a castle. I remember how we used to play there when we were little children, Nino and Nina and I."

Giovanni looked at him. He paused again. "If I had a hundred castles," he said, "I'd give them all to you."

"I know that, babbo," Benno said. And he went to help Gianna with their supper.

The Hot Fair of Champagne was held at Troyes each July and August, the Cold Fair in November and December. The summer fair was the most important of the year in all of Europe, attracting thousands of merchants and their clients from all over the world. Since his wife's death, Ser Gian had gone every year to both fairs.

His business had changed. He was no longer primarily a trader in cloth, but a dealer in money. Thus he set out with only a pair of horses, neither heavily laden. He and Nino picked up a bundle of scarlet silk — very valuable but not very heavy — at Lucca and continued along the main road to Pisa, where they had reserved space on a vessel sailing to Genoa and Marseille. They embarked on June twenty-first, reaching Genoa in three days and Marseille a week later. Their journey up the valley of the Rhone, from Lyon to Charmont and west to Troyes, became more and more a traveling gala as they approached the site of the fair. They were joined by dozens and then hundreds of travelers, each with his burden of goods to sell, his bags of money if he wished to buy, and his hopes and dreams. They arrived on July tenth, in time to register for the fair, which began on the fourteenth.

Nino was fascinated by the swarm of humanity, which was greater — or at least more frantic — than he had ever seen. There were hundreds of merchants and moneylenders, the "big" businessmen of the fair. But there were also thousands of visitors, from great lords and ladies and magnificently attired Churchmen, to country knights, their rusty armor refurbished for the occasion, to peasants who came either to sell or to buy a pair of chickens or a handful of peppercorns. Dancers, acrobats, jugglers, bears, and monkeys performed at street corners, and jongleurs sang on the church steps. And everywhere prostitutes, whether professionals from Paris or amateurs from the country round about — serving girls, tradeswomen, farmers' daughters — struck their own bargains. At the height of the fair the streets were even illuminated at night by flaring torches, which surprised Nino more than anything else. He liked to walk up and down in the dark that wasn't dark, and see the world from such a novel point of view.

Ser Gian set up his bench, or *banca*, in the area of the money changers, of whom he was one of a select few: there were by law only twenty-eight, a third of them Jews, most of the rest Lombards, as they were called, that is, Italians from Milan, Genoa, Florence, and a few other cities. Ser Gian was the only Cortonese, but he knew most of the others well, especially the Sienese, and with a few he had formed valuable friendships.

He himself had first come to Troyes with his father to sell dyed cloth, especially the beautiful red wool produced by the Florentine Arte di Calimale, for which his father had been one of the "foreign" dealers. For years he returned with cloth and other goods, which he sold in order to buy undyed cloth, which he sent back to Florence to be processed. As the years passed, however, great changes occurred in the way business was done at the Champagne fairs. Fewer and fewer merchants came with merchandise or money; instead, they brought promises, either oral or in writing, both to buy and to sell. The cloth of a reputable house didn't have to be seen; its quality could be counted on, and besides, it was guaranteed. The merchandise for which it was to be exchanged might already have been delivered to another place, such as Paris, where it could be consumed or processed further for still another use elsewhere.

Ser Gian discovered that his skill lay not in actual buying and selling but instead in helping others to do so. He therefore began to serve as a go-between, drawing up documents, figuring the percentages and profits, and pocketing his own profit for his services while others took the greater risks. His profit might be small on any transaction, but the total usually added up to a great deal during the six weeks of the Hot Fair and the four weeks of the Cold. As a result, he was becoming richer still.

With the money he gained, he was buying land or paying off old mortgages on land brought by his wife in her dowry. This was in spite of frequent remarks to Nino that land wasn't a good investment. In fact, over the years he had become unable to speak his mind to almost anyone, including his much-loved son.

Most of the merchants and visitors lived in makeshift ar-rangements, either sleeping on bedrolls in the cathedral, which remained open all night to accommodate them, or in tents erected in the surrounding fields, or in flea-infested huts and inns that, in the opinion of many, were worse than the open air. The more affluent regulars had their own apartments, which they rented the year round. Ser Gian's was in the home of an attractive widow, who adopted the son as she had earlier adopted the father. With this difference: She didn't take the young man to her bed. Nino was a little shocked when he first realized his father never slept alone while at Troyes, but he soon grew used to the idea, which his father never thought it worth the trouble to mention to him.

Nino went every morning to his father's *banca,* watching as he conducted his complex deals, calculating sums in his head or occasionally on his abacus, drawing up contracts, and conducting his clients to the Keeper of the Fair to have their signatures witnessed and a fair seal attached to the documents. Sometimes Ser Gian spent a morning changing money, which interested Nino because he liked to see all the different silver pennies, each having its own value (although the standard coin of the fair was the *denier de Provins*). Rates of exchange were posted, but the art of money changing consisted not in changing it at the standard rates but in making deals that depended on the source and dependability of one currency as compared to another and on the amount exchanged. Once a Cortonese merchant Nino knew came to exchange a large number of Cortonese and Florentine coins into deniers de Provins, and Ser Gian didn't give him an especially good rate despite the large amount. Nino asked him why.

"The Florentine money is better than ours," said his father, without a trace of sentiment about the coinage of his own city. "If all his coins had been Florentine, I would have given him a better exchange. He knew this as well as I did. Cortona is beautiful and I'm glad to live there, but I have no affection for its money."

One of the odd pieces of land in Ser Gian's wife's dowry was a debt-laden farm in the Isle de France, at Chermont, north of Paris. The land was good and supported a flourishing manufacture of cheese, but the burden of interest on the various debts, many of them undertaken in emergencies, made the farm unprofitable. Ser Gian had paid off most of these debts, leaving a few at affordable terms. The family that lived on the farm and administered the trade in cheese was therefore grateful to the wily Italian. The couple had two brothers, the younger of whom was Robert.

Robert arrived at Troyes late in August, ready to accompany Nino and his father back to Cortona. He was tall and slim with a languid expression on his thin, intelligent face that Nino liked as soon as he saw him. Yet his shoulders were broad, his body well knit. He was finely dressed, which Nino noticed at once; his own clothes were drab by comparison. A servant leading a donkey from his horse had come with Robert from Provins, forty miles from Troyes, bearing his possessions, which included a hauberk of chain mail, a helmet of burnished steel, and an assortment of weapons. His baggage also included a small box of books that Robert explained were of great value, especially to him — the last when he saw the look on Ser Gian's face. Squire Robert was five years older than Nino, five inches taller, and vastly more experienced in the ways of the world. It didn't take five minutes for his pupil to become devoted to him. It took Robert longer to recognize the talents and virtues of the younger man.

As Ser Gian expected, Robert began by teaching Nino French. Nino already knew a little, for he had learned what he could while at Troyes. But Robert said his accent was barbaric and he had to start all over again.

Nino wasn't averse, because he liked languages. But he was amused at what he considered Robert's typically French perfectionism. Robert, seeing this, gave him a severe lecture. Anything worth doing at all, he declared, was worth doing well. From that time on Nino concealed his amusement, but he never came to accept Robert's view of things, which was that anything you did well was worth doing. Sometimes he thought this was a basic difference between Frenchmen and Italians. Other times he thought it was just the difference between Robert and himself.

Nino liked French but he didn't respect it. French seemed to him rather soft and delicate as compared to the masculine roughness of Italian. He preferred talking to women in French, to soldiers in Italian. Of course neither possessed the majesty of Latin. It was appropriate, Nino believed, that Latin was the language in which you spoke to God, and he believed it should also be the language of kings. In later years he met a king and addressed him in Latin, but the king responded in French, with a puzzled look. This was a disappointment.

Robert also taught Nino, by precept as well as example, to dress in the modern fashion. Heretofore Nino had paid scant attention to his clothes, wearing whatever was available or the women of the household put on him. Robert showed him how to choose fine fabrics and found him a tailor in Arezzo, no tailor in Cortona being sufficiently skilled, he declared. The Frenchman tried to persuade Nino to wear the narrow shoes with long pointed toes that curled up and were attached by a thong to a band around the calf, just under the knee. These shoes were the rage in Florence, but Nino refused to wear them. Fashion was all very well, but it shouldn't give way to comfort; more important, it shouldn't give way to safety. The long pointed toes were a hazard — what if you had to run from a boar, for instance?

The new clothes weren't cheap, and Ser Gian complained. He wasn't really displeased; fathers ought to complain about such things as a matter of principle. Robert's morning lessons went beyond French and the art of dressing in the current fashion. He felt that Nino, no matter how skilled he might be at arms or how generous in temperament or how handsome, was deficient in the arts of social intercourse, or *cortesia*. These arts were not much practiced at Cortona, which, although thriving and prosperous, was still a provincial city where everyone knew everyone else and there was nothing remotely resembling a court. Robert believed Nino would sooner or later move in a larger world where *cortesia* would be important, and he drilled the boy incessantly in the social graces.

These included lessons in the rules of *honesti amandi*, or courtly love, according to the French master Andreas Chapelain, whose book was the bible of courtly lovers on both sides of the Alps. Andreas Capellanus, as Italians called him, had established how a man of this class or that should make love to a women of the same class or of one that was higher or lower. The rules were complex and for the most part seemed foolish to Nino, but to please his teacher, he tried to learn how to speak to a woman of the highest class as a man should who was a member of the nobility but not of the highest nobility, and so forth and so on.

Especially interesting to Nino were Andreas's remarks about the way a noble should address his love to a woman of the peasant class. "If you should, by some chance, fall in love with one of their women," Andreas wrote, "be careful to puff her up with lots of praise and then, when you find a convenient place, do not hesitate to take what you seek and embrace her by force. For you can hardly soften . . ."

"Andreas says that?" interrupted Nino as Robert read the well-known passage from *The Art of Courtly Love*, which he had carried all the way from Chermont.

"Says what?"

"You should take them by force."

"Of course he says that, and more. Listen. 'For you can hardly soften her outward inflexibility so far that she will grant you her embraces quietly or permit you to have the solaces you desire unless you first use a little compulsion as a convenient cure for her shyness.'"

"This applies only to peasant women?" asked Nino.

"Certainly. You must never use force with a woman of the upper class. She'll have nothing to do with you," said Robert, closing the book with a snap.

"I don't think Andreas knows much about peasant women," said Nino thoughtfully. "They're usually not very shy. It's gentlewomen who are shy, I think."

"On the contrary, *caro amico*. Gentlewomen have read the book so they know how to behave when a man addresses his love to them."

"And how is that?"

"Why, they should yield, at least if they've been addressed in the proper way. It's the role of a woman to yield and of a man to press his suit."

"Ah," said Nino.

Most of Robert's lessons were in the arts of defense. Nino threw himself into these with the passion that marked everything he really liked to do.

Robert proposed to teach him three things: to fight with a dagger, to fight with a sword, and to spar and defend himself with a quarterstaff. The first two weapons could be used in tandem, the dagger in one hand, the sword in the other; if the sword were lost or broken, the dagger could be brought into play.

As usual, the lessons began with precepts. Robert sat Nino down in the courtyard of the castellino and said to him, very seriously, "I want you to understand one thing, *mio caro,* before we start. And if you do not understand, or do not agree, we will not start. A man who wears a sword must know how to use it."

Nino laughed. Robert's portentous pronouncements always seemed funny at first. "Why would anyone wear a sword if he didn't know how to use it?" he asked.

Robert's face darkened. "You don't know the vanity of men," he said without smiling, for he didn't like to be laughed at. "I will say it another way and then perhaps you won't laugh. A sword is a challenge, like a woman's low-cut bodice. Sooner or later someone will accept the challenge. Both a man and a woman had better be ready and prepared to respond."

Nino considered this. "I think it's true."

"It's why I won't permit you to wear a sword until I'm sure you are capable of defending yourself against the likely response to your challenge in wearing a sword. Do you understand?"

Nino nodded. As usual he was sorry he had laughed.

Robert searched the city for an armorer who would satisfy his high standards, but as with the tailors he found none. So he and Nino rode to Arezzo and stayed for a week. With money provided by Ser Gian — a great deal of money, as Nino came to realize — they bought two swords, a dagger, a hauberk of shining chain mail reaching almost to the knee, and a helmet like Robert's, with a fringe of chain mail hanging down over the shoulders. To wear under the armor they purchased tunics of padded leather and leather hose with padding at the knees and other vulnerable points.

Nino was pleased but also a little disappointed. "I'd like to have a real suit of armor," he said.

"Chain mail is real armor," replied Robert, "and in many ways it's superior. For one thing, it's more flexible and you can move more easily. For another, it's cooler in summer and not so deathly cold in winter as plate armor. Besides, do you know how much a suit of plate armor would cost?"

Nino shook his head. "I guess a lot."

"A great deal — as much as our farm in France, the land, the house, the vineyards, for example. It's an investment for life and I don't think your father is prepared to make it, at least not yet. Besides, only a knight may wear such armor."

"I want to be a knight!" cried Nino.

"We will see what we will see," said Robert. He wasn't sure a Torreoni, the son of Ser Gian the money changer, would ever be a knight no matter how rich his father might be. Becoming a knight wasn't only a matter of being able to afford a suit of armor.

The first lessons were in putting the armor on, walking with it and moving his arms, and growing used to its weight. At first Nino disliked the restricted feeling; in time he grew able to move his arms as freely with the armor on as with it off.

Only when he was comfortable in his chain mail and helmet did Robert begin to teach him the use of his weapons. "A man who wears armor badly should not bear arms. Arms draw attack," he explained. "A man who is impeded by his armor will be easy prey, for armor alone is no defense."

He muffled the edges of Nino's long sword with strips of cloth and showed him how to strike and parry with this heavy weapon, held in two hands and almost as tall as he was. At first Nino was unable even to touch Robert with the sword, which was unwieldy, to say nothing of hitting him hard enough to hurt. After a month he was able, sometimes, to give as good as he got. After a year Robert said Nino was as skilled with a longsword as anyone.

"Except for a few Frenchmen," he added, "but you'd be unlikely to meet them."

They fought with the short sword (held in one hand, the other holding a dagger or a shield) both with and without armor; in the latter case they wore the padded leather tunics and the helmets. Nino preferred the short sword for it seemed to him more elegant and beautiful than the long sword, which depended more on sheer strength than on skill. There was much to learn about the short sword, both to strike and to parry, and Nino determined to become as skilled with it as any man, including Frenchmen. He practiced for hours every day and surprised his teacher by his progress.

At night he would unwrap his sword, which had been muffled for safety, sharpen it so he could shave with it, and feel its edge. The bright steel would sparkle in the candlelight. *Ave Maria* was engraved on one side of the blade, *Gratia Plena* on the other. He would kiss the hilt and say his prayers and then set the sword up at the end of his bedding so it was the last thing he saw before going to sleep and the first on waking.

Nino's dagger, a slender blade about eight inches long with a hilt of carved ivory depicting a gorgon with flowing locks, had been made in Damascus. Damascene blades were the strongest and sharpest in the world, capable of holding an edge longer than any other; they were crafted of strips of steel welded together and several times tempered in the forge. The dagger was weighted so it could be used not only to cut but also to throw.

The exercises Nino enjoyed the most, because of their element of playfulness, were with the quarterstaff. He and Robert made their own staves from small trees they cut themselves, scraped with their daggers, and smoothed with a handful of gravel and sand. A quarterstaff could be anywhere between six and twelve feet long. Robert preferred one about eight feet. You held it with your right hand on the middle and the left a quarter of its length from the end. The quarterstaff could both give blows and parry them. And then it could also be used as a walking stick.

It wasn't ordinarily a deadly weapon, although a man could be killed if he were hit hard enough along the side of the head. A skilled man with a staff would never let that happen. Usually, the weapons were used for defense even against sword, to make way through a melee, or to escape from robbers. Or, again, just for fun, because it was a pleasure, with someone who was skilled, to slide the attacking weapon down and then twist it from the other's grasp. Once in a while you could be hit, but a man had to be able to take that without flinching or running away.

Robert had a precept here, as well. "Let it be your aim in life, *caro mio,*" he would say, "that it shall always be the other man who runs away. However, foolhardiness is not a virtue."

Nino often thought back to his experience with Maria and of Robert's lessons in *honesti amandi.* Had he used force? He couldn't remember that he had. If anyone had used force it was Maria. Nevertheless, he continued to be impressed by Andreas's wise counsel. It seemed to make sense, for surely peasant women were different from noblewomen.

There was a peasant woman of the household whom he had admired for some time. This was Caterina, who often cleaned their room as well as serving their meals, assisting Mafalda in running the household. Nino knew she wasn't married; he also knew she had more than one man friend, for he had seen these men approach her, and once he had caught one of them as he left the house, very early in the morning. He said nothing to Caterina or to Mafalda, nor did they ever mention the man to him.

Caterina, although prettier than Maria, was still a large woman with sturdy arms and legs and a mane of black hair that she wore beneath a white cap. During warm weather she would ruck up her long skirt and show her legs bare to the knees and sometimes beyond. Once, when she saw Nino looking at her legs, she unpinned her skirt and let it fall, but there was a little smile on her lips as she did so. It was at this moment that Nino decided to test the wisdom of Andreas Capellanus, the master of the art of love.

They were alone soon after, and Nino went up to Caterina from behind, threw his arms around her waist and pulled her to him, knocking the wind out of her. "Whoosh!' she said. "You surprised me!"

Nino tried to spin her around so he could kiss her but she was stronger than he had expected and she pushed him away, sliding out of his arms.

"What is it that you desire, Master?" she asked softly.

"I desire to kiss you, Caterina," he said, trying to be as firm and forceful as Andreas would have recommended. He remembered he should also puff her up with praise and so he added: "Because you're so pretty!"

"You might have asked me first instead of grabbing me," she said. "Perhaps I wouldn't have refused. But now . . ." She turned away, a frown forming on her pretty face.

Nino was filled with desire as she stood before him, her hands at her sides. "Caterina," he said. "I like you very much and you're very pretty!" He moved toward her.

But again she fended him off. "Another time, perhaps," she said, her words thrilling him. "The next time you must ask me first!" she added.

Nino told Robert about this encounter. "I'm not sure Andreas is right about all peasant women," he said. "Caterina doesn't seem to be pleased when I'm forceful."

"Caterina in the kitchen?"

He nodded.

"But she hasn't repulsed you entirely. Perhaps she liked your forceful approaches after all, without admitting it. Probably you should try again."

"I will certainly try again because I like her very much, but I'll speak courteously to her, as if she were a lady. I don't see how that would do any harm."

"It would be completely discourteous," cried Robert. "She is not a lady and therefore you may not treat her as a lady. If you do, all real ladies will never forgive you."

"No real ladies will ever know," said Nino. And he went back to the kitchen after dinner, where once again they were alone.

"Caterina," he said, staring at her.

"Yes, Master," she replied, lowering her eyes.

"I'm not that, 'Master,'" he said. "I'm your friend."

"I am glad to hear that," she said, "although it is hard to believe it."

"I still want to kiss you," he said after a while.

"Perhaps you may kiss me, but not here where Mafalda can come in at any moment, or your sister."

"Where, then?"

"There is a room behind the storeroom. It's small and there's no window, but the eyes grow accustomed to the darkness. Sometimes I go there."

"Where is this room?" he asked, his heart beating faster.

"It's behind the storeroom. Sometimes I go there after dinner, sometimes not. You may want to seek me there." And she sprang to her feet and began to put things into the basin for washing. A moment later Mafalda entered. She glanced at Nino but she said nothing.

It was some time before Nino could find the room. A small door that opened behind high shelves led to a passage at the end of which was another door, only four feet high. He opened it and stared into the darkness. It was morning; he was sure Caterina wouldn't be there, which indeed she was not, but his body was immensely stirred nevertheless. He crept into the little room, where he found a bed of straw with a clean coverlet over it. He lay on the bed and stretched out his arms. His hands felt iron rings that had been imbedded in the stone over his head. He supposed animals might once have been kept here, perhaps before being slaughtered.

That evening he went to the room and waited for hours, until it was as dark outside as it was in the room, but Caterina didn't come. Nor did she come the next night, nor the next. But Nino didn't give up hope.

In fact he liked to lie in the darkness thinking of Caterina but also of many other things. His body ached for her but his mind sought the answers to other puzzles besides those of Andreas Capellanus. The deep darkness of the place freed his imagination to roam and he dreamed of places far away. And often he would fall asleep in the little room.

One evening, when he had been asleep for hours, he awoke suddenly, stirred by a sense that someone else was in the room. He sat up. A white figure, faint in the darkness, was sitting at the end of the bed. He was a little frightened.

"Caterina," he said softly, "is that you?"

"I am here, Master," she whispered.

He reached for her but she drew back. "Lie still and rest, Master, and we can talk, but very quietly, because sound travels easily through these stones."

"I'm glad you came," he whispered. "I've been here many evenings but you didn't come. Now you are here."

"Yes, I am here, Master." She was silent for a while as, obeying her, he lay quietly on the straw mat. Then she said, "Do you still want to kiss me?"

"Oh yes, Caterina, yes I do want to kiss you!" He rose up and reached out his arms toward her faint shadow in the darkness. But he couldn't reach her because she moved away from him.

"Do you remember what I said, Master?" she whispered. He wasn't sure but he thought she was smiling. He lay back, thinking. "You said I should ask you first."

"That is what I said, Master."

"May I kiss you, Caterina, for you are very pretty?"

"Perhaps you may, Master, or perhaps you may not. But if you promise to be still and not to move, perhaps I will kiss you."

"I promise, Caterina."

He lay still and she began to hum a little tune under her breath and then knelt on the straw bed by his side. He could just see her white face, hands, and dress. She reached out her hand — he could see the whiteness of it — and touched the belt that gathered his tunic around his waist. She undid the buckle and the belt fell away. He felt her hands touch the bottom of his tunic. They moved upward, unbuttoning the buttons as they went. Soon the tunic fell away. His body ached with desire but he didn't move.

"You are very good, Master," whispered Caterina. He felt rather than saw her face, a shimmering whiteness, approach his own. And then her lips brushed his.

"Do not move, Master," she whispered. Her breath was warm on his face and lips.

She kissed him over and over, her mouth open. Unable to control his body, he raised his arms to embrace her. But she immediately drew away.

"Do not move, Master."

"Yes, Caterina. I'll try."

Nor did he move, again for what seemed a delicious eternity while she hovered above him, kissing his mouth with her open mouth, while she slowly undressed him, drawing down his stockings and lifting his shirt, and while she took off her white dress and raised her shift — all this he could faintly see in the warm enveloping darkness.

Only when she lay upon him with her whole weight on his body, pressing him into the straw, her hands cleverly arranging their joining, only then did she whisper, urgently, "Now you may move, Master, now!" And she caught her breath and sobbed.

They lay together for a long time and then she released him. He realized he was holding her head against his breast. He couldn't remember moving but it must have been all right to do so, for she hadn't complained.

"Caterina," he whispered.

"Yes, Master."

"Cara amica. Dear friend."

She was silent, but he was sure she was pleased.

"Caterina," he said again. "Andreas was wrong."

"Andreas the cowherd?" she asked, startled.

"No, Andreas Capellanus, the author of the famous book about love. He said I should approach you with force."

"You could have had me in that way too, Master," she said softly. "But this was better."

He laughed. And the next day, when he told Robert the whole story, Robert laughed too. He roared and threw his hat in the air. "So much the worse for Andre le Chapelain!" he shouted. And he threw his arms around Nino.

"Amico mio!" he said. Nino was touched that he spoke Italian.

They sat for a while, savoring their friendship. "Do you know what Aristotle says about friendship?" asked Robert. His eyes twinkled.

"What does Aristotle say about friendship?"

"He says that among friends all things are in common, or should be," said the Frenchman gravely.

"Is there anything of mine that you want, friend?" said Nino. "You have only to ask for it."

"There's nothing I want for myself alone," said Robert, "but there's something I would like to share, to have in common."

"And what is that?" But suddenly Nino knew very well. At first he was astounded.

"Caterina?"

Squire Robert nodded, his eyes still twinkling.

Nino thought for a long time. Did he love Caterina? No, he decided, although he liked her very much and wanted her more than ever. Did he love his friend? Yes, more than ever.

"We shall share her," he said. "If she's willing," he added. "We must not force her."

"Certainly not," said Robert laughing.

"I'll ask her and see what she says."

The next time they were together and had made love in a new way devised by Caterina that involved the iron rings in the wall, Nino asked her. She thought a minute.

"Together or separately?" she asked finally.

Once more Nino was astounded. There was so much Andreas Capellanus didn't know. He too thought a minute, then he said:

"Both, I think." His heart stirred.

"I will think about that," whispered Caterina. But she assented before long and the three of them began to play together in the warm, dark, silent room, which was hardly large enough for all of them unless they were intertwined in one another's arms, which was usually the case.

A few months later, after one of their joyful episodes, Nino could feel that Caterina, as he held her, was crying softly. "What is it?" he whispered.

She shook her head.

"Tell us," said Robert. "Perhaps we can help."

She cried harder though she made little noise. Then she told them she was with child.

"Do you know who is the father?" Nino asked. He stroked her cheek.

"I know it's one of you," she said through her sobs.

"But you don't know which one?"

"I do not, Master."

"Then," said Nino, asserting his mastership, "we will consider that the child is both of ours and we will care for you and for it too. Will we not, *amico?*"

"Yes," said Robert without hesitation.

"I think you must go away," said Nino. "Is there a place where they will take you in?"

"I can go back to my family. They will accept me if I have money."

"You will have money," said Robert, whispering in the darkness. Caterina had stopped crying. And Robert took Nino's hand and together they pressed their hands against her belly as a sign and symbol of their loyalty to her and to her child.

And then they made love again, slowly and caring for one another's needs, because it was the last time.

Caterina's son was born at Natale, on the eve of Our Savior's birth. Nino and Robert were as good as their word, sending money to Caterina when she needed it and serving as godfathers at the christening of the little boy, whose name was Gianni. He cried out when the priest, who had overcome a certain reluctance because the mother did not seem to be married, immersed his little bottom in the cold water and made the sign of the cross over his face. Nino and Robert smiled at one another.

"I think our son will grow tall and strong," said Robert. And they marched back to the city along the old, winding road, singing as they marched, although it was very cold and there were a few flakes of snow in the air.

7

The Castellino

During his eighteenth year Nino grew several inches and gained thirty pounds, most of it muscle. This growth occurred almost overnight, as Mafalda said, and with equal suddenness he seemed to her, his father, and especially Nina, to have become a man. Even with the added inches he wasn't very tall, although somewhat above the average, nor did the extra weight make him broad or heavy; he was compactly built and very strong, his body lithe. He shaved his cheeks and chin and his dark hair fell nearly to his shoulders. His eyes shone under firm, wide brows, and his large curved nose gave his face a savage balance. He was still young but already formidable, Nina thought.

Even with that big nose he's as handsome as Benno, she said to herself one day when she saw them together. Benno is taller and has broad shoulders but, even though he's older, he hasn't filled out yet the way Nino has. Now, Nino is stronger, but I think Benno will be stronger later, he works so hard. What will become of him? Will he stay here? But what is there for him to do? If he leaves, where will he go and will he ever return? She sighed. I'll miss him, she said. He's like another brother — although Nino doesn't like me to say so.

She considered them a long time; they were working on the wall and paid no attention to her. They're different in lots of ways, she decided, but in one way they're the same. They're both determined. They'll both try to get what they want.

The spring of the past year had been dry; the wheat harvest was meager and vegetables withered on the vine or stalk. The drought had continued into the fall. Even the grapes were small and yielded little wine, for the peasants ate as many as they pressed, though they gave small nourishment. The Consiglio had bought grain in June and distributed it at a fair price when autumn came, but most landowners weren't so generous, and no one knew how the poorer folk would get through the winter if it didn't rain.

Severe hunger was already being felt in the country districts before Christmas; even the wild animals were fewer than normal, and there was no grass to feed the rabbits. All of southern Tuscany had been affected; other cities were even worse off than Cortona. As a result, bands of brigands had begun to prey on the countryside. Made up of men whose families were starving and who would starve themselves if they didn't find food to steal, they would swoop down on isolated farms and unprotected travelers. At first they hadn't harmed their victims, but in January several members of one band were identified by a person they had robbed; they were arrested, tortured, and hanged. The remainder decided it was safer to kill the people whose food and money they stole rather than let them live to accuse the outlaws.

By the end of February the brigands had become a plague. It was safe in the city, but Nina was warned not to take any of her accustomed walks outside the walls. Looking down onto the great valley from her window, she could see plumes of smoke rising in the still, cold air. She shuddered. Were those houses burning, and barns? Or were the fires the ordinary ones that could be seen almost any day?

Messer Uguccio, currently Podestà, decided a troop of soldiers had to be organized to rid the country of this infestation. He asked Conte Pietro di Pierle to lead, and Nino and Robert, who were reputed to be skilled with weapons, were asked to join. Ser Gian was reluctant to permit his son to go, but since Messer Uguccio had asked him and not the Conte, he could not refuse. Nino wanted to go in any case because the prospect was exciting, especially when Robert said hunting men wasn't very different from hunting wild boars. They were told to be ready in a week.

"We can be grateful for the time," Robert said. "We need to do some work on horseback." Nino had ridden all his life but he had never fought on horseback and he found that much of his newly acquired skill could not be transferred. He almost had to learn the short sword all over again when his left hand was occupied with the horse and couldn't hold a shield or dagger. They also practiced shooting their bows from a galloping horse. Nino was an excellent archer and he found this easier than swordplay. By the time the troop was to meet, they were both confident they would be useful members.

The recruits gathered in the piazza early in the morning. Nino knew the other men, who included the Podestà's young nephews, Ranieri and Ernando Casali; their father was dead, and Messer Uguccio, who was childless, had informally adopted them. Conte Pietro came riding into the square followed by his lieutenant, a fierce man called Baron Nerone. The Conte wore a massive helmet and a coat of brigantine, consisting of small steel plates riveted to a cloth garment extending from his neck to his thighs; Nerone wore a similar garment; both were black. Nerone bore a spear with a pennon of the arms of Cortona: a lion, black, on a field of gold.

The Podestà together with a small band of bagpipers had come to see them off; there was also a small crowd of friends and relations, including Nina and Benno. The Podestà praised their courage and willingness to risk their lives for their country. Their war cry would be "Cortona and San Marco," he declared, and the onlookers shouted these words as the troop set out in the cold, clear morning, trotting down the steep narrow street to the city gate.

When they could no longer be seen, Nina gripped Benno's arm. "Will they be safe?" she murmured. "Will they return?" He looked down at her white face. He did not touch her hand; he could not touch her. "They will come back safely, Mistress," he said. "Do not fear. They are well-armed, well-mounted, and well-led."

She nodded and they walked together to her house, where he left her, excusing himself by saying he had much work to do. He returned to his own house and sat for a long time staring into the fire. Gianna approached and placed her hand on his shoulder. "Giovanni is working in the outer barn," she said. Benno nodded and rose to leave. He looked back at her as he went through the door but he said nothing.

There were sixteen citizen soldiers, most of them young (half were still in their teens). None, apart from Conte Pietro, Baron Nerone, Robert, and a couple of regulars, had had any experience hunting men. Nino was intensely curious about the neophytes, especially the Casali, and he scrutinized their faces, weapons, and horses — as well as the way they rode them — as they trotted in rough formation. He decided he and Robert were as well armed and mounted as any but the professionals, and he thought they rode as well or better. He wondered if the others were as excited as he was. Looking at them out of the corner of his eye, he thought they were more afraid.

A small fortified farm near the tiny village of San Lorenzo had been attacked and most of its people killed. This was the first well-protected farm to be taken, and they went there to interview the survivors, who had hidden in the well. One was a woman, still speechless from shock and grief; the other was her son, a boy about ten. His name was Beppe.

Conte Pietro interrogated him. There were seven in the band, he said, and they came in the evening just before dark. One knocked on the door and asked for a crust of bread; since he appeared to be alone and unarmed, they opened the door a crack and handed him something. The others, who had been hiding, then forced their way in. The brigands stole a wagon loaded with grain — their only provision against the coming months — and before leaving killed his father and his older brother and three peasants, one a woman, although they pleaded for their lives and promised they would say nothing to anyone.

"I recognized one of them," said Beppe. "I was hiding in the well but I saw him. I don't know his name but I think he lives at Santa Caterina or nearby." His mother nodded.

"Come with us," Conte Pietro ordered, and he took the boy onto his horse, where he rode behind. They trotted through Vallone, where they commandeered a horse for the boy, and along the road to Sodo. There they turned off on a narrow track leading to Santa Caterina.

Nerone held up his hand then pointed to the ground. A heavy wagon had recently passed; the manure was still fresh. A faint trail of grain marked the way; there must have been a hole in one of the sacks.

The trail wasn't continuous but there were enough small piles of grain to make them confident they were following their prey. The trail turned and went through a big field. In the distance was an old granary that had been damaged by fire, its roof partly caved in. Quietly they surrounded the building and charged at a signal from Conte Pietro. But there was no one inside. Fresh manure indicated the wagon had been there recently, but it was gone together with the brigands.

The charge on the granary was the most exciting thing Nino had ever done. His heart beat louder than the sound of his horse's hooves as he galloped toward the ruined building, acutely aware of the others beside him, his head low over the animal's head in case there were men inside with bows. The disappointment at finding the building deserted was so great, he almost had to vomit. He thought back to those few moments. Had he been afraid? He didn't think so. Now he felt empty and sad. He wondered if the others felt the same way. Only Robert had a word to say. "We'll get them the next time," he muttered through clenched teeth. "They were here. They must be near."

Suddenly Nerone shouted from the edge of the forest. He had found the wagon, still loaded with grain. The brigands had fled. Nerone, a good tracker, thought he found a trail; then one of his men found another. The troop divided in two, one led by Nerone, the other by Conte Pietro. Nino joined the latter, and Robert.

They moved through the woods, slowing to look for clues. The trail seemed to divide again, and the Conte sent four men left while he led Robert, Nino, and Ranieri Casali to the right.

They halted by a pool in the great swamp they were now traversing and dismounted to let their horses drink. Ordinarily this area was impassable, the Conte said, but now, with the drought, they could move slowly through it on horses. Nino stretched; he was stiff after four hours on his horse. Suddenly they heard a whinny. They looked around; it wasn't one of theirs. Conte Pietro gestured for them to mount, his finger at his lips. He lowered his visor and motioned them to follow on a path leading away from the pool.

He went first, followed by Nino, Robert, and Raniari. The horses made little sound on the soft turf. After a few minutes they smelled smoke. Five or six men sat around a small fire in the middle of a clearing; in the background, their horses were tethered.

Conte Pietro indicated by hand signals the positions they should take around the clearing. Then the order came: "Cortona and San Marco!" and they charged into the open space, converging on the fire. The men scrambled to their feet, hands in the air. "Kill them!" shouted the Conte as he set upon them with his sword, slashing at them as they ducked and tried to run. At that moment Nino heard a sound behind him. A half dozen armed men on horses were bearing down on them from the rear, where it had seemed only riderless horses were tethered.

Nino turned to face the attackers, drawing his sword as they thundered toward him. He glanced around him. Robert was twenty yards to his left, Conte Pietro an equal distance to his right. Two horsemen headed toward Nino, who had time to notice neither wore a helmet of metal. One wore a rusty shirt of mail, the other a leather jacket. Both waved swords in the air.

He waited. He felt utterly calm, as though he were sitting at a table waiting to be served. Suddenly he rose in his stirrups and sliced at the man in the leather jacket, hitting him on the arm and almost severing it below the shoulder. With a backstroke he smashed the flat of his sword against the head of the other rider, who fell to the ground, blood gushing from his nose and mouth.

Nino glanced around him again. Young Casali was heavily involved with one of the attackers, a big man with an axe who was striking wildly about him to little effect. Robert was fighting with another, but seemed able to care for himself. The Conte was in trouble. There were men on either side of him wielding long, heavy swords that clashed against his helmet. He was fighting fiercely but it seemed to Nino he needed help.

Nino rode toward the three men without hesitation. He always remembered that: He hadn't paused for an instant. He rode up behind one of the attackers, who didn't see him in time to ward off a terrible blow to the back of his head. Conte Pietro soon dispatched his other foe, who was disheartened by the loss of his leader. Together they rode to Robert and helped him finish off his stubborn assailant. Without a word Robert raced to the side of the young Casali, and with a single blow dispatched his opponent.

The men who had been sitting around the fire had disappeared, but the Conte sounded his horn to call the rest of the troop and a search was instituted in the woods. Four of the robbers were soon captured; the fifth was never found. The captives were bound each to a different tree. Beppe rode his horse slowly in front of them, searching their faces when they tried to turn away. "That one killed my father," he said, his voice trembling. "And that one my brother."

"Hang them," ordered the Conte, sitting quietly on his horse.

Each of the men was placed on a horse, hands behind their backs and with their feet tied beneath its belly. A rope was tied around each neck and then passed over the low limb of a tree. When the rope was fast, the rope binding their feet was removed.

"You may say a prayer," announced Baron Nerone. The men, their eyes moving from side to side, muttered soundless words. A soldier stood behind each horse; at a signal the soldiers slapped the horses' rumps and they bolted, leaving the four robbers hanging, swinging each from his own tree.

It was utterly still. The brigands stopped turning after a few moments and hung in the still, cold air; the soldiers stood or sat on their horses without moving.

After ten minutes the ropes were cut and the four bodies fell to the ground. "Leave them," ordered the Conte. Motioning to Nino to ride beside him, he turned his horse's head toward home. Nino caught up and rode thigh to thigh along the narrow path.

"I didn't think to find such a fighter among the Torreoni," said the Conte when they had ridden for some time.

"My father is a merchant," said Nino, stung. "But my brother fought at Montaperti."

"He was there. I fought." He paused. "It doesn't matter. You came. You did well. If I hear it said you saved my life, I won't deny it." He spurred his horse as they were coming to a place where only one could pass at a time. He said nothing more to Nino, who fell back, his position next to the leader taken by Nerone when the trail widened.

The others had much to say. They chattered to one another, made plans, congratulated themselves. No one had been badly hurt though there were many bruises. In the frank way of soldiers, they were quick to praise Nino. Those who hadn't seen the fight were told about it, over and over, by those who had. Ranieri said Nino had killed three men and saved the Conte's life.

"It's not a bad thing to be the hero of your first engagement," said Robert, smiling at Nino as he trotted by his side. "To some that never happens — but the first time . . . !"

Nino smiled in return. He felt very proud of himself.

"Of course you might have come to my aid and not his!"

"But there were two to his one and he's old," cried Nino.

Robert laughed. "You were right. I was in no difficulty. And now I love you, *caro mio,* and I will serve you forever." And he laughed again.

Benno was waiting in the piazza when the vigilantes returned. He made sure Nino didn't see him, but he overheard the story from a man who was excitedly telling it to a companion. So Nino was the hero of this adventure, Benno thought. That's good, for Nina will be pleased. But it will make Nino even more arrogant, which is bad. He shook his head and went home. His father was alone, Gianna being out on some errand. He seemed to be sleeping but he roused himself when Benno entered.

"What happened? Did they all return? Is my young master unharmed?"

Benno nodded. He hated it when his father used that term. He told him how well Nino had acquitted himself.

"If you had been of the party, you too would have done well."

Benno sighed. "How could that be? I've had no training in arms, as Nino has. I have no arms, only my stick. I know nothing about swords and shields and armor."

Giovanni noticed the bitterness in his voice.

"If I were to leave Cortona," Benno mused, "I might become a soldier. Here I never could. I feel a great weight on my shoulders. I can't move my arms."

"There are other roads . . ." Giovanni's voice died away.

"You speak without conviction, babbo. We both know the truth, although we don't say it. Nevertheless, I'll keep my promise and stay till I'm twenty-one. After that who knows?"

"I hope you will never be a soldier," Giovanni said softly. "It's a perilous and fearful life."

"I know the perils as well as you. Yet there can be rewards."

When Nino told his father about the farm in the valley, Ser Gian suggested that they buy it to relieve the widow of her financial burdens. Nino rode down the mountain to tell Beppe and his mother. When he arrived he discovered Conte Pietro had already bought the farm for much less than it was worth. The desperate woman had accepted his first offer.

"And now his lordship says we can't stay here," said Beppe, trembling. "Mother doesn't know where to go."

"Come with me!" cried Nino. "There's plenty of room at Torreone and much work to do." He helped them pack their belongings and led them up the mountain, carrying the heaviest packages while they walked behind.

Later Nino learned that the Conte had given the farm to Nerone for his good service. But the Baron didn't want the house. He leased the place to a *contadino* who only wanted the land and didn't need the buildings, and after a few years they began to crumble.

From that time forth the castellino at Torreone became a center of young people's activities in the city. Nino and Robert rose at dawn and spent the early morning hours on French lessons and discussions of *cortesia*. If the weather was cold they sat near the fireplace where breakfast was served to them in midmorning by Mafalda, the mistress of the place, or Nunzia, the mother of Beppe who soon became a valuable helper for the older woman. After breakfast the two young men would go out into the courtyard whatever the weather — "War waits not on weather," Robert liked to say — to practice with their weapons until dinner, which was served to them in midafternoon.

After dinner they still didn't rest despite the fact that it was the custom to do so. During the day, Marco, son of Marcia, would have gathered stones, prepared mortar, set plumbs, and otherwise prepared for the afternoon's labors on the walls and other parts of the building still needing repair. Marco lived in a small house near the castellino to which he and his father and grandfather had "belonged." He was a good and dependable worker as were the two or three helpers he brought from time to time.

When it grew dark and they could no longer see to lay stones straight, Nino and Robert would descend and enter the hall, where a modest supper of bread and cake and a bowl of ale awaited. They often had company both at meals and in their practices and labors. Half a dozen young men came from time to time to share in Robert's lessons; the courtyard of the castellino was a good place to study under his tutelage. Nino was a generous host; he liked having visitors and made them feel comfortable when they were in his house.

Often, in the evenings, he and Robert would entertain guests with songs that they sang, either alone or in duets accompanied by their lutes. Robert, in addition to all his other skills, was an accomplished musician, and Nino had been taught by Giovanni as a boy and later by the monks. Now he learned songs from Robert both in French and Italian. He had a clear, true voice, and he sang with deep feeling; sometimes his own singing brought tears to his eyes.

Because they were generous with their time, their skills, and their food and drink, and because of the repute both had gained in the vigilante raids of that winter, they were popular among the young people of the city. Everyone liked them. It was a happy time.

Their most frequent guests were Nina and Benno, though for different reasons.

Nina came often to visit her brother in the castellino and she might spend a few days or a week there in the room he always kept ready for her; then, because she was jealous of the freedom he enjoyed, which was so much greater than hers, she would leave sometimes without even saying good-bye. But then she would come again.

When she was with Robert, she insisted on speaking French and he would instruct her. After breakfast she would sit against the wall, hunched up with her arms around her knees, and watch her brother and his friend strike and parry, listen to them grunt and gasp and shout at one another, and judge them loudly according to her own standards, which Robert claimed were different from his. It wasn't long before she demanded to be taught these arts, too.

At first they told her to go away. "These things aren't for women to learn!" cried Robert, scornful of her slender body and thin wrists. Unlike Nino, he hadn't yet learned how easy it was to underestimate her.

"Why not let her," Nino said after a while. "Perhaps she won't like it."

But she did like it and she worked hard like her brother, struggling to be as good as the men at their own games. Soon she was adept in the use of the dagger and the quarterstaff. She had no armor and Robert wouldn't let her practice with a sword. She didn't object for she understood that whoever carried a sword might have to use it.

Benno came almost as frequently as Nina because she was often there and he couldn't see her if he wasn't there too. He found it intolerable not to be with her, but it was an almost equal torment to be with her at the castellino in the presence of her brother. It was not that Nino was outwardly discourteous. If Benno was there at dinner time he would be invited to share the meal. But then, afterward, it was apparent that Nino felt Benno should pay for his meal by working on the walls. Ordinarily Benno wouldn't have minded; after all, he owed his labor to Ser Gian and his son. But the coldness of Nino's attitude made him shrink inside.

Sometimes Benno came in the middle of the day and practiced with the quarterstaff; he was skilled with the weapon, the only one peasants could possess. Later, he would watch Robert and Nino fight with sword and dagger. He couldn't join them, as Nino pointed out, because he didn't have a sword. Why not lend me one? Benno thought, although he never voiced this request, which would probably be refused.

If Nina was there he would sit with her and watch the two combatants, but he couldn't speak to her because he felt Nino was watching them. Yet he was even more miserable if he didn't come, not least because he believed Nina was completely unaware of the pain he felt.

In June Nina celebrated her sixteenth birthday. This was considered the age at which a woman attained her majority and the family shared the happiness of the event with a feast at Torreone. Nina received many presents, including a fine dress that had been her mother's (which she wore), the farm at Sant'Angiolo (which her father said would be a large part of her dowry), and a French book, one of his precious horde, from Robert. Nino gave her a dagger of her own because he knew no one else would do this and he thought he knew how much she wanted it.

The dagger was small with a double edge that could be honed razor sharp and a silver hilt set with little pearls. He and Robert had ridden to Arezzo, secretly, to buy it from the armorer. He had saved his allowance for it because it was expensive.

The dagger was wrapped in a square of fine red leather. When Nina unwrapped it, she stared at it for a long time then held it in her hand, balancing it. She knew how fine a thing it was. She stared at Nino, her eyes cold and serious. "Thank you, brother," she said. He never forgot this look, the intenseness of it, the total concentration. She wrapped the dagger in its covering, tenderly, like a baby, and placed it under her shawl next to her breast. Then she walked away.

Benno saw and followed her. She was standing by the gate looking out at the distant town. He hesitated then approached her. She heard his step and turned.,

"Did you see?" she asked, her eyes shining.

"I did. It's beautiful. But I didn't know you wanted such a thing."

"I didn't either," she admitted.

"I made you this, Mistress," he said, drawing an object from beneath his cloak. It was a tiny garden carved from hard wood with inlaid petals on a single flower. There was a little fence and a tree in the middle. It was no more than three inches by four, but it had taken him months to carve it and assemble the pieces of the flower.

"Oh, it's beautiful, Benno," she said softly, turning it in her hand so she could see the details of the carving.

He cleared his throat. "I wanted . . ." he murmured and then stopped. He couldn't say what he wanted because he wasn't entirely sure himself and because he thought she wouldn't really be interested.

She looked at him, holding the little carving in her hands. "I won't take it in the castellino," she said, "because then I'd have to share it with everyone." She looked for a place to lay it down. There was a stone near the road a few feet from the gate. "I'll remember it's here, Benno, and take it with me when I go."

Again she looked at him and touched his arm. "Thank you, Benno. Now we should go in, it's time for dinner." She preceded him into the courtyard where tables had been set up. He hesitated, allowing her to enter before he did. When he and Giovanni left, Benno noticed that the carving was still where she had left it. The next day it was gone — he had to come and see. But he didn't know whether she had taken it or someone else, perhaps supposing it a thing left by the wayside.

Nina never tried to explain to her father why she didn't go to church or what her views of being a woman were. These matters were hard enough to understand herself; she couldn't imagine making them intelligible to him. She also assumed Father Rafaelo was regularly reporting their discussions about religion and that he would probably put a better face on them than she could herself.

Nina loved her father despite his faults (as she liked to think) and would embrace him and kiss him sometimes and sit with him on the terrace overlooking the piazza and talk about safe things — the running of the households, the people in them, the accomplishments of her two brothers. These conversations occasionally came around to the forbidden subject: her future.

But she was now sixteen and many women of her age were already married. If she had been the elder sister, she too would have been married at an early age. She was grateful to her father for not pushing her, not pressing her hard, but she was determined to fight if he tried to marry her before she was ready. Her father was all too aware of her resolution although they never talked about it. He realized that in Nina he was dealing with a kind of elemental force that he might never be able to control.

Once Ser Gian, frustrated by the lack of anyone to talk to about his daughter, broached the subject with Mafalda; after all, he knew she was closer to Nina than he was and over the years he had grown to trust her to keep things in confidence. He asked Mafalda whether Nina had given any sign of a desire to be a wife and mother.

"Your mistress was sixteen when she married me," he said. "Elena was already thinking about being married when she was only fourteen." It was one of the few times in recent years he had mentioned the name of his lost child.

"Mistress Nina is different," Mafalda replied. "I don't talk to her and she doesn't talk to me, but I think I know her a little. What I know is, she can't be made to do what she doesn't want to do without killing her."

Ser Gian smiled. "It wouldn't kill her."

"I don't mean marriage would really kill her, Master. I mean, forcing her would kill something in her. Everyone likes to feel they chose their own life. Most people are willing to compromise. We realize we can't always choose, that others and events themselves sometimes choose for us. Your daughter doesn't know this yet and as a result she is unwilling to make any compromises with life."

"She's a foolish little thing," he said; but he wasn't sure it was true. As had happened more than once, he was impressed by the wisdom of this peasant woman who had spent so many years in his service.

Mafalda thought a moment. "Life will teach her hard lessons sooner or later," she said, "as it does everyone. But she is only sixteen and if she were my child — which she almost is, Master — I would hesitate to be the executioner of her dreams."

"What a strange expression!"

She lowered her eyes and paused again, then gathered her courage. "I admit it is a strange way to put it. But you, Master, you love her as much as I do and you don't want to hurt her. Perhaps patience, at least for a while . . ."

"I have to agree," he interrupted, "because I think you're right. But do you think she will ever feel she's ready to marry?"

He had trusted her and so she decided to trust him. "I am sure she will love a man and be loved in return," she said. "I do not think she knows love yet although it cannot be far away." Again she was silent, balancing. She looked at him. "I am not afraid she will not love a man and wish to give herself to him. What I fear is this, it may be the wrong man."

Shocked, he looked at her grimly. "What do you know that I should know, Mafalda?"

"I know nothing," she replied, again lowering her eyes. "I only know my young mistress." But she did know, or thought she did. Since she was not certain, it would be harmful.to speak if she was wrong. If she was right he would know soon enough.

When Nino would look back on his childhood and youth at Torreone, he would think with pleasure of things that had happened and of persons he had known and loved, not least Caterina. But what pleased him most to remember was not persons at all but stones, the stones he and Robert, over the course of a year or more, bought in the quarry down the mountain and that Marco, son of Marcia, brought up to the castellino on an ox cart and then carried up to the scaffolding to be laid along the walls they were rebuilding.

Marco was a good mason and he did much of the work, but Nino and Robert worked too although Robert complained from time to time that this was not fit work for a gentleman. "If a gentleman can't build his own wall, then I don't want to be a gentleman," Nino would say, to which Robert had no answer. And to be truthful, he too enjoyed building walls.

As it turned out, the building had not been in need of as much repair as Ser Gian had thought. Most of the walls were sound except for small places here and there, and the timbers holding up the roof and floors were still solid. Some roof tiles had to be replaced and window frames and sills rebuilt where rain had entered and frozen, cracking the mortar. And the crenelated wall around the court needed serious repair. Here Nino and Robert spent much of their time for months. And with the help of Marco, who cut down the trees from which they hewed the massive timbers, they built a new gate, the old one having been destroyed when the place was retaken from the Aretines. When it was finished, they affixed a new shield with the Torreoni arms.

Nino was proud of the gate, but all of the work pleased him and satisfied his old desire to be a *muratore*. He consulted with men in the city about mortar and from time to time went to watch real *muratori* working on the city walls or on some church or new house. He gained many ideas in this way. But he also had ideas of his own.

He especially liked the combination of the dark, rough stone of the mountainside with the white, smooth cut stone from the quarry. Cut stone was expensive and he didn't use much of it except in lintels. He made a new window in the front of the tower, which looked out over the court to the city in the near distance. This window had three narrow pointed arches and slender columns, all made of the white cut stone; the columns were carved at great expense by a Pisan mason. From a distance the aspect of this window, shining white against the dark stone of the old wall surrounding it, was beautiful, Nino believed. His father agreed.

"You're making yourself a fine house," he said to his son when he came a few weeks after Nina's birthday to inspect the works.

"Thank you," said Nino, although he would have preferred to have his father call it a castle instead of a house. Nino thought of his abode as impregnable, like a castle, and not as a mere residence.

"Do you like the arms over the new gate?" he asked.

"Very impressive," said his father smiling.

"I've had tapestries made and pennants to fly from the top of the tower when we've installed the last tiles and put the old mast in place."

"I look forward to seeing that."

"I want to offer a feast to all my family," said Nino, "and I've thought Ferragosto would be a good time." Ferragosto was the Feast of Our Lady, the anniversary of the day when she ascended to heaven to sit at the side of her Son. The fifteenth of August was still a month away, and Nino was sure everything would be finished by that time.

"You've forgotten, Nino, that we've agreed to spend Ferragosto at Pierle with Conte Pietro and his family," said the man. But his face darkened as it always did at the mention of the Conte.

"Yes, father, but I was thinking that we might make an excuse and celebrate the Assumption of the Virgin at my castle. I owe her a feast and you too, Father."

"We'll celebrate your feast at harvest time, Nino." He turned away so Nino would not see the look in his eyes.

"I can't change your mind?"

"You cannot!' said Ser Gian angrily. He strode across the courtyard to examine a piece of wall that had been especially well repaired. Perhaps he has a real talent, he thought, but because he was angry he didn't say so.

And then, because he wasn't an unkind man and he loved his son, he returned to Nino, who was standing downcast, and placed his arm on his shoulder.

"We'll have a wonderful feast at harvest time," he said again. "We'll all come to be entertained by you. We'll bring some things to eat and drink as we did on Nina's birthday, but you'll be the host and we'll be thankful to receive your bounty." And, because Nino still looked disappointed, he said:

"I think you are an excellent *muratore*. You've made fine walls — and the gate and window are wonderful."

The next day he went to Palazzo Casali and asked to see Messer Uguccio. He was shown into the great room where his old friend was sitting at a small desk by a window, looking out at the sky and the small white clouds drifting across it.

"Salve," he said. "Will you sit?"

There was a bench close to the desk; Ser Gian drew it even closer. "It's a lovely day," he said. "Perhaps you ought to be outside."

"Perhaps. But I can appreciate the beauty of the day from this window, and my legs . . ." The wounds received at Montaperti still pained him.

Ser Gian nodded. He cleared his throat. "I visited Nino at his castellino — the one you retrieved for us, my friend. I gave it to him and he's restoring it. The work is well done, in part by Nino himself. He likes to . . . pretend he's a *muratore.*"

Messer Uguccio raised his eyebrows.

"Even so, he's good at it, as appropriate or inappropriate as it may be."

Messer Uguccio smiled. "Whatever I may think, if I had a son I too would probably let him do whatever he wanted — within limits, of course. Practicing the ancient art of the *muratore* would not exceed them, I feel sure. After all Our Lord was a carpenter's son . . ."

"Indeed," Ser Gian responded. "Nino has nearly completed his restoration, and he told me he would like to celebrate with a feast at Ferragosto to which he wanted to invite you, of course. I was sorry to have to remind him of our promise to Conte Pietro. You don't suppose . . ."

"To turn back from the course we have chosen might be dangerous, Gian. The Conte believes he is being generous; we should accept his offer at face value even though we think there are unstated reasons for his seeming change of heart. And the help he has agreed to give Lorenzo is real enough. Even if he can't vote, he has followers who can."

"If in fact he does help him. The election is in three months."

"I agree that we won't know till then. However, I believe it's safe to assume . . . He wants your allegiance, Gian. He. . ."

"I'll never forgive him. I'll break bread with him for Lorenzo's sake and for the sake of peace in the city. But his men destroyed my happiness. I can never . . ."

"Perhaps not his men, Gian. Aretines, yes. I don't ask you to forgive — certainly not to forget. But you are a man of the world. Sometimes it is necessary to choose between evils . . ."

"There's so little good in the world," said Ser Gian bitterly.

"Yes," sighed the old man. "There is so little good in the world."

8

Ferragosto at Pierle

Ferragosto dawned bright and sunny, not too hot. It was a perfect day for a party if only the party were to be in a place you wanted to go to, with guests you really liked and other guests you wanted to meet and party with. In spite of all these negatives, it was a party you had agreed to go to, for some good and some not so good reasons. You had better put the best face on it if you could, even if you promised yourself not to enjoy it whatever might happen.

In the Torreoni family these feelings were nearly unanimous. Only Lorenzo, the older son now launched on a political career, was looking forward to it, and then only for its possible advantages. Yet even he was nervous. Conte Pietro di Pierle had promised help in the upcoming elections, but there was considerable doubt as to whether, first, he had the power to provide any really useful help, and second, whether he really intended to even if he could. Putting the best face on things was, Lorenzo already knew, something a politician had to be able to do. Shows of disappointment or fear of failure always aggravated the very events that had occasioned the disappointment in the first place. The first rule of politics was to keep on smiling, unless you happened to possess unchecked and arbitrary power. Tyrants didn't have to smile and could look as sour as they felt.

Nino disliked the whole idea of the extravaganza at Pierle. He would have preferred to host his own extravaganza on August 15th at the castellino and he thought he could do that sort of thing better than any disagreeable old man, no matter how rich. The food would be uninspired, he thought, the wine undistinguished, the entertainments embarrassing at best, and the speeches — he assumed the Conte and perhaps others wouldn't be able to resist the opportunity to make long toasts — would not only be boring but also of course insincere. In addition to everything else he would miss the chance to work on his walls in perfect weather: not too hot or too wet or too cloudy . . . Well, he thought, it's August and there are many nice days in August, and perhaps tomorrow will be even better than today. And to make himself feel happier, he asked Mafalda to help him dress as elegantly as he could.

"I will come to you soon, Master," she said, her mouth full of pins. "Now I am helping my young mistress, who needs me more than you do."

Indeed, Nina needed as much help as she could get. In the first place, she disliked intensely the preparations for a social gathering that other young women of her age so much enjoyed. She would have preferred to go to the Fiera dressed in her customary manner: that is, in such a way as to draw no attention to herself and certainly not as "pretty" women liked to do. More important, she had learned from Mafalda that the entertainments were to include a "pageant of beauties" in which she and other young women would be paraded up and down while old men leered at them and judged who was the most beautiful. She was sure she couldn't win such a contest and would have to stand by while the old women muttered unkind words behind their hands. Even worse, what if by some accident she did win? Then she would be forced to sit on a silly throne and look pleased to receive the insincere congratulations of the losers and the pretended adulation of men, young and old, most of whom would dislike her because they knew how much she disliked them.

On top of everything else, she was tired. Mafalda had washed her hair the night before and arranged it, with the help of a professional "dresser" from the town, in a complicated (and she was certain ridiculous) coiffure that made it impossible for her to lie down; she had therefore sat up all night and gotten very little sleep. And now Mafalda was packing up the ointments and powders that would go to Pierle and be applied to her lips and eyes and cheeks at the last moment. And also, she thought irritably, to her breasts, which her mother's silk dress had been altered to reveal in an almost shameful way.

She cringed, remembering the dresser's remark when she first tried on the dress. "Very pretty, *cara,* very attractive. And now don't forget, if a handsome young man should happen, just *per caso,* to drop some crumbs of bread down between them and then ask you, after sincere apologies, if you will let him retrieve them — remember that you may permit him to do so, but you should be careful not to let him fondle you too obviously, because that would suggest things you don't want suggested. A word to the wise!" the woman had added with a wink.

"I'll be sure to wear my kerchief," Nina had responded.

"But you mustn't! That would be completely inappropriate! You are going there to be seen and admired, not to be hidden."

Perhaps Ser Gian had the strongest feelings of all. Messer Uguccio had pointed out that it was most likely Aretines who had kidnapped his daughter. The Aretines were gone now, although the Bishop was still demanding punitive taxes that made it harder to undertake profitable ventures. Even so, the Aretines had been let into the city, in the middle of the night when people were peacefully at sleep, by traitors from within who had then joined in the slaughter and looting. Who they actually were, those traitors, was still not clear. True, several Aretines had claimed responsibility for the act, but Ser Gian and others believed the claims to be fraudulent and designed to cover up the guilt of a pack of Cortonese Guelfs who had mercilessly opened the gates to the wolves. True again, no proof had been discovered that Conte Pietro had had anything to do with the onslaught. If he was in the city that night, no one had come forward to say so, and he of course had denied all the allegations, insisting it was merely because of his Guelf sympathies — which he had never denied — that he was suspected. And he had even responded to Messer Uguccio's inquiries about the whereabouts of the Torreoni girl in a sympathetic manner.

There were times when Ser Gian felt he was wrong to continue stubbornly, as Messer Uguccio had implied once or twice, to believe the Conte was a black-hearted villain. The city was prosperous again, although not as prosperous as before; the papal interdict that had been the Bishop's excuse for his villainies had been lifted, with the result that Cortonesi could marry and die again in the bosom of the Church; and there was peace. But peace, Ser Gian believed, was more than just the absence of war. This peace had no stable foundation; it could be betrayed again at any time.

Why was he going to Pierle, then, instead of to Nino's castle for a more sedate family celebration? It wasn't just for Lorenzo, and it wasn't for the sake of the uneasy truce that pervaded all the city's activities. Mistrust underlay every contract, every handshake, every marriage, even every kiss of peace among friends. Italians were notorious, Ser Gian knew, for their age-old addiction to partisan strife. They had never learned how to agree to disagree.

Good men could differ in their view of what was good and what ought to be done. Good men could press for what they believed. But they didn't have to kill their opponents because their opponents didn't agree with them. Every Christian said, when praying to the Lord, "Thy Kingdom come, on Earth as it is in Heaven." The Kingdom of God was surely not rent by partisan strife even if the Holy Church sometimes acted like it. The prayer to Our Lord was a plea, not a promise. Yet the mere saying of those words should have an effect both on those who said them and those who heard them. Thus Ser Gian was going to Pierle, against his own will and that of his family, as an act of contrition and in the hope for a better world in Cortona, and Pierle, and everywhere else.

It was still early when the family set out. Ser Gian and Lorenzo rode at the head of the procession, followed by Nino and Nina and her dresser, and Mafalda and Carlo and Giovannni and his son, and Robert, Nunzia and Beppe, and a few other servants and retainers. There were no soldiers; they were hostages to peace and good fortune, Ser Gian said. They carried baskets and panniers of provisions, gifts for their host, and other necessities including Nina's little basket of cosmetics. One horse was laden with the clothes they would wear later in the day; Nina in particular refused to use a woman's saddle and therefore couldn't wear her fine dress until they reached their destination.

The journey required several hours. When they rounded the last curve, the great Rocca suddenly came into view, awing the travelers with its height and rough power. But flags flew from the battlements and pennons hung from the windows, and a band of trumpeters announced their arrival. The drawbridge was down, the portcullis up, and the Conte and Nerone stood in the opening, smiling a welcome. The new arrivals were led to the peasant houses, newly cleaned and whitewashed, in which they could rest and change their garments, and Carlo took the horses to a stable. He returned to find the family ready for their grand entrance.

Other guests were milling about outside the Rocca; it was now two o'clock. Greetings were exchanged and eyebrows raised as it became evident that the Conte had made a clean sweep of *Cortona bene* — that is, all the persons in Cortona who amounted to anything. Country nobles mingled with city magnates and merchants, soldiers conversed with men of the cloth, and landowners of whatever party, Guelf or Ghibelline, seemed to be talking business in a way that had been rare in recent years.

The only notable personnage who was absent was the renowned Bishop Guglielmo. He had been invited, Conte Pietro told someone who passed this around, but had been unable to attend. He wasn't sorely missed by anyone.

Again the trumpets sounded, and the girls and women left their quarters and gathered at the foot of the drawbridge. There were perhaps forty of them, of whom a dozen were of an age and station, Nina thought, to be included in the pageant. Hastily she looked around her, critically evaluating this one and that. They were all prettier than she was, she decided, and better dressed. She sighed in relief; probably she wouldn't even be asked to walk with the others around the courtyard of the Rocca, which had also been decorated to the extent that it appeared almost attractive.

Tables had been set up in the middle of the space, with long benches running on either side of them; the high table, perpendicular to the others, stood on a platform at the shady end of the area. Another platform facing the first held an armchair adorned with colored cloths; on either side pages stood holding ornamental spears. The trumpeters found places on the steps leading to the upper floors. At a signal from the *maggiordomo,* a fanfare announced the arrival of the Conte and his party, who took their places at the high table. The Conte and Nerone sat in the middle; to his surprise, Ser Gian was asked to sit next to the Conte with a man he hardly knew, who introduced himself as Ugo Bordoni on his right hand, at the end of the table. Next to Nerone sat Messer Uguccio and another noble whom Ser Gian did not recognize.

When everyone had found his or her place — men facing women all down the long tables — another fanfare announced the arrival of the wine, beer, mead, and water, and of the first of many dishes that were, Nino had to admit, surprisingly good. Two hours were devoted to the repast, which was interrupted from time to time by speeches — none by the Conte — and toasts, and amusing interludes provided by acrobats, dancers, and singers. The last of the entertainments was provided by a group of five girls from Arezzo who did cartwheels all around the courtyard; they were dressed in short skirts and their audience, which by this time had become sleepy and tired, was jolted awake by the discovery that the girls wore no underclothes. The women pretended to cover their eyes but the men clapped and whistled and threw coins to the girls, who took their places on the steps beneath the trumpeters. At this point, chamber pots were brought so the guests could relieve themselves, after which they returned to their places.

The Conte stood as a ferocious fanfare echoed around the high walls. "Welcome, guests!" he said, loud enough for all to hear but not too loud. "I am happy you have come to dine with me today and happy the weather has also been welcoming. I would like you to remember this day with pleasure and I have arranged for a small gift of no great value in itself except as a memento." He paused while pages trotted along the tables distributing scarves to the women and gloves to the men.

"And now," the Conte proclaimed, "the promised contest. Which of Cortona's damsels is the most beautiful; on whom will I have the honor of bestowing this golden apple?" He held the object high above his head; the sun caught it and flashed its brilliance to all eyes.

The pages indicated the place where twelve of the youngest girls and women would stand facing the high table; Nina, her nerves trembling with a kind of dread, was positioned near the middle. Out of the corner of her eye, she glanced up and down the line. Most of the competitors she knew, but there was one, hardly more than a girl, with lovely soft blond hair and a surprisingly full figure that her dress emphasized rather than concealed, whom Nina had never met. She's certainly the most beautiful of all of us, she quickly decided, with more relief than discomfort. Her decision allowed her to relax, and she stood straighter, arms at her sides and her head held high, satisfied that she looked as well as she could even if she wasn't the best. There was a little smile on her lips as she realized she was certainly not the worst looking of the group; another quick glance suggested she might be one of the prettiest four or five.

But it's of no account, she said to herself. All of them may care a lot; fortunately, I don't care at all.

The contestants were asked to walk slowly in a circle before the judges and then, one at a time, to turn slowly around in their original places. This is ridiculous, Nina thought, but it's also fun. Maybe I've been wrong to be so standoffish. Many of these girls could be my friends but I've never encouraged that. I will from now on. She felt she would especially like to know the beautiful blond girl who would surely win; she wondered who she was. She had noticed how she walked and turned with a special grace. The judges will see that too, Nina thought.

They were eight men, none of whom was the father or brother of any contestant. Slips were given to each judge on which he marked his choice, after which a page collected the markers and gave them to the Conte. He looked at them for some time, shuffling them in his fingers. He turned to Nerone and said a few words; the man nodded.

Conte stood as another fanfare echoed around the walls. "A very strange thing has happened," he announced, smiling, "but before I tell you what it is, I ask each of the contestants in turn, starting on my left hand, to come forward to claim your prize." The girls looked at one another; what could this mean? When the first girl reached the high table and curtseyed, the Conte extended his hand. In it was a small object, not much bigger than a grape; it was a copy of the golden apple he had held aloft. To each girl he murmured a few words of thanks; only when all had returned to their places did he rise again.

"The judges," he explained, "were asked to choose not one but three of you, with the three ranked in order, first, second, and third. I'm happy to say that not a single one of you failed to be chosen by at least one judge as at least the third most beautiful of all. But, counting first choices as three, second as two, and third as one, three clear winners have been selected."

He paused and wet his lips; the trumpets sounded again. "Tina Manzoni, please step forward. You are the winner of the third prize." Nina knew Tina; they had played together in exile. She watched her advance to the high table. Yes, she's very pretty, Nina thought; I should have realized that before. But who will be second and first?

Tina curtseyed again, and the Conte presented her with another golden prize, this one in the form of a cherry. She returned to her place, blushing, both pleased and disappointed, Nina could see.

The trumpets sounded again. I'm growing tired of those trumpets, Nina said to herself. The Conte waited, letting the anticipation swell. Finally he spoke. "I told you a strange thing had happened. It is this: Two of you have tied for first place. Each has received the same number of first, second, and third place votes; the total is therefore the same." He waited again.

"Please come forward, Angelica Bordoni." The blond girl, with a quick glance around her, took a few steps and then waited, unsure of where to stand. "And Mariana Torreoni, please come forward, too."

Nina was stunned; her heart beat fast. She too looked around; the expression on her face said she begged the others' forgiveness, that there must be some mistake. But she stepped forward and stood next to Angelica. They didn't look at one another.

"Fortunately," said the Conte, smiling broadly, "the tree that bore the golden apple bore another as well, and I have plucked it. Here, Angelica, is your prize; may you use it to win the right swain, and may he not be Paris of Troy. And here is yours, Mariana; may you not love the same man as Angelica." He threw up his hands. "And now," he called, "let us applaud all these winners, and especially these three, and most especially these two. Is there another city in Tuscany that can boast such beauty in its damsels?" The entire company was standing, laughing and clapping their hands. Nina stared at the Conte. Then, urged by a page, she followed Angelica to the other stage; where there had been one chair there were now two. She took her place and only then turned toward her companion. Her small smile invited a smile in return.

"I was sure you would win," Nina whispered. "I was surprised by what happened."

"I thought you would, or one of the others. Are you pleased?"

Nina thought a moment. "I'm not sure. Are you?"

Angelica shook her head. "I don't like to sit here with everyone looking at me. But I'm glad I'm not alone." At the urging of one of the pages, she held out her hand and Nina took it. The trumpets bellowed again.

More wine was poured and their health was drunk. Some of the guests lined up to congratulate the winners. Nino was one of the first; he joked with Nina but his pleasure couldn't be hidden. He kissed Angelica's hand and looked into her eyes. "I'm happy for my sister and for you. Any other decision would have been unjust." Others followed him and, toward the end of the line, Benno. He was dressed in a dark tunic Nina hadn't seen before; Gianna had made it for him.

It was hard for him to speak to either woman. He kissed their hands and Nina introduced him as her friend. When he said, hesitating, *"Amica,* Mistress," Angelica looked quickly at him. Nina lowered her eyes, which were full of tears.

Conte Pietro was enjoying the results of his *trucco*. It had worked out exactly as he had planned, except that the Torreoni girl had gained more votes than he had expected. She had even received two first-place votes, although all the others had gone to the Bordoni girl, who he had expected to win every one. There was no question she was a beauty; her blue eyes and blond hair were stunning and her deliciously rounded figure made his mouth water.

But the Torreoni girl was also a beauty. Her face and figure lacked the perfections of Angelica's, but she had striking good looks even so. Her flashing eyes and thick black hair were of the sort that made a man look twice when he passed her. As he watched them chatting together after their first uncomfortable moments, Nina's animation demanded attention. In ten years, he thought, she might be the more beautiful and probably the more interesting.

He had arranged it, with Nerone's help, so he could see them together, isolated from the crowd. He had wanted them both to be pleased and excited in order to see what effect that would have. They seemed in no hurry to leave their little decorated thrones. So much the better; he was enjoying himself just looking. He had given orders; the pages would keep them seated until he had paid his respects.

Which of them would he prefer to have as his third and last wife? If he were absolutely free to choose, the choice would be hard, he thought. Perhaps . . . He turned over the possibilities, the difficulties. If he could take either one of them at this moment, it might well be Mariana Torreoni.

The trouble was he wasn't free to choose, at least not at this moment. Angelica was his for the asking, he believed, even though her mother had apparently sworn to oppose the marriage with all her strength. But what was her strength compared to his and her father's? The girl's own desires need not be taken into account.

Mariana was a different matter altogether. He was aiding the elder brother and would continue to do so. He had made approaches to the father about business matters and had not been rebuffed, although so far the matters had been trivial. He had not mentioned the daughter. What answer would he receive if he did?

Probably a direct approach was out of the question. It might stir up the hatred that still underlay the difficult smiles Ser Gian had for him when, as happened infrequently, they met. It was regrettable about the older sister. He had had nothing to do with that, although at the time it had not displeased him; now he was sorry it had happened. But you could never turn back; you always had to start from where you were.

There was one thing about both young women that seemed to be in his favor. As far as he knew — he had made discrete inquiries — neither was spoken for; neither had lost her heart to another man. He felt that Ser Gian would be able to see the great advantages to himself and his family if . . . He shrugged his shoulders. Was there anyone who might act as a go-between? He would have to think about that.

He strolled across the courtyard and approached the little thrones. The girls immediately stopped their animated chatter and looked down at him as he ceremoniously knelt at their feet. "Madonna Mariana, Madonna Angelica," he murmured as he raised their hands to his lips. "You have honored me by your presence and by your beauty. Please know that you will always be welcome in this old gray fortress, which today you have made delightful." He stood. "Thank you both. I was so pleased by the vote, which was entirely just."

He held out his hands, and they accompanied him to the portal. A single trumpet sounded and pages hurried to where they stood. "I would like you both to stay as long as you wish, but I see that your family, Mariana, are preparing to depart, and yours too, I expect, Angelica. God go with you both."

They turned and ran across the bridge, holding hands and laughing. They didn't look back until they were on firm ground again. When they turned to wave, they saw him standing, all alone in the great doorway, raising his hand in a salute. Both were struck by how sad he seemed.

A few weeks later Signora Bordoni brought her daughter to Case Torreoni. She and Donna Lisabeta had once been friends, but the marriage of the fiery southerner to a minor landowner and that of Donna Lisabeta to a merchant of the city had separated then in more ways than distance could explain. Signora Bordoni had conveyed her sympathy to Ser Gian when she heard of his wife's death, but for many years there had been no contact between the families.

She had hoped to see Ser Gian and speak to him about her plans, but he was not at home. Mafalda asked her to wait if she wished and offered her something to drink. Both mother and daughter accepted a cup of cool water and Mafalda went in search of Nina.

"You have a visitor, Mistress."

Nina came reluctantly from the kitchen where she had been making bread. As soon as she saw Angelica she was sorry she hadn't stopped to at least wash the flour from her hands. Angelica was well dressed and looking more dazzling than ever, with a cap of fine French lace and jewels at her throat and ears. Nina bowed and Angelica curtseyed; then they burst out laughing.

Angelica introduced her mother. "My daughter has learned much during her five years at the convent," she said, "but as yet she knows little of the world. She's going to spend a few weeks at the home of her aunt, her father's sister. She lives nearby. You're the only person of her age that she knows. She and I are hopeful that you might be able to help her find some new friends . . ."

Angelica looked at Nina woefully. It was all so hopelessly formal and idiotic. Although she had been looking forward to seeing Nina again, she was sorry she had come.

"I don't know many people," Nina said. She was unhappy about the idea of being a chaperone to someone she had only met once.

"Perhaps we shouldn't stay, mother," said Angelica. "I can see that Mariana is busy; we're disturbing her. Perhaps another day . . ."

Nina sprang to her feet, feeling guilty. "No," she cried. "Stay for a while; it's a beautiful day. We might take a walk. Would that be all right, Signora?"

The woman nodded. "Of course. Will we remain in the piazza? We don't want . . ."

"I don't mind," said Nina. "Would you like to?" she asked Angelica, who smiled.

Nina ran to her room and changed her clothes and combed her hair. I'll never make myself as pretty as she is, but at least I don't want to look like her servant, she said to herself. She returned to find Mafalda and Angelica talking about the gala at Pierle; they remembered it very differently, Angelica thought. She went with Nina to the door and down the steps, walking with her back straight and her head held high, almost gliding as the nuns had taught her. Nina felt awkward in her presence.

The three women walked slowly around the piazza, which was almost deserted because the market had ended and the *passeggiata* had not yet begun. At the corner of the street the Signora said she would leave them while she went to help her sister-in-law with the dinner. "Don't stay out too long. And thank you, Mariana. I do hope we haven't disturbed you."

The two young women started to make another turn around the piazza. "I was baking bread," Nina said, by way of explaining her disarray.

"Oh, I like to bake bread," said Angelica. Nina was surprised. "I learned to bake different kinds at the convent and now that I'm home I bake every week."

"The women don't bake bread for your family?"

"There aren't many women. There are three soldiers' wives but they work mostly in the fields and vineyards. The wives of the peasants are always busy. My mother used to bake, now I do it. I suppose she'll go back to it while I'm here."

"That's a beautiful dress," said Nina. "Did you make it, too?" She couldn't stop glancing at it and admiring its fine materials and workmanship.

Angelica smiled.

"I should have gone to that convent," Nina said laughing. "I don't know anything."

"They say you know how to fight like a man. I'd like to know that."

"You would?" Again Nina was surprised. "I don't know how to fight very well. My brother Nino — you remember him?"

"I met him at Pierle, but we didn't have time to talk. He's older?"

Nina nodded. "Two years. Nino lives at Torreone in a castellino our father gave him. It's all he'll have because he's the younger brother, but it's a fine house and I like to go there. Nino and Robert the Frenchman — you remember him? — practice with swords and staves every day and they let me watch and even practice with them sometimes. But you

137

mustn't think I know a lot about it, and I couldn't make a dress like that or like the one you wore at Pierle."

"It's not hard. I'll show you if you like." Angelica found it hard to believe Nina would want to make a dress like hers. She was so slim and strong, graceful in her movements, like a cat walking along the top of a narrow wall never once fearing to fall. Her face is beautiful, Angelica thought, although her skin is dark from the sun as mine has never been allowed to be and although her hair doesn't seem to have been combed very recently. She must be comfortable in those clothes instead of in a long hot dress.

"Would you like to go to Torreone?" Nina asked suddenly. Half an hour before, she wouldn't have thought of asking this newcomer into her private world. But she found she liked Angelica even more than she had at Pierle. She was so beautiful — Robert and Nino would like to see her again.

Angelica nodded quickly. Half an hour before she wouldn't have thought twice about refusing. She had disliked the idea of being brought to the house of this rich city family primped and dressed for show. But Nina was interesting . . .

After telling Mafalda they planned to walk to Torreone and might not return for an hour or two, the two young women climbed the steep path to the Montanina gate and started on the narrow curving road. The watchmen cried out a greeting to Nina and added a whistle or two for Angelica. Nina glanced at her, surprised that she took no notice of the frank admiration of these rough men.

It was a lovely October day, cool in the shade but warm on the sunny road. The chestnut trees were already dropping their fruit and the olives, their silver leaves twisting in the slight breeze, were spotted with green, brown, and black fruit. The grape harvest was over, but a few clusters of deep purple grapes still hung from some of the vines, either waiting to be picked later for *vin santo* or just overlooked and now forgotten.

It was quiet as it usually was in the afternoon. A distant dog barked and a pair of doves cooed their persistent, maddening moan of love. In the far distance a narrow plume of smoke rose from a countryman's fire.

They passed a small herd of swine grazing alongside the road. "The swineherd, Giovanni, is my friend," Nina said. "Since I was a very little girl he's taken care of me."

"They're wearing bells like cattle." Angelica's father kept his swine in a filthy crowded pen as did most of the farmers.

"Giovanni says pigs like freedom as much as we do. They don't get lost because of the bells. He makes the bells and the leather thongs around their necks. He also says they like music and he sings to them." Nina looked around. "I don't see him now, otherwise we could stop and talk." She paused for a moment. "I don't know if it's because of the songs and their freedom, but they grow to be fat and taste good. I try not to be friendly with any of them."

"You mean because of . . ."

"I hear them scream. It's necessary but I hate to hear it."

"I don't like to see my mother wring the chickens' necks. They run around for a while without their heads and then fall over. The men laugh at it." Angelica looked at Nina, who returned her gaze; they smiled in complicity.

"Benno is Giovanni's son," Nina said. She hadn't meant to mention him but it seemed natural to do so.

"Benno?"

"The man who came to congratulate us — the last one in the line."

"I remember. He called you Mistress."

"He always does, although I tell him he doesn't have to. He and I are friends. We have been since we were children."

Angelica didn't reply, and Nina was a little sorry she had mentioned him. But I would have eventually, she said to herself. Anyway, there's no reason why I can't talk about him because he really is my friend.

They walked on, arm in arm, content in one another's company. They rounded the last curve. "That's Torreone," said Nina. The old tower, newly refurbished, rose from the side of the mountain with a kind of splendor in the full afternoon light.

"It's not so little!"

"It's little compared to lots of places. The Rocca at Pierle, for instance."

Angelica said nothing, but the blood left her face and she looked stricken. "Did I say something to offend you?" Nina asked, concerned. "If so, I'm sorry. Please forgive me."

"It's nothing," Angelica replied, but as they walked on Nina felt a shadow had fallen between them.

They approached the open gate. Angelica looked through into the courtyard and beyond to the tower with its battlements now outlined against the deep blue October sky. "I prefer this," she said firmly.

Nina hesitated. "Before we go in," she said, "I meant to tell you. The Conte called me Mariana and so did your mother. Actually, Benno does too, sometimes. Everyone else calls me Nina."

"I should call you Nina?"

"I think so. Mariana always makes me feel strange, although of course it's my real name."

They entered the gate. Nino and Robert were in the courtyard apparently just finishing their daily practice with quarterstaves. They threw down their weapons when they saw they had visitors.

Nina led her friend forward. "Robert de Beaumont, you remember Angelica Bordoni," she said, conscious of the formality of the introduction. "Nino, you remember Angelica? You came to see us both . . . You do remember, don't you?" This last because Nino was staring at the newcomer, a dazed look on his face. "Nino!"

"Angelica," he mumbled. He bowed, as did Robert, who was smiling broadly. "You are very welcome to our poor abode," Robert said. Gallantly he ushered the two young women to a bench, out of the sun but where they had a good view of the way it struck the tower. "We are happy to have such a good excuse to end our labors. Can I bring you a cup of wine?" He didn't seem to be able to stop talking — but perhaps this was to cover the confusion of his friend, who ought to have been acting as host. Nino stood still, paralyzed.

"Wine!" he suddenly shouted. He ran to the open portone. "Ho there! Wine for our guests! And something to eat — the best we have!" He returned wiping his hands. He removed his helmet and drew the shirt of mail over his head, throwing it down in a pile on the stones. "Whoof! I'm glad to be rid of it." His bare arms, tanned to the shoulder, glistened with sweat when he removed his heavy jacket.

Angelica stared at him. She had said nothing despite Robert's efforts to engage her in small talk. She looked about her at the courtyard filled with arms and equipment, at the open door of the stables, at the wide ramp leading to the portone, at the window in the tower. Nino followed her eyes.

"That's my new window," he said, but he told her no more.

Robert continued to fill the vacuum with his chatter, in Italian and, from time to time, in French. Once when he addressed a remark to Angelica in French, she responded in that language. She had learned it from the nuns. "Your accent is good," Robert said. "I know, because I'm French."

"*Moi je sais bien*," replied Angelica, smiling for the first time. It was easy to smile at Robert, who amused them all with his jokes and chatter. The wine came and the remains of a cake they had had for dinner. They ate and drank; then, as the shadows lengthened, Robert sang songs. Nino didn't sing as he usually did. Nina also noticed he seemed to have difficulty looking at Angelica; he sat with his head down. He seemed to her to be suffering.

Nina was growing irritated; she was being left out completely. Robert was flirting with Angelica, who was smiling at him but really paying no attention — her attention seemed to be on Nino, to whom she nevertheless said not a word. He was obviously in a bad mood; he was also being a bad host. Nina was sorry she had come and was especially angry with Nino. She began to try to make Robert flirt with her, laughing at his jokes and chatting with him, saying foolish things. Nino noticed it and was annoyed with her. Why was his sister making a fool of herself? He felt all the more beset, overcome by a paralyzing languor.

Suddenly Nina stood up. "They'll be expecting us to return!" she said to Angelica as though Angelica had been the one delaying them. Indeed they had been at Torreone for two hours without noticing the passage of time. They would have to hurry, for the sun was near the horizon and the gate would soon be closed. Robert and Nino accompanied them to the gate. Nino took Angelica's arm whenever they came to a rough place. She didn't object although she had had no difficulty walking the other way.

The two young women waved through the gate as it was being closed. Robert and Nino were still standing there, Robert looking cheerful, Nino looking sad.

Nina apologized for her brother as they walked down the path toward home. "He can be such a gloomy person sometimes," she said. although she realized this wasn't true. "Usually he's nice. I'm sorry he was such a bad host today."

She was unprepared for Angelica's response, for her new friend suddenly began to sob, her face in her hands. They had to stop while she found a kerchief and wiped her eyes. Her shoulders slumped, her cheeks streaked with tears, she was the picture of dejection; Nina's heart went out to her.

"I'm so sorry," she said softly. "I didn't think our visit would displease you."

"It didn't displease me," Angelica said. She straightened. "I'm the one who should be sorry. I apologize for my behavior."

"Tell me what's the matter," said Nina. Angelica shook her head. She took Nina's hand and pressed it, but she said nothing. By the time they reached her aunt's house she was as cooly beautiful and in control of herself as ever.

Nina walked slowly home; she was puzzled. Why had everyone acted so strangely? Something had happened to Nino, for he was ordinarily such a cheerful host. The way he

142

had looked at Angelica! As if he wanted to spring upon her and eat her! Suddenly she wondered if he had fallen in love. Had it started at Pierle? She remembered how he had looked at Angelica then, but they had exchanged only a few words, and today even fewer. She had heard others speak of such love at first sight, as they said, but it had been meaningless to her. I can't blame him, she thought, for she's certainly beautiful and she carries herself so well. But he doesn't really know anything about her. Can you fall in love with someone just for the way they look? Robert may have fallen in love with her too. Although even in her inexperience she realized he had just been playing. Her brother was another matter.

Nothing explained Angelica's reaction. She had made a great impression on Nino, maybe on Robert too. With them as friends she wouldn't lack for company in Cortona. But she had wept when they talked about the visit. There was a mystery about her. I'll find out what it is, she thought as she quickened her pace and reached home as dusk lay over the city.

Nino was silent almost all the way back to Torreone, and Robert didn't see fit to interrupt his thoughts. But as they neared the castellino, the Frenchman said in a cheerful voice, "That's certainly a good-looking girl. She will be a welcome addition to . . ."

Nino gripped his arm, digging into the flesh. "Did I make a fool of myself?" he whispered hoarsely.

"Only a little," said Robert, laughing. "But I think she rather liked it." He began to sing one of his songs. He didn't believe in being serious about women, especially young ones.

Nino wouldn't let him go. "What shall I do, Robert? Tell me what to do!"

"Do!" Robert chuckled. "Why, look in your Andre le Chapelain. He'll tell you what to do, when to do it, and what the result will be."

"This isn't a matter for joking!" cried Nino. "I don't need your foolishness."

Robert saw his friend was in real need. "You are in love then," he said gently. "And you want to know what to do about it."

Nino looked down. "Always it was a kind of game. At Pierle that's what I felt. Now I have the feeling that it's not a game anymore."

"You had better treat it as a game," said Robert, suddenly as serious as his friend, "or you are likely to lose out to someone else who does." But he recognized, as they stepped through the gate and into the courtyard, that he wasn't sure of this. In truth he had never believed in love or felt it. What would I do if I were in love with a woman? he wondered.

He looked at Nino standing in the middle of the courtyard staring at the cups that had held their wine and the birds pecking at the remains of their cake. Robert went to him and put his arm around his shoulder. "Come inside and have supper," he said. "Tomorrow we will work very hard with the long swords in the morning, and then in the afternoon we will plan what to do."

9

The Tomb of the Old Ones

Nino seemed a changed man. He fought with Robert with a grim determination that often led to his hurting the Frenchman in their practice bouts with swords and staves. Robert responded by fighting harder himself. One result was that both became more skillful than ever, especially in defense. If they had not done so, one of them might have killed the other.

Once, in a bout with unmuffled short swords, Robert struck Nino hard on the nose guard of his helmet, the blow opening a cut on his cheek. Blood ran down over his collar of chain mail. But Nino paid no attention. He continued to slash and parry, mouth drawn tight, eyes hard. Afterward he refused to let Mafalda treat the cut, saying it was nothing. When it healed it left a scar he bore for the rest of his life.

Robert had little useful advice for his friend in the matter of Angelica. He told Nino he should be patient and try to see and be near her, but he could think of nothing else. Nino dressed carefully in the late afternoons and went into the city. He haunted the street where Angelica lived with her aunt and strolled in the piazza in case she walked by, but she seldom went out, apparently, at least not during the evening *passagiata* when everyone else walked about, chatting in their best clothes. When he did see her, it was only for a moment or two. She would respond to his attempts at cheer with stern looks and few words.

Even so, he believed she liked him. There was something else, something he didn't understand. Because he didn't understand it, he was troubled, even a little afraid.

Nina and Angelica met frequently. They found it was easy to be silent with one another, merely sitting and thinking. This was welcome to Angelica, who didn't want to reveal her heart to anyone, and also to Nina, who didn't know how to reveal hers. Even so they felt close to one another. Neither had other friends they really liked; it was as though they had been intended for one another.

Angelica noticed Nina did not go regularly to church. She mentioned it one day.

"Regularly? I never go," Nina admitted. "I have a sort of dispensation from Father Rafaelo."

"He's not the priest at your church, Santa Maria?"

"His church is San Cristoforo, the little one on the way to Porta Montanina. He's old and poor and no one respects him. I like him very much — perhaps," she added, smiling, "because he's an outcast like me."

"You? The beautiful daughter of the Torreoni?"

"I'm not beautiful — even though . . ." She smiled, remembering their joint triumph. But she was serious. "There are those who have no love for my father."

"They say he's rich." It was an opinion Angelica had heard expressed.

"I don't know whether he's rich, but I believe there are a few Cortonesi who owe him money. That doesn't please them."

Angelica considered this. "It's not his fault they need him and he helps them," she said.

"You're right. If he refused, they would dislike him even more. But it's not because of him I'm an outcast. It's because of me. I don't like the way they live, and they don't approve of the way I do." Nina was surprised at herself. She had never said this to anyone.

"Who is 'they'?"

"You know. Almost all the people — all our friends except Nino and Robert and Benno."

"You've mentioned Benno, but I haven't seen him since Pierle."

"Is that true? He's always so busy, he has so much work to do. Anyway, he's Giovanni's son. He's my friend, and Nino's too," she added a little defensively, knowing it was no longer true. "We were brought up together and he's like another brother."

"The son of your swineherd? Is he a swineherd too?"

"He cares for the pigs when Giovanni's busy. He also does many other things. He's capable and I like him." Nina realized she was unable to describe her relationship with Benno even to her friend; as a result, she blushed. Angelica noticed but didn't press her.

"I was talking about the others, the people I've introduced to you," Nina went on after an awkward moment. "With their clothes and jewels and velvet shoes turned up to their knees. They look like silly birds clucking and strutting in the piazza in the evening. They're good for nothing and don't know why they're alive." Her seriousness amused her friend.

"I can see them now," she said, "those peacocks and peahens, wobbling their heads when they walk. When they talk they sound like pigeons, burbling and bubbling in their throats."

"I knew you would think so," cried Nina. "You're just like me." She was delighted.

"No, dear Nina, I'm not," said Angelica gravely. "You can better afford those opinions than I can. I know what I must do in life and I'm willing to do it. The choice of being an outcast is not open to me. I wonder if you can understand this?"

"I think you can be anything you want because you're beautiful and accomplished. Perhaps you're not as rich as you'd like," added Nina gently, "but that's not as important as you think.'

"Women can't be anything they want," Angelica replied bitterly. "I may not know much about the world but I know that. As for riches, they're more important than anything else. Poor women especially are little better than slaves."

"Slaves!" Nina stared at her friend. "I don't think so. Wealth doesn't make you free. My brother Lorenzo, who will inherit everything, will have to marry the woman Father has chosen even though he likes someone else better. I'm a little bit free, and Nino too, because Father allows it. He might change his mind. I'm always afraid of that! I'd fight if he tried to marry me to a man I hated; I think I'd rather die. Or I'd go into a convent even if I could never come out again."

"Will you be free to marry the man you want?"

Nina looked down, confused.

Angelica took her hand. "You don't have to tell me. But would you do that, go into a convent, even if your whole family depended on you?"

Nina stared at her. Her mind was racing. She had heard the rumors — what did they mean?

"Naturally, that's not my situation," said Angelica quietly, and they went on to speak of other, easier things.

Benno, son of Giovanni, was now twenty years old. He had long since become a man and he did a man's work and more in his father's aid, whom he was rapidly replacing as the most trusted of the Torreoni *coloni*. He was respected and liked by most people for his good looks and cheerful demeanor as well as his skill with animals and tools. But with all his surface cheer, he was not happy.

He wasn't only unhappy because of his love for the odd and unpredictable daughter of his master. That was the prime cause, doubtless, for he still knew his love was inexpressible and impossible, and apparently his father continued to agree about this although they hardly ever spoke of it now. Nor had his love abated. If anything, it was stronger then ever; it lay inside him like a heavy weight on his heart that was sometimes so overwhelming he felt weak. But even if he hadn't loved a woman he could never have, he would still have been unhappy. For he was ambitious, and as long as he remained at Cortona, working with his father and his pigs, he could no more expect to realize his ambitions than to gain his beloved. Thus he felt that he lived in an invisible prison from which he would never be able to escape.

He no longer brought flowers to Nina every day, but he served her in many small ways and knew she was pleased by his attentions. He even thought she liked him, perhaps a lot. But he was equally certain she looked down upon him and pitied him for his inferior station. He felt this especially strongly when they spoke Latin to one another, which they usually did when they were alone. To be able to read and write Latin was such a strange talent for the son of a swineherd! He mostly kept it a secret, and as a result even this talent didn't make him feel better about himself.

He seldom saw Nino anymore except when he had work he could not avoid at Torreone. He tried not to see him because he suspected Nino had guessed his feelings about his sister. There was a coolness between the two young men, good friends as they once had been, that was painful for them both. And this was all the more so after the meeting between Nino and Angelica, when Nino became difficult for everyone to deal with.

One afternoon, late in the year, when Benno was walking from Cortona to Torreone for a few hours of work he had been asked to do on the castle walls, he saw Nina in the road ahead of him. He hurried to catch up and they walked together the rest of the way.

They talked in Latin about Christmas and other inconsequential things, but Benno's heart churned within him. His fingers curled as his hands hung at his sides with the desire he felt to take her in his arms and hold her and cry out that he loved her. He glanced at her walking easily beside him with her quick, eager step, but when she looked at him he turned his face away to hide the tears that filled his eyes — tears of frustration and hatred of his life, which he didn't know how to change.

Because Nina knew something of his feelings, she did pity him. But she didn't know how to speak to him about his feelings, or her own, which were troubling because they were so confused.

Nino was standing in the open gate when they approached and he was able to observe them closely before they realized he was there. They were not walking together or touching one another in any way, yet he could see, for the first time, the electric web that bound them. He had never seen two people so intent on one another. And suddenly he knew, beyond any question, they loved one another and probably were lovers.

He was filled with uprushing rage. All his own frustration was converted, instantly, into hatred for Benno, their friend, the son of their faithful servant who had betrayed his trust. And his sister, his beloved little sister, had been ruined by this devil they had taken to their hearts.

He welcomed them as though nothing had occurred. He and Benno worked until dusk made it dangerous on the wall. Then, after asking Benno to return the next afternoon, Nino went into the house. He chatted with Nina as if he were the same man he had always been; but she saw he had changed. She asked him what troubled him. Was it Angelica? She flinched as she saw the fury in his eyes.

"Angelica is nothing to me," he muttered. "But I wonder about you, sister. Are you honest?"

She paled. "What do you mean?"

"You and Benno. You're good friends?"

His tone was icy cold, and she shivered. It didn't seem to be a question and she didn't know how to respond.

"That's true? You're good friends?"

"Of course we're friends. We've been friends since we were little children. You and Benno, too . . ."

"You're right, Nina. Benno and I are good friends. He's also our *colono*. He belongs to us, he's our man. He owes us everything he is and has. You understand that?"

She stared at him, her face set in anger. "I don't believe that," she said after a while.

"You don't believe it?" He laughed bitterly. "I can see you don't. You think he's worthy of you, sister. Well . . ."

"Worthy of me! What do you mean?"

"You know what I mean. I've seen you with him. You've forgotten who you are and who he is. You're a little fool!"

"You think . . . you think that . . ." She was so angry she stumbled over the words. "There's nothing between Benno and me! We're friends still, as you and he used to be. You've forgotten how it used to be and you're very wrong to do so. He's not 'our' man, he's his own. You're cruel to think so ill of him!"

He raised his hand as if to strike her and she shrank from him. It was the first time she had ever feared him. His face was contorted as he stared at her and then turned away. "Go!" he said over his shoulder. "Say your prayers and think over carefully what you are doing."

Nino and Robert were working with quarter-staves when Benno came through the gate the next afternoon. It was cold and all three men were dressed in heavy garments. Nino wore no armor. He hailed the newcomer.

"Ai, Benno!" he called. "Come to work, have you? And where is Nina? She is not with you as she was yesterday?"

"I do not know, Master. I have not seen her."

"Strange! Well, so be it. Benno. I hear it told that you are skillful with these staves. Is there truth in that?"

Benno was surprised. It was true, he was respected as an opponent by the younger men in the countryside. Bouts at quarter-staves were a common event in rural festivities and he was usually the winner if he chose to compete. But Nino knew all that and they had often fought mock battles with the weapon.

Suddenly, Benno realized what was happening. Nino was challenging him for some reason. He nodded without speaking.

"Come and try a bout with me, then!" cried Nino. "We will see which of us is the stronger and more skilled."

Benno could not refuse although he hated the prospect of either winning or losing. He chose a staff and took up his position. Robert, who had been silent and seemed unhappy, agreed to serve as referee. He raised his arm, then dropped it.

Nino sprang forward, face twisted in fury. He struck and struck again with all his strength. Benno tried to defend himself, but his heart was so heavy he could hardly lift his staff to ward off the blows, much less hit his master hard enough to hurt him. He was skilled at defense, but Nino's ferocious onslaught would have overcome a man even more expert than he. Suddenly his staff flew from his hands, twisted away by Nino, and a moment later Benno found himself upon his back, Nino crouching above him, his heavy staff held against his throat.

"So who's the better man, Benno?" whispered Nino. He didn't want Robert to hear. "You're nothing. And I think I'll kill you." He moved to draw his dagger. But the horror of such a death made him pause. It was long enough to save them both.

"I won't do so, Benno, if you leave tonight," he said, his voice hoarse and low. "If you're here tomorrow, I'll kill you. Do you understand me?"

Benno's voice was also hoarse because of the pressure on his windpipe. "Leave here? Tonight?"

"By sundown, before the gates close. The night is long and you'll have time to go a long way. I don't care where as long as it's far. Or I'll kill you. It's your choice."

Nino jumped to his feet, for Robert was approaching. "You have fairly won," he announced, laughing a strained laugh. He turned to the man lying on the stones. "Are you all right, Benno?"

Benno struggled to his feet. He nodded to Robert and bowed to him. He turned and bowed to Nino, then walked out the gate and along the road to Cortona. He hadn't said a word.

Robert watched him until he disappeared. Then, without looking at Nino, he said, "You were angry, my lord."

"Justice required it," Nino responded. "He is a scoundrel." And without any further word of explanation, he strode away. For perhaps the first time, Robert did not dare to speak to him.

Benno walked home quickly. He was trembling with shock and anger, sweating, and then in the cold air he began to shiver. He felt his head and neck. He hit me hard, he said to himself, but I'm not badly hurt; it'll hurt worse tomorrow.

Leave Cortona! He ordered me to leave Cortona. This afternoon, before they close the gates. How long do I have? Two hours? Three?

The threat to kill me — was he serious, angry because I hurt him? I don't remember even hitting him, and anyway he was angry before the fight began, before I got there. Perhaps he meant to kill me in the fight then changed his mind. If so, I was lucky. Why did he want to kill me? What made him change his mind?

If I stay I'll have to fight him again, this time to the death. I can't kill Mariana's brother. And I, I don't went to die. So I must leave Cortona. Leave babbo. Leave her.

Is there any way I can see her before I go?

Giovanni was sitting in front of his house, eyes closed. Benno sat beside him. For a few moments he said nothing. He thought his father was asleep. Let him rest. He won't be able to rest when he learns what I'm going to do.

But Giovanni spoke first. "You're home earlier than I expected, Benno. I thought you would work on the wall until dark."

"I didn't work on the wall, babbo."

Giovanni opened his eyes and sat up. "What's the matter?"

"Everything and nothing, babbo. We had a fight . . ."

"A fight? With whom?"

"Nino. He challenged me and I had to fight. With staves. I didn't want to beat him but I couldn't have anyway, because he was like a mad dog. I think he wanted to kill me."

"Why, Benno? Because of Mariana?"

Benno hesitated. There was no time for anything but the truth. "Perhaps. Probably. He saw us together yesterday. Of course we did nothing. I've never said a word to her or touched her."

"He knew, looking at you. You and her. Just as I knew, a long time ago. Just as others know and are sorry."

"They pity me!" cried Benno, grief welling up in his throat, and rage.

"I'm not sure they pity you. Some think you're foolish but all are sorry for your pain."

"Do you think I'm foolish, babbo?"

Giovanni didn't answerer the question, and reached to touch his shoulder. "What happened in the fight? Are you hurt? There's a bruise . . ."

"A little, nothing important. But I'm going to leave. I can't stay here now."

Giovanni turned pale. "Leave!"

"I can't live this life, so near her, yet infinitely far. I cannot! Do you understand, babbo? I don't want to leave you, but I must."

"He's driving you away, that boy who I loved."

"He ordered me to leave," said Benno quietly, "but I'm not leaving just for that. There are so many reasons. There's nothing for me here; you know as well as I. Many young men are leaving, going to the cities to make their fortunes, babbo. I don't know if I can make my fortune, but I have to try. I couldn't live with myself if I didn't try!"

"What will you do? Where will you go?" He was trembling.

"I don't know. Florence, Siena — a city where I can lose myself in the crowd. If they don't find me in a year and a day, I'll be free forever of the Torreoni. We've even talked about this."

"They won't try to find you. The Torreoni. When will you leave, then? Preparations have to be made. It's a hard time for traveling. Will you wait till spring?"

"I have to leave tonight."

"Tonight!"

"Nino . . . those were his orders. He's right. I have to leave immediately."

"You needn't obey him. He's no longer your master," said Giovanni bitterly. "Or mine." He paused, thinking. "You'll go to Florence, then. And you'll take a letter from me to a man who used to be my friend. Is he still my friend? Is he even alive? I don't know. But it's all I can give you."

"What man? Have you ever spoken of him?"

"He's a priest. Or he was; now he's more than that. It's twenty years, Benno. A friend of mine and of your mother's. If he's alive and if you can find him and if he'll see you — none of this is certain — he'll be able to tell you some things you must know." He paused. "Go get me a piece of paper or parchment. And that pen you used when you were studying with the old priest. Go quickly!"

Benno stared at his father. He rose unsteadily and went into the house. On the shelf by his bed was the piece of parchment on which he had written the Lord's Prayer years ago. The other side was blank. The ink in the small inkpot was dust, but he mixed the powder with a little water and the goosefeather pen still worked. He returned to the bench, holding these meager materials. "There was nothing else to write on." He sat down. "What do you want me to write?"

"I'll do it," said Giovanni.

"But . . ."

"Hush," said his father, taking the parchment and spreading it on his knee. He held the pen awkwardly in his cold fingers, getting the feel of it. Muttering under his breath words that Benno couldn't understand, he dipped the pen in the ink and drew a wavering line on the seat. "Be patient, Benno. I'll have to do it slowly."

Bending over the parchment, he began to write, forming the letters with painstaking care, his hand shaking. The letter was short — only a few sentences — but it took him an hour. Finally he sighed and folded the parchment. He wrote a name and address on the outside fold.

"There," he said. Benno took the letter, turning it in his hand, staring at it.

"Don't read it now. Wait till you're a long way from this cursed city."

"No!" cried his son. "For she's a part of it."

"That's true, Benno, and the best part." He raised himself to his feet. "Now you must gather your things together — I fear you have little enough to carry — and say your farewells to Gianna, who has loved you like a son. I have an errand to do. I'll be back in an hour." He glanced at the sky. "There's time. I'll walk with you partway down the road." Tears came into his eyes.

Giovanni hurried to Casa Torreoni, knocked on the door and, breathless, announced he must see the master. Ser Gian appeared immediately, for Carlo had said he must come without delay.

"Giovanni," he said, and waited.

"My son is leaving. There's been trouble. I don't know exactly — perhaps others will tell you. My young master . . . Nino . . ."

Ser Gian nodded. "I've heard. There was a fight; it became more serious than it should have. But surely Benno doesn't have to leave because of it!"

"He has to leave," said Giovanni, nodding his head quickly. "He takes my heart with him but that's not important. I've come to ask you for one more thing."

"Anything!"

"You know the little stone house on the mountain where I used to sleep when I was tending the swine in the high pastures? Now, I want to go there because I can't stay here. Yet I don't want to leave Cortona, and you, Gian. In the summers I can still tend the swine up there and I'll do whatever else you ask as long as I don't have to come down . . . here."

Ser Gian swallowed. "You don't have to go anywhere," he said.

Giovanni didn't reply.

"Is that house livable?" asked Ser Gian after a moment. "The nights are cold on the mountain. How will you keep warm? What will you have to eat?"

"We'll manage, my woman and I."

After another pause, Ser Gian nodded. "The house is yours, Aldo. And if you like, I'll come to visit you from time to time and we'll sit in the sun like two old grasshoppers and chatter about the past." He embraced Giovanni then handed him a small purse. "He has to take this; it's his wages."

"No more?"

"No more."

The swineherd didn't turn to go. "Is my young mistress here?" he asked. "May I see her?"

Ser Gian stared at him for what seemed like a long time and then disappeared into the house. Soon Nina was at the door, her face as pale as snow.

"My son is leaving Cortona," said Giovanni. He spoke quickly, words tumbling off his tongue. "Tonight. We'll go down the road to Sodo. The big gate will close, in half an hour. Shall I take a message to my son, Mistress?"

Nina found it hard to speak. Her father had just told her the news but she hadn't really believed it. "Tonight?" She was bewildered but she didn't ask why for she thought, suddenly, she knew. "Tell him," she said. "Tell him . . ." She paused. "He's taking the road to Sodo? In that case, tell him nothing, dear Giovanni." She hurried into the house.

As they walked down the cobbled street to the Santa Maria gate, father and son said little to one another. Giovanni told Benno that from now on he and Gianna would live in the mountain house. Benno didn't question the decision; he only said he would always know where to find them. When they passed under the high arch of the gate, he turned and looked back. Then he began to walk rapidly down the road.

At the big curve below the cemetery, Giovanni stopped. He held his son in his arms, then stepped back and looked at the young man's face.

"There's one thing I must tell you, Benno. It's the most important of all. Your blood is as good as hers. I've told you, never forget it." He walked quickly away up the steep road and disappeared before Benno could ask him what he meant.

The moon, nearly full, had risen and now silvered the stones of the city walls and the valley far below as Nina made her way down the road to Sodo. She was grateful for its light, for she could keep the two men in view ahead of her, but she was careful to stay far enough behind so they wouldn't be able to see her even if they looked back.

It was utterly still in the cold December air as she walked on the road, startled from time to time by the shadows thrown across her path by the gnarled old olive trees. She was frightened and she kept hoping Giovanni would turn back so she could run to catch up with Benno. But the swineherd went on and on and therefore she did also.

Finally the two men stopped in the middle of the road and she saw them embrace. She saw Giovanni say something to Benno and that Benno seemed surprised. Then, suddenly, Giovanni was hurrying up in her direction. She ducked behind a wall and watched as he approached and passed her. She saw his face clearly in the moonlight and could tell there were tears still on his cheeks.

She waited until she could no longer hear his footsteps. Benno was out of sight; he must be walking fast. She ran, breathless, down the road, but it was a long time before she caught up with him.

Suddenly she saw him as he headed for a curve that turned into the hill. She knew the area well; they had often explored it. There was a shortcut, and she scrambled over the rough ground and came out on a little rise. The road was now below her and there he was, his long legs striding quickly. He wore a dark cloak, carried a pack on one shoulder, and swung a long heavy staff as he walked.

She crouched on the top of the wall and whispered as he passed: "Amicus!" It was the name she called him when they spoke Latin. She heard him gasp, then saw him cross himself. He stared around him, a wild look on his face.

"Up here, Amicus," she whispered. He looked and saw her. Dressed in black, she was almost indistinguishable from a bush or a stone, but her face shone white in the moonlight.

"Thanks be to Our Lady," he whispered, and started to scramble up the steep embankment till he reached the low wall. She reached out to help him but he climbed without her aid. She rose to her feet and he stood before her, arms at his sides. But he ached to touch her.

"Mariana!" he sighed.

"Amica had to come to say good-bye to Amicus," she said, laughing and crying at the same time. "So I'm here. Good-bye, Benno. I will miss you very much." She held out her hand.

It was no longer possible for him to resist the desire to touch her, to hold her, but he wasn't practiced at embracing women, so he reached for her roughly and grasped her to him. He needn't have feared, for although she too was unpracticed, she moved easily into his arms. He held her close and each felt and heard the other's heart beat. Her cheek was wet and, her hood being thrown back, her hair smelled of flowers or the moss of spring pastures.

"Mariana," he whispered again. Then they heard a sound and started. "We can't stay here on the wall," he said softly. "In the moonlight we can be seen for miles. Come," he took her hand, "the old tomb is nearby. Let's go there." She followed him, meekly obeying what he asked as she had seldom done.

They had discovered the Etruscan tomb years before when they were gathering blackberries. It was guarded by a great bramble, although from one side an entrance had been cut by a peasant who lived nearby. It was a magical place and stories were told about it by the country folk. Some said it was a tomb of the Old People, before the Etruschi; others said it had been a temple of Greek pagans; still others believed it to be a place sacred to witches, followers of the old religion.

Moonlight sifted down through the bramble as they picked their way to the entrance and found the low doorway into the tiny, ancient building. The floor was of packed dirt, the walls of enormous stones of the kind the Old People had used and that could still be seen in places at the bottom of the city walls. Part of the roof had fallen in long ago, and moonlight filtered down upon the two as they stood together, arms tightly round one another, as still as trees with branches intertwined.

He kissed her cheeks as he held her. Her tears were salty and he licked his lips. "I'm not Amicus," he whispered. "Mariana, I'm something more, or at least different."

"I know," she whispered against the rough wool of his cloak.

"And you? Are you, too, something more or different?"

She didn't answer but she held him tighter, pressing herself against his body from her knees to her shoulders, feeling his hardness, his manhood, something she had only thought about, with misgiving and a kind of wonder. And she felt herself melting into something new and different from what she had been. She began to sob but didn't let him go.

"Mariana," he said again; he couldn't say her name often enough. "I have no right to ask and I'll understand if you don't even answer me. But . . ." He hesitated.

"Yes," she whispered. "Yes!"

"You knew what I wanted! You'll wait for me!"

She looked up, her cheeks drenched. "If you promise to come back."

He swallowed hard; he hadn't expected it, he hadn't even let himself think it. It was what he had hoped beyond hope. "I swear it! I'll come back with an army and carry you away."

She laughed but didn't stop holding him. "Don't bring an army. Don't take me away. I like it here! We were children here and you brought me flowers. But come back. Promise!"

He held her for a long time. She didn't want to let him go. She thought if he threw her down on the cold ground and did to her what men did to women, she wouldn't resist; she would give herself to him. Whatever he wanted she wanted. Her heart was full of joy, for it had opened suddenly to a love she had never been able to imagine. Now it was easy to love where before it had seemed impossible, full of difficulties, complications. She murmured his name, kissed his neck, caressed his face with her cold fingers. Then she raised herself and kissed his mouth. At first their mouths were cold, then quickly hot and full of desire.

While he kissed her he reached inside her cloak, pressing her to him, passing his hands over her body. She shivered but not from cold, for her lips burned against his own. He touched her everywhere, her most secret places, and all the time their lips were glued together, their eyes closed, seeing with their fingers.

Finally, trembling, he withdrew his hands and held her roughly. "Are you my woman, then?" he whispered urgently, his lips buried in her hair.

"I think I've always been your woman, at least since I became a woman — and since I stopped being in love with my brother," she added laughing, then frowning. "My brother! He's a villain and I won't forget it."

"You must forget it," he said, holding her hands and staring into her eyes. "You mustn't stop loving him. Even I haven't stopped except for a while today. He loves you. He was protecting you."

"From you!"

"Yes, from me, but from a person who no longer exists. I was meek, frightened. Because I thought I couldn't leave you, I was willing to lose you. Now I'm leaving in order not to lose you. Do you understand?"

She nodded.

"He's still your best friend and you'll need him."

She had started to cry again. Sobbing, she fell to her knees and took off her cloak, spreading it on the soft dirt ground, carefully smoothing the wrinkles.

"What are you doing?"

"I'm making a bed for us as the peasant women do when they spend a night with their men in the open. They use their cloak for the underneath, next to the ground, and the men spread their larger cloak over them both. Come!" She held up her arms.

He trembled, his legs gave way. Sinking to his knees before her, he took her cold hands in his own. "I want you more than anything I ever dreamed of," he said, "but I . . ."

"Well then," she interrupted, "come and take me. I'm yours." She lowered her head, waiting.

"Oh Mariana!" he cried. "I know I must not, we must not. I've thought about it for years, night after night for years. When I come back we'll have whatever we want of each other. I'll come back if I live, for if I live I'll succeed, and then I'll be proud to go to your father and say I want you, and he'll say yes to me. I know it! But . . ."

Again she interrupted. "If you live!"

He nodded, serious, holding her steady with his hands and eyes. "I'll be a soldier. I know I'll be a good one for I'm skillful and strong and I'm not afraid. I'll serve some master for a while and then I'll be my own man. I'll be fortunate, I know it. And I'll bring my fortune home and lay it at your feet." He paused, feeling her tremble, from cold and fear.

"If I came back too soon," he said gently, "I wouldn't be able to stay."

Without a word she struggled to her feet. She leaned to pick up her cloak and wrapped it around her. She looked at him.

"Do you want me, then?" she whispered. "And it's just because — because you must not?"

"I've loved you, Mariana, all my life," he said, smiling a little as he saw her waiting for reassurance. "I'll love you all the rest of my life and I'll never love anyone else. Therefore if I lose you I'll lose love itself, and for me, I think, that would mean I could no longer live. I'll come back and when I do I'll stay, and you'll be my woman and, I hope, my wife — and the mother of my children. Do you know, Mariana, I've even dreamed of our children and given them names!"

She laughed. "And what are their names?"

"That's another thing for which we must wait," he said, suddenly serious.

She reached inside her tunic. "I brought you this," she said, bringing forth an object wrapped in red leather, though it seemed black in the clear moonlight. "There are flowers in it, too, if you look. I had little time . . ."

He unwrapped the dagger Nino had given her for her birthday, holding it in his hands, staring down at it as though it were alive.

"You will need it, I think, although I hope not, more than I. The steel is good. Nino said so."

"What will you say to him if . . ."

"Nothing. I'll say . . . He won't ask me, he's lost in his anger and frustration. I don't think we'll speak much to one another from now on."

He shook his head, holding her hands, willing his strength to flow from his body into hers so she would be able to wait for him and endure all she might have to suffer while he was gone. He knew what difficulties faced them even better than she. Then he turned away. She followed him, climbing through the bramble. He walked quickly down the road and did not look back.

"Fare thee well, Bernardo, son of Giovanni!" she called softly as he disappeared around a curve. For a long time she could still hear his footsteps and a sound of singing. She turned her head to hear; he was singing her name, that was all, over and over.

Halfway back to Cortona, Giovanni stepped from behind a tree and met her in the road. "I feared for you this cold night."

"I didn't think you saw me!"

"I didn't, but I thought you would come so I've been waiting. He's well away?" She nodded, and he threw off his old cloak and wrapped it around her, for now she was shivering so hard her teeth chattered. She leaned against him and they climbed the hill together as they had more than once. He led her through the dark secret passage at the top of the city wall and left her near her house. When he said good night to her, he, too, called her Mariana.

She stood in the street, staring at the house, remembering that other night when Giovanni had brought her through the wall, the night when Nino had left her to go to the monastery. There was an emptiness around her heart, for then she had thought only of him, of Nino, and now she thought only of another man. She shivered again and climbed on the bench and scratched at the shutter as she had done that other time.

The shutter opened and the outline of Mafalda's head was there, beckoning. "In with you!" Nina scrambled through the opening, although it was harder now because she was no longer a litte girl.

Mafalda was speaking to her; she didn't understand. "Quick! Give me your underthings! I'll wash them. No one will know."

"Wash them?"

"The blood. It comes out if you soak the clothes in cold water and then wash them. Quickly! And then I'll give you something to eat, child."

Nina embraced the old woman who was all the mother she had ever known. "There was no blood,'" she whispered. "I offered myself but he didn't take me."

"Didn't take you! Why?"

"He said I would need the strength of it, that it would keep me strong until he comes back. He promised, Mafalda!"

"What did he promise?"

"To come back. And I promised to wait for him."

Mafalda led her to a chair and brought her bread and cheese and milk and then a foaming cup of ale. She stroked her hair and stood by her while she ate. Afterward she led her to the mat on which she used to sleep and sat by her, caressing her face, her shoulders, her hands.

Nina began to cry, almost silently, her shoulders shaking. Mafalda said nothing but only held her pressed against her body. After a long time she went to sleep, but Mafalda continued to hold her, keeping her close, keeping her safe, promising her own promise, that she would stay with her until the end.

10

The Monsignor

When Bernardo reached Sodo, nestled at the foot of Cortona's mountain, he could tell by the moon that it was nearly midnight. He had friends in Sodo, but he didn't want to share his plans; also, his excitement kept him from feeling tired. He walked on through the little village on the way to Montecchio and Arezzo. The bright moonlight made every stone and pebble visible, allowing him to walk swiftly. He passed several farms, and even the watch dogs seemed to be asleep. He was alone in a vast silence, alone with his tumultuous thoughts.

He felt such joy that he wanted to shout at the top of his voice that he loved Mariana and that she loved him. Love made him light-headed and he began to speak as he walked, addressing the moon and the stars.

"Is it true that she loves me? But how can she love a man such as me, she who is the possessor of all virtues and beautiful and wealthy too, and I the son of a swineherd? Yet she loves me because she gave herself to me. I didn't take her because I must care for her now; when I'm far away I have to leave her able to defend herself from blame. But by God I wanted her!"

Other thoughts intruded. He carried another heavy burden now, that of his promise. *I told her I would succeed, but how? Will I be killed, far away; will I die in a ditch whispering her name, waiting for death? She'll never know what happened or why I didn't return. She'll wait for me, wondering why I have forgotten her, while life passes her by and she has no chance for happiness.*

He stood uncertain in the middle of the road. He started back but then he stopped again, knowing there was only one way he could go. He slept that night in a farmer's *capanna* at Mezzavia and arrived five days later at Florence. He had worn down his shoes, but the light of his joy burned as bright as ever. Nor had he been troubled on his journey, for a young man in an old cloak and with a heavy stick is not worth the danger of a challenge.

Bernardo had never seen a place as big or as busy as Florence. The streets were full of people, both men and women, and children as well, all of them in a hurry to be somewhere else. Horses were everywhere and great ox carts laden beyond the limits of safety carried merchandise of every description. A few soldiers lounged in the *logge* lining the streets, and groups of clerics picked their way among the crowds, but most people seemed to be engaged in buying and selling in the numerous markets and, less formally, on street corners as well.

For hours on his first day, he walked up and down, looking and listening, fascinated and excited. He bought a meager meal that cost more than he expected and rented a pallet where he could sleep come nightfall. Then he sat down on a bench in the big piazza, surrounded by traffic of every sort, and took out his letter. He turned it over and over in his hands, then opened it for the first time.

He was disappointed to discover that he couldn't read what was written. It looked like Latin and it seemed to be Latin, but it wasn't quite Latin. Was it a kind of Latin he hadn't been taught, or was it another language entirely?

At first he thought it might be because of his father's writing; he hadn't written anything for years. But the more he examined the letters, the more he realized they were clearly written; they just didn't mean anything to him.

He turned over the letter and saw, written on the fold, an address: His Excellency Monsignor Malpenti, Santa Croce, Firenze, it said.

Santa Croce. That's a church. I know I can find it. Bernardo had become accustomed to talking to himself. But a Monsignore! How will I find him and speak to him?

He asked directions and found the church in an area of small shops and workrooms where the cloth that had made Florence both rich and famous was dyed. Searching the twisting streets, he found two men who knew the Monsignor's office was at the top of a flight of stairs.

"He's not here today," one of them said. "Anyway, he wouldn't see you. Who are you?"

"My name is Bernardo and I've come from Cortona with a letter for his Excellency."

"All the way from Cortona! Hear this!" the first man said to the other. "All the way from Cortona. This fellow is an adventurer!"

Embarrassed, Bernardo persisted. "May I ask your honors if you can tell me when his Excellency will be here?"

"In the morning," he grunted. "Perhaps tomorrow, perhaps the day after."

Bernardo came the next morning, but the door at the top of the stairs was closed. He came again the next day and the day after. On the fourth day, the door was ajar. His heart in his mouth, he knocked and hesitantly entered a large room. At a low table in front of a fireplace with a cheerful fire sat a fat man, writing. He was dressed in black silk lined with fur and wore a round black hat with a narrow brim. On his fingers were several rings.

Bernardo fell to his knees. "Excellency," he murmured.

"Yes? What do you want?" The fat man did not look up.

"I have a letter." Bernardo had remained on his knees but the man beckoned to him and he approached, kneeling again to kiss the proffered fingers.

"Who is the letter from?"

"It's from my father, your honor."

"And who is your father?"

"His name is Giovanni and he is a swineherd. He told me he was once your friend."

"I have never had a swineherd for a friend," said the fat man. "Your story is curious to say the least."

"I don't think he was a swineherd then," Bernardo said. "I don't know what he was. I've come to you in the hope that you will tell me about my father, and my mother, too."

"Your mother? Did I know your mother too?" The fat man smiled. "Was she a milkmaid by any chance?"

Miserable, Bernardo reached in his tunic and handed the letter to the Monsignor, who took it and stared at it as if it must be tinged with pig manure.

"Have you read the letter, young man?" he asked.

"I tried, but I couldn't, Your Excellency."

The monsignor glanced at the address and unfolded the piece of parchment. "I'm sorry to tell you if you don't know it already," he said severely, "but this isn't a letter. It's the *Pater Noster*. Naturally you couldn't read it because it is in Latin."

"Yes, your honor, I knew that," Bernardo said, his eyes pleading. "I wrote it. The letter is on the other side."

"You wrote it? Can you write Latin, young man?"

Bernardo nodded. For the first time the Monsignor noticed how tall and strong the young man looked, how handsome was his frank, open face. He wore an old cloak and his shoes were all but worn through, yet there was something about him that belied the appearances. He might well be the son of a swineherd, but he also might not. He shook his head, turned the parchment over, and began to read the letter. When he finished he looked at Bernardo, then read the letter again.

"You don't know what's in this letter, Bernardo?" His tone had softened.

"No, your honor."

"I'm not surprised, because it's written in a language your father and I invented many years ago. I don't think anyone else could read it, except perhaps one other man. He didn't teach you, then?"

"I didn't know my father could read or write until a few days ago. He never taught me anything of that sort."

"Yet you know Latin?"

Bernardo nodded. He didn't have the strength to explain.

"You say you didn't know he could read or write? That's strange, very strange. Because once your father was a scholar. He knew Latin and French and some Hebrew and Arabic, for he studied the theologians. You didn't know?"

Bernardo shook his head.

"You say your father is Giovanni, just that, Giovanni. That's not his name. You don't know his real name?"

Again Bernardo shook his head. He was trembling with excitement and apprehension.

"Your father's name was Aldo, Aldo di Benci. He wasn't a swineherd, far from it. He was a younger son of an important family of this city. There are still Di Benci in Florence — if you asked, you would find them. But perhaps you shouldn't do that. We'll think about that." He grew silent, staring at the young man standing before him, then noticed that he was trembling. "Here," he said, tossing a pillow from his chair. "Sit down and we'll talk." He watched as Bernardo almost fell onto the pillow. "Have you eaten today?"

"No, your honor," Bernardo admitted.

The Monsignore called and a servant appeared. "Bring my visitor some bread and cheese and wine," he ordered. "And tell no one to disturb us." The servant returned after a very few minutes, during which the Monsignor said nothing. The servant departed. "And close the door after you, if you please!"

He waited until Bernardo had finished eating. Then he said, "Well, Bernardo di Benci — for that's your real name because you are your father's son — I'm not sure how to begin. So I'll start by asking you some questions. You've lived with your father at Cortona?"

Bernardo nodded.

"And he was, and is, a swineherd?"

"For Ser Gian Torreoni, a lord of Cortona."

"Of course," said the Monsignor. "I knew him, too. He's the other man who could have read your letter. He's now a merchant, a buyer and seller of cloth?"

"And of money."

"Yes, of money. Which is usury. If I were a better Churchman, I might disapprove." He paused. "How old are you, Bernardo?"

"I'm twenty, your honor."

"Of course — you must be. And for those twenty years your father has served Ser Gian as his swineherd, and no one knew he once lived a different life."

Bernardo shook his head. "At least I didn't, nor did Gianna. She's my father's wife, but not my mother. He told me that. I don't think anyone else knew." He thought of something that had troubled him. "Perhaps Ser Gian knew . . ."

"He did," said the Monsignore. "Now I ask you, what do you think made your father change from being a scholar, a young man not much older than you are now and with a brilliant future — what made him give up all that to become a swineherd? Surely it was a strange choice for the man he was?"

"I don't know."

"But what do you think?"

Bernardo looked down. His mind was whirling, his thoughts disjointed. "It must have been something terrible, something that made him very unhappy," he said finally. "It could only have been something like that."

The Monsignore continued to smile at him, but not unkindly. "You say he's married?"

"She is the daughter of a peasant and she cannot read or write, but she has cared for him and she also took good care of me for as long as I can remember."

"I'm glad to hear it. He wasn't fortunate in . . . women. Then, my young friend, you didn't know he was a priest?"

"A priest!"

"A priest, a Dominican, one of the Dogs of God who nip our Franciscan heels when we don't behave. Just the same, he was my friend, Aldo, Gian, and I, we three. Now I am a monsignor, Gian is a wealthy money lender, and Aldo is a swineherd called Giovanni." He waited, but Bernardo said nothing.

"He told you this wife — Gianna is her name — wasn't your mother. He told you nothing else?"

"No, your honor. I asked him but he wouldn't tell me. After he told me that, he never said another word."

"It's no wonder, young Bernardo. I'm sorry to be the one to tell you, but your mother is dead. I hope she is in Heaven."

"You hope . . . you're not certain . . . ?" Bernardo had noticed the hesitation in the choice of words.

"I'm not certain anyone is, but I'm equally uncertain any particular person is *not* in Heaven. We can discuss theology another time. Now we are speaking of your mother." He paused, looking into the fire.

"My father said you were her friend."

"Yes, she was my friend and I was hers." He said no more, nor did he look at Bernardo.

The Monsignor sighed deeply. "Your mother was not married to your father, although I believe she loved him very much, and he loved her." He looked at Bernardo for the first time since he had begun to speak of her. "Why were they not married?"

"I don't know. Unless . . ."

"Unless she was already married to another man? That was so, Bernardo. Her husband was much older and very rich. When she married him she was only thirteen. Do you not pity her?"

"Oh God, Excellency, tell me the truth!" Bernardo cried.

"The truth is, soon after you were born, your mother's husband discovered you were not his son, and he killed her. That is the truth, although not all of it."

"Killed my mother? Murdered her?"

"With his own hands."

"Where is he?" cried Bernardo, struggling to stand up. "Is he in Florence? What is his name? How can I find him?"

"Please sit down, Bernardo. We'll see if those are things you should know. I'll tell you one thing: He isn't in Florence. And another: I don't know whether he is alive or dead."

Bernardo fell to his knees. Shaking, he held his head in his hands. "But you do know my father didn't kill him?" he murmured.

"He did not. He wanted to but we held him back, Gian and I, for Aldo would not have gotten her back and he would have lost his own life. Your mother's husband was a great nobleman. They would have tortured any man who even tried to kill him, whatever his reason, and hanged him from a hook in the wall of the Bargello. We couldn't bear to see that happen."

Bernardo continued to sway back and forth. He raised his head. "You said there was more to the truth." His voice was grim.

"There is more for you to hear, Bernardo. I told you your father was a priest." Bernardo nodded. "He was her priest."

"Her confessor?" Again he had started to tremble.

"Her confessor. Thus they had many opportunities to be together, alone. I hope you will forgive him, because I did, long ago."

"He shouldn't have done it." His mouth was dry.

"He shouldn't have done it, and her father shouldn't have married her to such a man, for all that he was a Marchese and a Prince of the Empire, and perhaps God shouldn't have created the world, but if He did not, and they did not, you would not exist and we would not be talking here. You haven't forgiven him?"

"He must have been . . . greatly tempted." Bernardo knew how sacred was the relationship between a confessor and his charge.

"They were both tempted, whether or not by the Devil, I don't know. Your father was handsome and kind, your mother was young and unhappy. There was no hope for them. So they fell hopelessly in love."

It was impossible for Bernardo to imagine his father in that state. But he thought of how he had loved Mariana when he too was without hope. Had his father felt the same way? "I won't stop loving my father, and respecting him," he said after a while. "It's not for me to judge him."

"No, it's not. It's for God to judge all of us." The Monsignore was looking away again, into the fire, then at the window with its small distorted pane of glass. "Do you have any idea how your father felt?"

"When they told him she was dead?"

"No one told him. He received a package, a basket."

Bernardo was filled with dread. "A package?"

"A large package wrapped in cloth like a gift. It contained two things, one living, one dead."

"I don't understand," Bernardo whispered, keeping his eyes on the Monsignore, who had swung around to face him.

"The living thing was a child, a month old. Who was that?"

"Me?" Bernardo was gasping for breath.

"You. The other was a severed human head."

Bernardo fell forward onto the floor. For several moments he was unconscious. He sat up, dazed. There was blood on his forehead where it had struck the stone. He touched his face, then wiped his fingers on his cloak.

The Monsignor was looking down at him. He hadn't stirred from his seat. On his face was suffering, as though he knew how terrible the world is. "There was also a letter. From your mother's husband. 'Here is your bastard,' is what it said." He didn't tell Bernardo the rest of the letter, for he believed it would be too cruel.

"He cut off my mother's head!"

The Monsignor nodded.

"And sent it to my father?"

He nodded again.

"May he be damned for all eternity!"

The Monsignor didn't reply.

"And my father did nothing?"

"There was nothing he could do. You fell to the floor, but you did not know her. He loved her; she had borne his son. He went mad for a time and Gian took him away, together with the child. When he came back to life — his madness was a kind of death — he remembered the child that had been in the package. You. And he swore he would devote his life to you because you were hers. Evidently he has done that, Bernardo."

"Whatever they did, my mother and father," said Bernardo through his teeth, "they didn't deserve . . . that."

"No," said the Monsignor quietly, "they didn't deserve that."

Bernardo began to cry, then he raged, then he cried again. Finally he became aware of the Monsignor's hand on his arm; he was sitting beside him on the floor, holding him.

"I'm sorry," Bernardo said, his head hanging.

"I'm sorry too. I've been sorry for twenty years. All that time I've wondered about Aldo, your father. He said he was going away — I didn't know how far he had gone — not just to Cortona, but to another person, another life. I've heard little from Gian, nothing from your father until today. He and Gian were always close. Even so, it's a strange thing for him to have done."

"I think I can understand why he couldn't tell me," said Bernardo after a while, "but if I hadn't found you, I wouldn't have known."

"That was the chance he took. I too understand; it was hard enough for me to tell you."

"Thank you, Your Excellency," said Bernardo, swallowing. "I owe you much for your generosity. You could have turned me away."

"I could have done that," said the Monsignore simply. Perhaps I should have, he thought. But how could I not tell him?

Bernardo hardly heard him. "To think," he mused. "Ser Gian must have taken care of me while my father was … dead, as you say."

"He found someone, a woman. I believe her name was Giovanna, or Gianna. Perhaps your father's wife is even more your mother than you think." Bernardo sat, nodding his head.

"And now the question is, what will you do? I wouldn't return to Cortona for a while."

"I can't go back to Cortona."

"You can't?"

He regretted he had said even this much. He didn't want to say anything about Mariana or her brother. "I left home to seek my fortune, as a soldier. I can't return with nothing; they would laugh at me."

"The letter says more." Bernardo didn't reply.

"I won't press you." The Monsignore sighed again. "Out of the love I bore your father, and pity for them both, I'll help you as he asked me to do. I will write to Ottone Visconti, Archbishop of Milan. I'll try to find you employment, or he will, in his continuous wars. What advantage you make of this, or don't, is up to you." He paused. "Have you been a soldier?"

"I have not, but I've won some bouts at quarter-staves — and lost some, too."

The Monsignor smiled. He was feeling much better now that the hard part was over. He liked this tall young man with the broad shoulders and the honest face. "Well, I suppose that is something. I believe soldiering is one profession in which an amateur can succeed, if he's brave and determined. Let us hope that happens."

He drew a clean sheet of parchment from a leather case, dipped a silver-handled pen in a silver inkstand, and began to write. In a few minutes the letter was finished and he folded it, dripped wax from his candle, and sealed the letter with the ring Bernardo had kissed.

"It won't be easy to find his lordship even with this letter, but you found me and I suppose you can find him. You have much to think about and preparations to make. To begin with, buy a new pair of shoes." He stood up, put his hands on the young man's shoulders, and stared into his eyes. "Aldo's son!"

Bernardo knew he would soon start to cry again.

The Monsignor reached into his purse and handed him a few coins. "These will get you to Milan," he said. Bernardo started to object, but he raised his hand. "Go! And Godspeed!" Bernardo went to the door. He looked back; the Monsignor was sitting at his little table again, writing. "Your Excellency," he called out, "I have one question. May I ask it?"

"One only!"

"Why didn't he kill my father, too? He could have."

The Monsignor looked up. "For a long time I too asked myself that question. But then I realized the truth, which is that the punishment that cruel man inflicted on my friend was worse even than death."

"I will never forget that," said Bernardo, and went through the door and closed it silently behind him.

11

Fathers and Children

Signor Ugo Bordoni came to Cortona a few days before Christmas to borrow money from Ser Gian Torreoni. Ser Gian was not generous in his terms, but Bordoni borrowed the money anyway. He was desperate but he was also exultant, since he believed his pressing financial troubles were nearly over. Before he returned home, he stopped at his sister-in-law's house to see his daughter.

Angelica was at the well, and he waited impatiently, drumming his fingers. When she appeared, he was struck, as always, by how beautiful she was and how elegantly dressed. He had castigated his wife on numerous occasions for spending too much on their daughter's clothes, but his wife had always replied, in her controlled and rather contemptuous manner, that no expenditure on that girl was too great, but anyway there had not been much expense because Angelica was an accomplished seamstress and could make a silk gown out of a cabbage leaf. Her white linen dress and the kerchief around her head — which she removed when she saw him — set off her golden hair and blue eyes. Because she was so beautiful and because of the things his wife said, and because he was never at ease with his daughter, he was even more abrupt than usual. "You're missed at home," he said sharply. "Your mother has too much work to do."

"I'm sorry, Father," said Angelica. "But it was my mother who chose to send me here." She carried her two pails into the kitchen and returned immediately, wiping her hands on a towel.

"Apart from that, how is my mother? And the others?"

"All well, all well — no thanks to you. We all work too hard. And the vines didn't produce as well this year as last. I have had to borrow some money." He paused. "This time from Ser Gian Torreoni. I had heard he wasn't too hard on poor countrymen, but I was wrong."

Angelica's pale face showed no emotion. "I'm sorry to hear it," she said.

"And are you doing everything you should do, and nothing you shouldn't, daughter?"

"I believe so, Father. I have met many young persons, as my mother wished. I have even become friends with the daughter of Ser Gian, Mariana. She has been kind to me, introducing me to many in the city."

"That's more then I can say for her father."

Angelica did not reply.

"In fact I'm pleased you are her friend. It's said her family — her father and brother — have ambitions. Who knows? Perhaps one of them will be Podestà one day."

"Anything is possible," said Angelica.

"But it's all the same to you!" The refusal of his wife and daughter to care about anything he cared about was a constant irritation to Signor Ugo.

"I'm sorry, Father. I have displeased you by my opinions."

"It is not your opinions that displease me, daughter. It is the fact that you have no opinions. Except about clothes, perhaps."

Angelica really would have liked to please him, yet she knew from bitter experience that if she expressed any opinion about one of the subjects he considered his male prerogative — politics, for instance — he would explode in a fury and attack her for her presumption. So, to change the subject, she said, "I've made a new dress. Would you like to see it? The material was very reasonable," she added. "Mariana showed me where to buy it."

Because he really did not want to fight with his daughter, although he always ended up doing so, Bordoni held his tongue and restrained himself from any remark about the excessive expenditures on clothes he believed were made by all women.

Angelica reappeared in a few moments attired in a long dress of pink silk with a high, starched white collar of linen. She wore a necklace but had not taken the time to smooth her hair; however, this one bit of disarray only added to the splendid effect. She turned in front of her father, then curtseyed. She stood, waiting for his response.

"Hmm," he said. "It's good looking." In fact, her beauty in the stunning dress, her air of queenly repose, made his heart come up in his throat. His pride in her was so great he almost felt he loved her. But he had no words to express these thoughts.

"I shall wear it to the Christmas festivities at Palazzo Casali." Again he was profoundly impressed. He knew the Casali were the greatest family in Cortona and lived in the finest palazzo. His pride in his daughter for having been invited made him weak. But he couldn't say so. "I hope you don't get it dirty," was his reply. "You will have better opportunities to wear it when spring comes."

Angelica grew even paler. Silently, she went into the house and returned in her white linen, her face composed. "I'll pay careful attention to not getting it dirty, Father," she said.

"I know you will, daughter. You're a good girl." He was happy because he had alluded to the forbidden subject without producing a storm of objections. He held out his hand and she curtseyed again and kissed it. "I'll take your good wishes to your mother. She'll miss you this year at Natale."

Angelica stood at the door and watched him walk up the street to the piazza, where his horse was tethered. She knew she shouldn't feel it and she wished she did not. But she hated him. Tears came, but she didn't raise her hand to wipe them. She stood at the door for a long time, staring into the cold street with unseeing eyes.

In Casa Torreoni there was a small room into which Ser Gian normally admitted no one but himself. It was his counting house, where he kept his books and wrote letters that he sent to other cities in Italy and even more distant places. The room had no window but there was a cabinet with doors painted to resemble an outdoor scene. On a branch with small green leaves, a bird sat and seemed to sing to the white clouds drifting in the blue sky.

On the few occasions when she had been admitted to the room, Nina had always been mesmerized by the cabinet doors. When she was a little girl she had thought she could actually hear the little bird's joyous song. Even now it was easy to imagine that the leaves and the bird and the clouds were real.

She was perched on a stool in front of the desk where her father sat. He had met her on the stairs and asked her to come into his study.

"We've never talked much together in private," he said. "Just the two of us." Even though he had planned this conversation, it was hard for him to begin.

"No, Father."

"Perhaps we've both been in error, Nina," he said gently. "Suddenly, when I look at you, I realize you've become a woman. Yet I've still thought of you as a little girl."

"I'm not a little girl any longer."

"That's what I wanted to talk to you about."

Nina believed she knew what the subject of this talk was going to be. She steeled herself.

A faint smile showed on her father's face. He knew what she was thinking. He didn't know what effect the news he would tell her would have. Probably she would be as surprised as he had been. What he didn't know was what change recent events might have produced in her.

"From time to time — too rarely, perhaps — you and I have mentioned the prospect of your marrying. I know

Mafalda has sometimes spoken to you. If your mother were alive she would have spoken to you often and you would probably have wanted to talk to her. Alas, she is gone and I have to fill her shoes as well as I can."

"What are you saying, Father?"

"I'm saying, first, that this is a matter you and I ought to be able to discuss. You're my only daughter. You've reached the age . . . Who you marry is important to me."

"I realize that."

"In the past, when we mentioned this subject you were adamant in saying you didn't want to marry anyone. I put that down partly to your youth. Now that you're sixteen, I think I have to ask you seriously whether that's still the way you feel."

"I don't know, Father."

"You don't know? That's a change, isn't it? Previously you said you did know. You were certain that you never wanted to marry."

"I meant I didn't know. I still don't know."

"Can I take this to mean you haven't yet found the man you want to marry? Until you find him you don't want to marry anyone else. Is that right?"

"I suppose so." She looked down.

"Well then, I want to talk to you about a certain man. He is rich, powerful, not bad-looking although older than you. He has been twice widowed. Although he is Guelf he says he wants to give up all partisan activity and become a simple citizen of our city. This may or may not be true, but it's what he says. He is a nobleman, his title depending not from the emperor but perhaps from His Holiness; it may be permanent even if he retires from politics. His wife will be a noblewoman, a contessa; she or her child, if it's a boy, will be his sole heir; he very much wants a son . . ."

She interrupted: "A contessa?"

He looked at her. "That's what I said. Since he's a conte his wife will be a contessa. And he wants to marry you."

Her face was suddenly completely pale; her mouth was dry; she could hardly swallow. After a long moment she was able to ask, "Do I know this man?"

"You do."

"His name is Pietro? Conte Pietro?"

"It is."

"Oh, Father." She reached out, but he withdrew from her; she wanted to fall into his arms and be a child again; he knew this and would not let her. She sat on the little stool, head bent, shoulders shaking, and wept. She covered her eyes; she couldn't stop the tears. He waited. He would wait as long as necessary.

Finally she raised her eyes and looked at him, her eyes full of pain. "He spoke to you? He came here and asked . . ."

"He did not. He approached me through an intermediary. If I give any sign of a positive response, he will certainly come to discuss . . ."

Again she interrupted: "The money . . ."

"Well, yes, the money. And other things. As you know, he has been an enemy of our family; at least I've considered him to be. I may have been wrong. The intermediary thinks I may have been. If . . . He and I would have to discover some common ground. That might be possible, I don't know . . ."

Her eyes glittered. "How much are you willing to sell me for, Father?"

If she had stabbed him in the heart he could not have felt a sharper pain. He reached out to her, but this time it was she who withdrew. "Nina," he said softly. "*Figlia mia.*" He looked at his hands; the fingers were clenched.

He tried to speak in a calm, low voice. "It seems that he believes you to be beautiful and accomplished. He's right. He knows that his person, because of his age, may be unattractive to you; he says he would try to overcome that and would treat you tenderly and with love — as you deserve. He says he would make you the queen of his household, the Lady of Pierle, renowned far and wide for your *gentilezza*. He says if you outlive him, which is likely, you — or your son — will be rich.

He says it will be the only desire of his heart to make you happy."

She closed her eyes and pressed her hands together. *"Santa Maria, madre di Dio,"* she murmured, *"prega per noi . . ."*

They were both silent for an interminable moment.

He cleared his throat. "You haven't . . . answered. What shall I tell the intermediary to tell Conte Pietro?"

"You may tell Messer Uguccio," she said. He started. "You may tell Messer Uguccio . . . You know my answer, Father."

"You're absolutely and unconditionally certain? You understand that this would be, in the eyes of the world, a brilliant match. With you as his wife, the Conte could look forward to a position of power in the Commune; you would have helped create an alliance that might insure peace for many years. Your son might become . . . Do you want to take time to think? Is there any possibility?"

"You know my answer, Father." He reached for her hands, and she gave them. He held them, looking into her eyes; now his eyes were full of tears. Strength flowed from one to the other. She mouthed the words, "Thank you." He swung away and looked at the painted scene. "Do you sometimes think you can hear the little bird sing?" he asked gently. "I do."

"So do I."

He swung around again, his face serious; it was as though it had been wiped clean, a tabula rasa. "I want talk to you about Bernardo," he said softly. He wasn't surprised to see her blush.

"The son of Giovanni?" He had taken her completely off guard.

"The son of Giovanni. Benno, the son of our swineherd, who is no longer our swineherd because he has gone to live in a hovel on the mountain where I hope he won't freeze to death. That was one bout at quarter-staves I wish had never happened!"

Nina pursed her lips and said nothing.

"To repeat, I want to talk to you about Benno — Bernardo. I'll be frank and I want you to be frank, too. I won't lie to you and I don't want you to lie to me. If you promise, I'll promise not to press you to answer any question you don't want to."

Nina lowered her head, accepting the bargain.

"Do you know where Benno is?"

Nina looked up quickly, her gaze level. "I do not."

"Nor do I. When did you learn he was leaving Cortona?"

"When you did, Father. Giovanni told me."

"Do you know why Giovanni told you?"

She hesitated. "Because he knew I cared about his son."

"That's true. But I meant, he couldn't have told you if I hadn't permitted it. He asked to see you. I called you and you went to him."

She nodded.

"Do you know why I did that?"

She hesitated again. "Because you knew I cared about Benno."

"I did know that, Nina. I also know you left the house that same evening and were gone for several hours. I learned this by accident. No one betrayed you."

Nina colored again.

"No one knows that except me, and perhaps Malfalda. Another accident." He paused. "I assume you met Benno somewhere in the city and spent several hours with him. It must have been in the city because you could not have come back into the city after nightfall. And he must have spent the night and left early the next morning." Ser Gian paused again. "I'm not going to ask what happened while you were together."

She lowered her eyes, trembling.

"When I said you have become a woman I meant not only that you have grown tall and beautiful. I also mean you've become, to the extent possible, mistress of yourself. You have obligations, to me, your brothers, Father Rafaelo, and others as well. But your first obligation is to yourself. Not all admit this to be true, especially where daughters are concerned, but it's the Church's teaching as well as common sense. I want you to know that I know it, Nina."

She was astonished. It was what she deeply believed but no one had ever said it to her, certainly not her father.

"Do you understand me?"

"Very well."

"Then I want to ask you one question and I expect you to answer it since it can't compromise you. Do you consider Bernardo the son of Giovanni to be an appropriate husband for you?"

She was more astonished than before. For a while she couldn't speak. She looked at her father waiting for her reply.

Her first realization was that in the euphoria of her new love, she had not even thought about the question. She had daydreamed about the children Benno named and she had thought more than once about what would have happened if he had let her make their bed and lain with her in it. Those thoughts might imply a positive response. But did she really think of Benno, could she really think of him, as her husband? She knew she could not and this made her so sad she began to cry again, hardly making any sound.

Still he waited patiently.

"I do not," she whispered; he could hardly hear her.

"Do you mean now, or never, Nina?"

She looked at him, her eyes flashing through her tears. "I mean now. I can imagine . . ."

"Circumstances very much changed?" He completed her sentence. "I admit I also can imagine such circumstances, though that may surprise you. But they haven't changed yet, have they, just because he left Cortona?"

"No, Father." She had promised the truth.

"That's what I wanted to discuss. If you agree with me about that, as I believe you do, then you'll understand if I ask you to be very careful what you do and say, perhaps even feel. And I ask you to promise one thing, and one only."

She continued to regard him silently, a little suspicious.

"If you change your mind about it, will you tell me? Do you trust me enough to promise me that?"

She nodded. Tears filled her eyes again.

"Then I promise to deal with you fairly and . . . honestly about it. And now that's enough about it."

She started to stand up, but he motioned her to stay. "I forgot. We still have some business to do. What shall I say to the Conte?"

"*Oh Dio.* You can't say I'm promised to another man?"

"Are you?"

"I'm not sure, Father. You've made me see . . ."

"The world being what it is, I don't think I can tell the Conte you are promised to the son of my swineherd." She started to speak but he held up his hand. "I said enough of that. But I have to tell the Conte something."

"Tell him I'm uncertain whether I want to enter a religious order. I need time."

"Is that true?"

"I have considered it — more often before Benno left. Not since."

He thought for a moment. "Here's a question you don't have to answer if you don't want to. If that bout at quarter-staves hadn't happened and Benno were still here, and things were as they were before and the Conte made his proposal, would your response have been different?"

"No!" She needed no time to consider.

"Do you dislike him so much?"

"Oh Father, it isn't that I dislike him so much. I don't loathe him. I remember when we left that day, Angelica and I, we both felt sorry for him. But I don't want to marry an old man even if he does have a fortress and riches and soldiers and trumpeters and half-naked dancing girls. I don't want to be the mistress of Pierle. I want to stay here, in Cortona, in this family and my own family. I want to be close to you and Nino even though he was cruel. What Conte Pietro wants is a pretty ornament to show off to his friends. I wasn't born to be an ornament." She thought but didn't say, He ought to marry Angelica. She's more beautiful than I am and she wants so much to be rich!

She drew a breath. "When I came in to see you, I was prepared to fight for myself. I was afraid you might force me to marry . . . somebody. I had no idea it might be him. I said to myself I would rather die . . . that's not really true. I love you, Father, and I want to please you. I realize I've been a wilfull, difficult daughter. I ask your forgiveness for that." She smiled at him because he was smiling at her. "But I don't want to marry Conte Pietro di Pierle."

"I believe you've made that clear." He laughed. "But the problem remains. We have to say something that won't offend him too deeply. He's like a *vipero*. You have to walk around it very carefully and not taunt it into striking. *Viperi* can kill and so can he." He paused. "I'll think of something, and if you have any ideas, let me know." She stood up and went to the door. "And by the way, how did you know the intermediary was Messer Uguccio?" he asked, grinning.

"It couldn't have been anyone else," she said, laughing. She was still trembling, just a little, but she also felt light and happy. "Mafalda was preparing some chickens," she said. "I'm so hungry!"

Two days before Christmas, Ser Gian rode to the castellino to inspect his son's new window. It was no longer merely a large hole in the tower wall. The marble framework Nino had ordered from Arezzo was in place; there were three arches, with slender hexagonal columns, and delicate tracery at the top. He had also ordered glass, which was being leaded into three casements, the outer two of which would open. A window seat had been built so two or three persons could sit and look out. In the central casement Nino's coat of arms, a lion couchant on a white field, was being worked into the leaded glass.

Ser Gian was impressed. Nothing in Case Torreoni, which was larger and more luxurious than this ancient castle, could compare with the new window for elegance. Nothing in the city could.

"I've never seen a window like it," he told his son. "It must have been very expensive."

"The expense wasn't so great," Nino explained, "because most of the work was done here. The glass . . ." He chuckled. "It was my present to myself for Natale. The style is French; they build new houses and churches this way. Robert sent for drawings."

"That's so," mused Ser Gian. "I meant I had not seen such a window in Italy or at least not in Tuscany."

"The important thing is, it's beautiful. Then you like it, Father?"

Ser Gian walked up and down the courtyard to observe the effect from different angles. "It is in every way elegant and fine," he said finally. He sat down on a bench, where the winter sun had warmed the wall a little. He shivered. "Even here in the sun it's cold," he said. He drew his cloak around him.

"Come inside by the fire," said Nino. "There's plenty of wood." He started to call Beppe, to tell him to build up the fire.

"Let's sit here in the sun and talk," said Ser Gian. "I would prefer not to be interrupted." Nino glanced at him, disturbed by his serious tone. "How old are you, Nino? Eighteen?"

Nino nodded.

"You're a man. You have Torreone and a small income from it. I said there wouldn't be more, but I've arranged to transfer to you your mother's French properties, which are also not very prosperous, but they'll add to what you have to live on. I've given them to you instead of Lorenzo because of Robert, who has an interest in them."

Nino was moved by his father's generosity. He was sitting with his legs together, leaning forward with his elbows on his knees. He reached and pressed his father's arm.

"I don't think there'll be much more, at least from me. Of course there would be more if you were to join us in our affairs. Are you still . . . reluctant?"

"I'm sorry, Father. It's true, I don't yet know what I want to be, but I do know I don't want to be a priest, on the one hand, or a merchant, on the other." He looked at his father anxiously. "I don't believe buying and selling is ignoble," he said. "But I don't think I would succeed. I may never succeed at anything except . . . windows!"

Ser Gian said nothing for a while, then continued. "Your brother is more ambitious than you are. Our family is growing in importance here in Cortona. The Cortona properties your mother brought to our marriage have increased in value and Lorenzo's and my affairs have been . . . satisfactory." He was reluctant to reveal his secrets even to his favorite son. "Your brother, as far as I can discern, is well-liked. He hopes to have a career in politics."

"Will he stand for election to the Consiglio?"

Ser Gian nodded. "The Casali and others have approved his candidacy. Eventually he hopes to serve in some high office." Nino whistled under his breath. His mind raced, imagining his brother as one of the city's rulers, if only for a short time — they were elected for only half a year.

"In the course of events it may be necessary for me to serve in some position to open the way to Lorenzo," said his father.

"You? Could you do that?"

"Do you mean, could I be elected?" He was smiling. Nino was embarrassed.

"I believe I could. The prejudice against money lenders has abated, especially in the city, where everyone has something to do with money. Among the country nobles it's still strong, but they can't vote."

"I didn't know they couldn't vote."

"You haven't been paying much attention. By the law only city men retain the franchise and not too many of them. Men like Conte Pietro still have influence, of course, but they can't vote. If they could, I would never be elected."

"The Conte doesn't like you?"

"That's putting it very mildly. I'm anathema to him," said Ser Gian, crossing his legs. "I represent everything he hates. I admit his disapproval of me is no greater then mine of him. I try to be fair, to understand his view of things. But the way he treats his *coloni* as slaves, his cruelty to man and beast alike . . .

I've also offended him. I think he can't forgive me, and I can't forgive him."

Nino had seldom heard his father speak with such feeling. "Is there something I can do to help you and Lorenzo?" he asked.

"Perhaps. You might begin by learning to keep your temper." Ser Gian was smiling, but Nino could see the words hadn't been said in jest. "That is, you might think twice before banishing any more young men from Cortona who are well-liked by the people even though they might be of a different class."

Nino looked away. Anger and shame fought for dominance in his soul. He had colored, and he couldn't look at his father. His throat was dry and he couldn't speak.

"Perhaps you thought I didn't know about it? Everyone knows. Everyone knows everything, Nino. Even what you said to him, and what you said to Nina. Neither Benno nor Giovanni belongs to us or to me, which would be closer to the truth if they were in fact slaves. You know little about Benno, nothing about Giovanni, if you can believe it. And little about me, Nino. I'm making you very uncomfortable. I mean to. I never want to hear again that you have said to anyone else what you said to Nina."

He paused, and Nino, who had gotten his face more or less under control, turned toward him. He was surprised to discover that his father was not so much angry as troubled, even hurt. "There are murmurs, Nino. It's said that my son is a tyrant like Conte Pietro. That might please him, if he heard it. It doesn't please those who support Lorenzo and me."

Nino's feeling of justification for his act had not long survived his conversation with Nina on the day after. Recently he had begun to feel ashamed of what he had done, not least because Nina had stopped seeing him altogether. But he too had been surprised and hurt by his father's words.

"I assume it's not true?"

Nino looked at his father and saw that his face had softened. *He wants me to tell him it's not.* He cleared his

191

throat. "It's not true," he muttered. "I regret that some people think of me as a tyrant." He didn't add that he regretted what he had done.

"I believe I don't have to say anything more to you about this, Nino. In the end what happened may turn out to have been for the good. What kind of life could Benno have had here at Cortona? He was no ordinary peasant, as you must be aware, because everyone else was. They treated him as though he were almost a — I don't know what to call him. The son of our swineherd — yes, he was that. But our swineherd was no ordinary swineherd, either. There's a streak of gentleness in him, almost of nobility. Don't you sense that? You did when you were little. Benno had it too, don't you agree?" There was a look of suffering on his face.

After a moment he smiled. "Come now, perhaps it's not so bad after all. You shouldn't dwell on it. I see that you know it was unwise and I can only urge you to remember that reputations are built on small things, not great ones."

Nino shook his head as though to clear it. Then, partly because he desperately wanted to change the subject, he remembered that he didn't want to miss this opportunity to talk to his father about the matter that was closest to his mind.

He drew himself up. "Does Signor Ugo Bordoni vote in the elections?"

"No. He too is a member, although a minor one, of the country nobility. He too has refrained from living in the city, so he can't vote. I'm not sorry because he would vote against us. He's tied to the skirts of Conte Pietro by more than mere affection, if in fact there's any of that. But why do you ask?"

"I wondered what you thought of him."

"Nothing especially good. He's both mean and foolish. I've recently loaned him some money. The security wasn't good, so I had to ask a high rate. Naturally he wasn't pleased but he borrowed the money anyway. If he pays me back, it will be worth the risk. But again, why are you interested?"

"I know his daughter Angelica."

"Yes?" Ser Gian, who had been feeling relaxed after his scolding, was suddenly all attention.

"Yes, well, Nina brought her to visit one afternoon not long ago and I've met her since in the piazza. She lives near our home. She is . . . she's very good-looking."

"She's certainly that. There's no more beautiful young woman in Cortona, if any can compare to her. Except for Nina, of course," he added, thinking back to the pageant. "I didn't know you were all that well acquainted with her."

"So you don't know everything, Father," said Nino smiling. His father's quick response made him regret the remark.

"Is there more I should know?" Ser Gian's dark eyes bored into his son's, trying to see beneath the surface.

Nino swallowed. He realized he couldn't retreat now nor did he really want to. "I've never cared greatly about a woman before, Father. I think I care . . . that way about Angelica Bordoni."

"Care greatly? What does that mean? She's not a suitable match for you, Nino. Her father, as I've said, is a fool, and he's much in debt, to me and others. On the other hand, her mother is a woman of spirit. That's something. She was your mother's friend."

"I'm the younger son," Nino persisted. "I may marry as I wish even if it's not to your — to the family's advantage?"

"Yes and no. Your brother would have to approve. I'm not sure I would. Have you spoken to the girl?"

"She'll have nothing to do with me."

"Ah!" said Ser Gian. He sighed. "I'm sorry, but perhaps it's just as well. It was my impression she was already spoken for."

"Spoken for? What do you mean, Father? You must tell me!"

"It's only a rumor. Actually I know nothing." Ser Gian didn't want to go on, and he was silent despite Nino's prodding.

He really did know nothing despite the gossip. He only repeated that there were rumors and rumors were not to be trusted. He returned to the subject he had been discussing, although Nino had lost all interest. "Once on the scent of political power," his father said, "one finds it hard to stop. Thus it is with Lorenzo. I would like him to succeed. And my own affairs would prosper if my son . . ." He looked at Nino. "I'm sorry," he said again. "Is the girl that important? Haven't there been others?"

"Yes!" cried Nino. "But not like this: I feel as if I'm being tortured, as if my head were in a vise. I don't know what to do."

"I can't help you," his father said. He rose to go. "You'll join us for the feast of Natale? Angelica Bordoni will be there. Nina invited her."

"I don't know," said Nino glumly. "I'll see you at church. Robert and I will come to the city and sleep at the house."

12

Christmas 1272

The threat of snow hung over the city all through the day before Christmas. The sky was dark and cloudy with occasional flashes of lightning. Men who came down from the mountains for the feast day said it was already snowing there and that the streams were frozen. In the main piazza, crowds huddled under the *logge* of the houses surrounding the square. There was the usual Christmas Eve market but it was over before noon, as it was so cold the peasants could not remain outside with their produce even for the sake of the small profits they might make since there were few customers. By the dinner hour the square was deserted.

Nino and Robert had arrived during the morning. Nino sent his squire to Casa Torreoni while he remained in the square. He enjoyed the solitude for it accorded with his mood. He walked up and down, his heavy cloak wrapped tightly around him and his woolen cap pulled down over his ears. He stamped his feet from time to time to warm them. He kept wandering into the nearby street where Angelica was living with her aunt, in the hope that she might emerge and speak to him. He had decided that, come what may, he would not let Christmas pass without revealing his feelings.

The hope that Angelica would respond any differently than she had was faint indeed. But Nino was disturbed by what his father had said regarding a rumor that she was 'already spoken for.' He did not want to ask anyone what this might mean for fear of appearing a fool. In any case he wanted the truth from Angelica herself. Whether she would tell him the truth was another matter. He already knew how difficult it was to break through her self-imposed isolation.

Was she in love with another man? He didn't think so, his instincts told him her heart was free. Was she promised to another even if she didn't love him? This was possible, but it seemed unlikely given that she had been permitted to live in the city for these months, alone and far from her family. Had she forsworn marriage, like his sister? This he also doubted. Had she promised to enter a convent, then? But she had recently returned from a convent where she had spent five years and she didn't seem to be particularly devout. What then could it be?

He believed Angelica was more interested in him than it appeared. In part he believed this because he wanted it to be true. But hadn't there been hints? He thought of their last meeting, when he had overtaken her in the piazza. Usually she had avoided him, but not that afternoon. And he had asked her if there was hope for him.

"There is no hope!" she had cried. "For you, or for me."

But he believed her words hadn't conveyed her meaning. He was sure of it, recalling her look as she had spoken them. What could that look mean unless it meant she loved him. Why, then, was there no hope?

These thoughts preoccupied him for an hour, whereupon he went in to dinner. It wasn't a feast, which would wait for the next day, but it was pleasant just to be with the family again. Lorenzo was there with his sturdy new wife, for whom it was the first Torreoni Christmas; he introduced her to everyone as though they had never seen her before, although most of them had known her for years. A city woman, the daughter of a prosperous tradesman, she was just the sort of steadying influence Lorenzo needed, his father thought. Nino agreed.

Nina seemed cheerful and Nino wondered if she had forgiven him. They continued to sit at table all the afternoon; it was too cold to go outside. They sang, played games, and teased one another. Finally the women left to rest in the big bedroom and the men lay down in front of the fire for naps before it was time to go to church.

It was customary to form a procession in the piazza and walk down the hill to the church of Santa Maria Annunziata, the procession led by all the city's priests. The Torreoni family huddled together against the chill wind, the candles of the priests, in lanterns raised on poles, swaying in the night ahead of them.

Nino was half asleep as he walked, shivering, unhappy. Suddenly he was wide awake for he realized it was no longer Nina who walked beside him but another woman, her face covered by her hood. He kept glancing at her until she turned. She smiled, her eyes dancing in the lanterns' cold light.

"Angelica!' he whispered, wondering how she had managed to come so close without his noticing. She took his arm as they picked their way over the cobblestones. He remembered how she had held his arm when they walked back to the city from Torreone.

Inside the bitterly cold church Angelica remained near him, kneeling on the cold stones between him and Nina. He could hardly wait for the long service to be ended. He was delayed by greetings and didn't see her at the door when he reached it; he ran to catch her in the street, calling out to her as she disappeared around a corner. When he too rounded it, there she was, leaning against the wall, smiling as before.

He tried to take her into his arms but she twisted away. "This is folly," she said in a low voice. 'If someone were to see us . . ."

He bowed. "Donna Angelica," he said in a voice loud enough for anyone to hear, "may I have the honor of escorting you to your home on this cold night?"

"Thank you, Messer Nino," she replied, taking his arm. They walked together up the hill, feeling one another's nearness but saying little. Nino's heart was full. He could hardly believe it, but what he had hoped was true: Angelica loved him and no one else.

"You're coming to dinner tomorrow," he said finally, smiling to himself, almost laughing out loud.

"I've been invited by your sister to dine with you. Then we will go to Palazzo Casali. I've heard the festivities are lovely."

"There are musicians and everyone dances, except the old people of course. You'll dance with me?"

She nodded. "But you must first dance with your sister."

"Certainly!" Nino felt he loved Nina more than ever because she was Angelica's friend and had brought her to him.

"Here's my house," she said, turning to smile at him one more time. She reached and kissed him lightly on both cheeks. "I'll see you tomorrow then. May the joy of Our Lord's birth remain with you always."

She turned to go but suddenly looked up. "It's snowing!" she cried. "Look at the snow in the piazza. How beautiful!"

He glanced at his sleeve. Already the flakes were turning it white. He raised his eyes to her, pleading.

"I'll ask my aunt," she said, laughing. "How often does it snow at Natale?" She reappeared a moment later. "I said you and Nina . . . "She laughed again. He had never seen her so happy. She took his arm and walked with him back to the piazza, now filled with people enjoying the snow. They strolled up and down, pausing to greet friends but most of the time talking to one another. Nino had a thousand questions about her life at home, her days at the convent, her dreams for the future. One was uppermost in his mind even though he feared it would offend her, make her retreat again into the far distance she had occupied for two months.

"When you said . . ." He paused. "About hope, that there is none. For me, and . . . for you." The words were hard to say. "I didn't understand. Please tell me what you meant."

She grasped his arm tighter and sighed, but said nothing.

"Please speak to me," he said. "My life depends on what you say."

"Oh, Messer Nino," she said softly, "don't tell me that."

"It's true: It's very true." He stopped to bow to an acquaintance. When the couple had passed he continued. "I don't see how . . . I think of you always. I even talk to you when I'm alone. Robert thinks I'm a little mad and perhaps it's true, too."

Again she pressed his arm against her.

"I beg you to tell me what you meant."

She sighed again. "I meant . . . I'm not free."

"You are promised to another" His voice was harsh.

"I'm not free," she repeated. "I'm a woman. I owe much to my father . . ."

Her voice trailed away. "I would like to be your friend," she said quickly, "as I am your sister's."

"I am your friend.' he cried. "But forgive me if I say . . .'"

"I won't forgive you!" she interrupted. "Don't say anything more. Let us be friends as I sincerely wish us to be."

His frustration was so great he couldn't speak for several minutes, during which he became occupied with more bows and greetings. Finally they were alone, at the far side of the piazza, and he began to talk to her about himself, about his own past and his own hopes.

She listened intently, holding his arm. When he paused, she said: "Do you know, Messer, what happiness is?"

He looked at her, wondering, hoping.

"I think it is just to be walking in the piazza, in the snow on the eve of Natale, talking to a friend such as you," she said. "I have few friends, perhaps only two, your sister and my mother. You are a third." Her voice was so low he could hardly hear her.

He leaned forward and saw, even in the dim light, the gleam of tears.

"Angelica,' he murmured. But he said no more for suddenly there was Nina running toward them through the snow, shouting that she had found them. She took Angelica's other arm and they walked quickly, prancing in step with one another.

Nino's heart was so full of happiness, his love for Angelica was so large and splendid, his throat pained him. But he wanted to speak to Nina, too, to ask her to forgive him and love him again as she always had until Benno's departure — until, as he quickly said to himself, I so unjustly sent him away.

He cleared his throat. "Sister," he said, over Angelica's head, "on this beautiful night, at this beautiful time, I wish . . ."

Nina interrupted. "Oh, I know very well what you wish, brother," she cried. "It's what you always wish. You desire to do what you desire to do and then to be forgiven because you're so charming. Shall we forgive him, Angelica?" she asked, laughing.

Angelica smiled. "I think we must," she said, "for he is indeed very charming. Only, I don't know what for . . ."

"Then you are forgiven, brother, but only because it is Christmas." Nina looked. The piazza was quickly emptying, as the last of the lovers of the snow realized they were wet and cold and sought their firesides. "It's time to go home," she said, guiding both Nino and Angelica toward Angelica's street. They reached it in a few moments — too soon by far for Nino.

He raised Angelica's hand to his lips; he wanted to cover the ice-cold fingers with kisses. But his sister watched, smiling a little, so he bowed, saying good night. "Good night, Messer Nino, good night, Mariana." The door was open and Angelica moved through it. Brother and sister stood in the door way, entranced by her beauty as she turned to smile.

"Did you mean it?" Nino asked as they walked home.

"I did. You were wrong and I was very angry but I don't want to stay angry forever. I hope you're not angry at me."

"I'm not," he said, "although I was."

She waited a moment to control her indignation. "Do you ever think of that man, that friend of ours for so long, and wonder what he's doing, Nino? Wherever he is, is it snowing there too? Does he have a place he can go for shelter from the wet and cold?"

Nino didn't look at her. "I do think of him," he muttered.

"Do you think of Giovanni and Gianna in that little cold house? Do you think of what you took away from them?"

"No, but . . ."

"But what?'

"Nothing." He continued to walk with his eyes on the ground.

"On this night of Our Lord's birth, brother, it behooves us all to forgive one another even as He did, long ago."

"You mean . . . Benno?" He was astonished by her remark.

"He too. But I meant Jesus."

This was dangerous ground. Anyway, Nino wanted to talk about Angelica, even though he had lost most of his joyousness. "We had a good talk," he said lamely.

'A long one, Nino. I noticed. So did everyone."

"We're friends," he said firmly. "Friends may walk in the piazza in sight of all." He paused. "I like her very much."

"I too am fond of her. She's not only beautiful but also good and intelligent and skillful with her hands . . . She's everything a woman should be," she finished, looking at her brother.

"Oh, Nina, you love her as much as I do."

"Do you love her, then, brother?"

"With all my heart!" He saw her serious look. "You're surprised?"

"Not very. I suspected." Nina was silent for a moment, her eyes on the ground as they walked slowly. "I don't know . . ." she murmured. She raised her head. "I'll pray for your happiness, for you are dear to me. Will you pray for mine?'

He held her arm. "You are dear to me," he said. "Yes, I'll pray for that." He wanted to say something more about Benno but he could not. He did not wish to discover that what he suspected was true and he feared Nina would tell him if he asked. At any rate, they were close to home. He had time to say only: "She told me she has few friends beside you and me."

"Then we must take care of her, brother," said Nina as the door opened and they felt the warmth on their faces.

It snowed all night and by morning there were several inches on the ground and on the roofs and walls. There was concern about the olive trees, which would be damaged if the cold lasted. Ser Gian also wondered if Giovanni and his wife were warm enough in the mountain hut; in fact, they had come down to their little city house for the holiday; only Nina knew this. The boys and young men organized a snowball fight in the piazza and then rolled up a huge ball of snow that they carved into the shape of a wild boar. Then they shot arrows at it until it fell to pieces.

Angelica and her aunt arrived at Casa Torreoni shortly after noon. Under her cloak Angelica was clothed in white linen trimmed with fur; a small gold cross glittered on her bosom. Nino swallowed hard when he saw her. "How beautiful you are!" he whispered as he kissed her hand and then rushed off to change his clothes. He donned leggings of fine white wool, a new tunic of glorious purple velvet, a belt with a silver buckle, and a soft white hat with a long feather. On his feet were white leather slippers; despite Robert's urging he still refused shoes with turned-up toes.

Nina too was beautifully dressed in a green gown she had made herself under Angelica's tutelage and with a string of small pearls wound through her hair which, thanks to Mafalda, was tidier than usual. The rest of the family were also elegantly attired in their best clothes and wearing their finest jewels. At least it seemed so to Ser Gian.

"Do you suppose it's the influence of Angelica?" he said to Nina. "And this is only for a simple dinner at home. What will we wear to Palazzo Casali tomorrow?"

She smiled at him, amused by his innocence. "We'll think of something," she said. "Angelica certainly is pretty."

"Nino's evidently quite fond of her," he said. "Has he said anything to you?"

She smiled again. "Would I tell you if he had?"

All told some twenty persons sat down at the long table to be served by Carla, Mafalda, Nunzia, and the rest of the servants. Beppe was the cupbearer; sweating, he kept everyone's cup full of wine, beer, or mead, as they chose. The "simple dinner at home" required several hours to consume, for it consisted of many courses starting with chicken, duck, and rabbit, some of them brought from Torreone, followed by oysters, beef, and veal, and finally capped by two whole roasted pigs for which places at the table were cleared by the enthusiastic and apparently still hungry diners. There were bowls of cabbage, beans, and turnips; baskets of cheese and fruit; and an enormous slab of Mafalda's bread, baked the night before, at every place around the table.

The hall at Case Torreoni was more than twenty feet long. High narrow windows on one side of the room were covered at this season by oiled paper that let in some light and kept out some of the cold. A roaring fire blazed in a fireplace on each of the long sides of the room; braziers at the ends helped a little to meliorate the chill that was all-penetrating at any distance from the fires. Torches sputtered and smoked at the room's corners and candles dripped wax on the table from heavy silver candelabra. The only "silverware" was a knife laid at the places women and children sat; men brought their own knives, long and sharp and drawn from scabbards on their belts. Although most Cortona families still placed their food directly on the table in front of them or on a slice of bread, the Torreoni used large pewter plates; they were proud possessors of half a dozen. This wasn't enough for everybody, but children didn't need plates and others could share.

The table itself was very long but hardly more than two feet wide, enabling guests on either side to converse with one another easily. Ser Gian and Nina, who was acting as hostess, sat in armchairs facing one another across the middle of the table; everyone else was crowded onto benches. Ser Gian was flanked by his daughter-in-law and her mother; Nino and Lorenzo sat on either side of their sister. Angelica had been given the place on the other side of Nino, while her aunt sat far away on the other side of the table.

The bench was short and forced them together so that Nino felt her presence. He toyed with his food, too nervous to enjoy it. "You don't eat," said Angelica, smiling at him over her wine. "Are you well?"

"I'm well," he murmured, trying to swallow a piece of rabbit that seemed stuck in his throat. "But . . ." He paused.

"But what?"

"It's . . . only . . . I wish we weren't here."

"Where should we be? I'm glad to be here in your family."

"Oh, I'm glad of that, too. But I wish everyone else wasn't here."

"Just you and me on Christmas Day?" She smiled again, her eyes dancing. "That would be a sad feast."

"Oh yes, very sad," he mumbled, miserable because she persisted in not understanding him. He drew himself up. "What I really wish is that we were at Torreone."

"Everyone? Or just our sad little Christmas party of two?"

"It wouldn't be. It would be the happiest party in the world." He had raised his voice, and he realized his father, sitting across the table, had noticed. "We were speaking of Christmas parties in the past," he told him.

Almost imperceptibly Angelica moved closer to him so he could feel her shoulder against his shoulder, her hip against his hip. His hand had fallen under the table and she found it with her own and pressed it. He was stunned, as always when she touched him. He realized she had begun a lively discussion with Nina about the dresses of some of the guests.

After a few minutes she turned to him again. "Thank you, Messer Nino," she said, her low voice thrilling him.

"Why do you call me that?" Despite her nearness he still felt a chasm between them. Desperately, he wanted to bridge it. She shrugged. "What should I call you then?"

"My name is Nino."

"If you want I shall call you Nino, but not in public. Then, I must speak to you formally, as I would to your brother. Yours is a great family, mine is not."

He shook his head. Their conversation, though occasionally showing promise, was getting nowhere. "Angelica — I like to call you that."

She smiled and he leaned toward her, but at that moment Ser Gian rose to pronounce the first of many toasts: "Alla famiglia!" The noise of laughter and cheering was so loud, Nino and Angelica could not speak to one another without shouting.

Finally the other women followed Nina into the bedroom, where mats had been arranged on the floor so they could rest before dressing for the ball. Nino watched Angelica leave. Once she was gone, there was no more pleasure for him at the table and he slipped away to lie on a mat near the kitchen fire, as he used to do.

Palazzo Casali was twice as large as any other home in Cortona; it filled the entire end of the main square. A balcony extended from one side to the other so members of the family could participate in the business of the piazza without becoming mere members of the crowd. In a building around the corner some dozen horsemen were quartered with their steeds and servants. As the city's wealthiest family, the Casali were the target of threats; they never left the piazza without an armed guard. This largest house in the city also contained the largest room. Known as La Sala Grande, the big room, despite its being in a private home, was used for much public business. The Consiglio usually met in the smaller Palzzo del Capitano del Popolo, but if many persons were to appear before it, or sometimes just for convenience, it met in the Sale Grande, seeing that one or another member of the Casali family was usually the Council's president, the Podestà, or both. Public dinners were held there as well; it was the only room where a hundred persons could sit and eat together, and it was also the place where Cortona's *popoli grossi* met and celebrated Christmas, as they had done for many years.

The room was sixty feet long, with a ceiling twenty feet high supported by massive beams, each a forest tree. Wooden shutters opened onto the balcony, but these were closed during the winter. Narrow slits allowed some light to enter, but also enough cold air to keep the room drafty. Two enormous fireplaces provided some heat, but on a cold night such as this one, guests would have to be either very warmly dressed or very active. The old people chose the former, the younger the latter, and the dancing was therefore often wild. The orchestra consisted of half a dozen bagpipers, two drummers who banged away with a will, a few men with long shepherd's pipes, and four fiddlers each with an instrument of a different size and shape, who nevertheless managed, rather miraculously, to play together although not necessarily in tune. There was also a tall young man who clashed his sword on a large bronze pot at appropriate moments; when this happened, the dancers would cheer and kick up their heels.

Most of the dances were group affairs, the men in one long line facing the women in another; sometimes the dancers formed a square, men and women alternating. Other dances demanded capering by teams of men or complicated, rapid footwork by pairs or foursomes of women. The Podestà led the first dance, a formal square, with his wife who was dressed in a gown of heavy silk with fur at the wrists, throat, and around the hem. Thereafter this couple, far from young, stood on the sidelines and turned over leadership to the Magister Ballium, a young cleric in a fantastic costume of red, blue, yellow, and green who wasn't yet certain whether he wanted to remain in the Church or devote himself to a life of pleasure. His clerical sponsor had advised him that it was a choice that didn't need to be made but he was afraid this might be a trap.

Nino and Robert were both good dancers and they joined nearly every dance, taking partners when that was called for, otherwise dancing alone or with groups of men. Nino's first partner was his sister, who teased him whenever he indulged in a particularly flamboyant leap or gesture. Whenever he could, which meant whenever she allowed it, he danced with Angelica.

She was clearly the star of the evening. She had changed into her new pink dress and wore all her jewels, which glittered on her fingers and wrists and ears and on her bosom, swelling in the low cut gown. (It had been slightly altered since her father had seen it.) Her eyes danced along with her feet and she was obviously enjoying the attentions of all the young men and most of the older ones, for she was remarkably beautiful and relatively unknown to Cortona's higher society.

She had been taught some formal steps by the nuns but had not learned the quicker folk dances the young men and women knew; these she sat out, or rather stood out, in the corners, surrounded by men who simply wanted to be near her. Nino stood by through one agonizing long dance during which he was unable to address a single private word to her; thereafter he took part in these dances, throwing his body with abandon and leaping and clicking his heals like a goat, Nina said. Despite his frustration he was having a wonderful time, especially after he saw Angelica watching him during one especially splendid caper. "Bravo!" she mouthed silently. He jumped all the higher and was rewarded by applause.

Supper was served at midnight. Uguccio's nephews offered their arms to Angelica, but Nino was able to stand near her at the banquet table covered by dozens of rich dishes together with large pitchers of wine, and after she had spent a polite ten minutes with her hosts, she excused herself and joined him.

He tried not to stare at her bosom. Suddenly she was embarrassed. "I'll get my shawl," she said.

He too was embarrassed; he had been staring at her as though she were just another attractive young woman. He felt no better when Robert joined them; he didn't want even his best friend to share their few moments of intimacy, yet he hardly knew what to say to her. The sense of carefree happiness he had felt earlier had vanished. Angelica, perhaps understanding this, sent Robert for her shawl.

"I must speak to you," Nino whispered.

"I'm here. Speak." She smiled, in some concern.

"1 mean alone."

"I don't see how that's possible," she replied nervously.

They were standing by one of the slits in the wall. "The sky's clear now and the moon's nearly full. Come onto the balcony."

She hesitated but then followed him, her face troubled. Nino had often been at Palazzo Casali and knew of a small door opening onto the balcony. There was consequently no need to open one of the high shutters, which would have brought the entire company outside. It was warmer now and the moon shone bright on the roofs, here and there gleaming with the remains of the snow. They stood together for a long moment, silently absorbing the beauty around and below them.

He reached for her hand and she allowed him to take it, pressing his fingers with her own. He moved toward her, but again she turned away. He didn't persist, knowing she was right to avoid his embraces in this place. But she still held his hand.

"I don't know how to say this," he murmured hoarsely. He hesitated. "I think there is hope. May we not . . ."

"There is no hope, Nino," she said, her voice so low he had to lean toward her. "Why do you torture me with that word? I live without hope. I've lived all my life without it. You make me think . . . But I must not."

"You love me. I know it. And I love you. That's why there must be hope." He felt her fingers press his so they hurt but she did not reply. He took her silence as consent to what he had said.

"We could run away. Tonight," he whispered, his voice hoarse with urgency. "I have horses at Torreone. Robert and Beppe would go. . ."

"Don't torture me!" she cried, her voice choking.

"Torture you? I want you to see . . ."

"They would find us. They would kill you and take me back. I tell you. I'm not free. I have never been. Except to be your friend. I love you as a friend. You and Nina. Please understand."

"But you don't tell me why you aren't free." He felt without any hope, like her. He both wanted to know and not to know.

"I can't tell you," she said, more calmly. "You must trust me and understand me, without knowing."

"Tell me one thing," he said after a moment. "I will accept your answer and do what you say. But I must know this. Do you love me as a friend — or as a man?"

"What's the difference?" She smiled faintly.

"You know the difference. You don't live with a friend, share your life with a friend." There, he had said it. "I want to live with you, Angelica, and share my life with yours. That's the difference."

"I know that difference, dear Nino," she said softly. "But whatever I say will make no difference in what will happen — what has to happen. Do you understand?"

He looked at her, uncomprehending. But he nodded glumly.

"Well then, I love you as a man. Do you have any doubt of it?"

He swallowed hard. His hands were icy cold yet his body felt hot; he wanted to throw off his clothes and be utterly abandoned and free. Yet he could not move.

He stared straight ahead across the dark roofs of the city. "Then there is hope, Angelica. It can't be otherwise!"

Her reply if she made any was lost in a torrent of shouted words from behind them as a crowd, led by the two young Casali, surged onto the balcony and surrounded them. "Here they are!' they were shouting. "The lovers on the balcony."

13

Nina's Room

Nina's room, in which she had slept for years, had once been Nino's. He had slept there until he left home to go to the friars and then to Torreone. It was still his favorite room in the house. High under the eaves, it was hot in summer and cold in winter and its irregular shape meant it could accommodate very little furniture. It made up for these defects by being cozy, a nest. There was a tiny window looking out over the valley; it was closed in winter by a panel of wood with a metal grill in the center that allowed a small amount of light to enter. The ceiling was high on one side and sloped downward, the heavy roof beams obtruding into the room and making you duck near the outside wall. A shelf and a chest under the window held Nina's few possessions as they had held Nino's. The door opened against the narrow bed, which had been made for Nino and had also passed to Nina when she inherited the room.

Nina treasured it, privacy being rare. Most of her friends lacked rooms of their own. Even her elder brother and sister had not had their own rooms as children. Here she could think her own thoughts, read, sew, dream, be foolish if she wished. One of her treasures, another rarity, was a broken piece of mirror, a gift from her father. It was part of a mirror he had bought, at great expense, in Troyes from a merchant of Venice, where it had been made. On the way home it had broken in three pieces, the largest of which he had given to his wife, the others to his daughters. There were few mirrors in Cortona, even broken ones, and Nina's gave her pleasure especially since it had come into her life just at the time when she was beginning to pay attention to her appearance. She would take it down from the shelf and stare into it; sometimes she talked to it, which was part of her private foolishness. Since her room had once been Nino's, neither felt any reluctance to share it and he often went there to talk to Nina when he was in the city. They had spent many hours in the room until the banishment of Benno strained their relationship. Tonight, as he lay on his mat in the kitchen, rolled up in his cloak against the cold, he thought of the room and tried to remember when he had last been in it. It was months ago; he couldn't recall just when.

He was thinking of the room because Nina and Angelica were sleeping there together, and the thought of their nearness and especially the nearness of Angelica had kept him from sleep, tired as he was after the dancing. Angelica's aunt had gone to bed early, and in order not to disturb her it had been arranged that Angelica would go home with Nina to spend the night. Anyway, because she had changed there before the ball, her clothes were at Case Torreoni.

Nino thought he must have slept for a while but then he had wakened suddenly, intensely aware that Angelica was in the house, in a warm bed, lying next to his sister. He didn't know what time it was, but it must be late. Yet at this time of the year nights were long. He wondered if Angelica was awake, too, perhaps for the same reason. Was she lying in bed, staring at the ceiling as he was and thinking about him? She had told him she loved him as a man. She must have understood what it meant. He wasn't just a friend; he was more to her as she was more to him.

He remembered her fingers pressing his as they talked on the balcony. He felt a surge of joy, but soon fell back into despair as he recalled her words. She had said he was torturing her, that there was no hope for them even if, even though, he thought, they loved one another.

It was hard to understand. He had had little experience of wanting something and not getting it. All his life he had been able to have what he wanted if he wanted it enough. Now he wanted Angelica more than he had ever wanted anything. Was it possible he couldn't have her? And she loved him, too. Was it conceivable that their mutual desire would be denied?

What was love? Was it anything more than desire? He loved his sister, who was an attractive young woman, but he didn't desire her. He loved his father, but he certainly didn't desire him. Yet he liked being with both his sister and his father. He looked forward to their meetings and remembered them with pleasure. Was his love for Angelica like that? Yes, but also more.

Of course he desired her. He wanted to hold her and make love to her, more than any woman he had ever known. Did he also want to care for her in the tender way he used to care for Nina? Yes, this too, he thought. He was suddenly intensely aware of the loneliness Angelica must feel. Her family — she didn't like them, at least her father. She didn't remember with pleasure her life at home. She seemed to want something she couldn't imagine having. Was it him? Yes, but it was also something more, or different. She was unhappy because she couldn't have what she wanted most.

What stood in the way? He didn't know, but then, as he thought, he did know. There was something in her that stood in the way. She couldn't let herself be happy in the way he was happy, or had been until recently. Was this because she was a woman and he was a man? No, some very deep sadness stood in the way.

Was there any cure for it? He wasn't sure, but as he lay there he began to believe he could cure it. His love for her could make her happy and therefore able to love him in return. Thinking these thoughts, he became even surer Angelica and Nina were awake and perhaps even talking about what he was thinking. And so he decided to go and see them while the house was still asleep.

It was so dark in Nina's room he could hardly make out the bed, much less the persons in it. In fact the bed had been moved and he stumbled over it, making a noise. He saw a figure stir in the bed and he heard a whispered word.

He sat on the bed's sturdy frame. "Nina?" he whispered.

"Nino?" Angelica whispered, rising on one elbow. Her hair, washed of color in the faint moonlight, fell about her face.

"Is Nina asleep?" he whispered. "I don't want to wake her. I'm sorry I woke you — I thought you might be awake."

"What are you doing here, Nino?" Angelica, who had been sound asleep, couldn't get her bearings.

"I came to talk to you and Nina."

"She's not here. After we went to bed we talked for a long time and then she went away. It was as dark as pitch. She said she wanted to take something to Giovanni."

"To Giovanni? Up on the mountain?" He realized he and Angelica were alone, really alone, for the first time. But he was worried about his sister. "Why couldn't she wait till morning?"

"I asked her about this bed and she said Giovanni had made it. Then we talked about him, and Benno. She felt guilty because she hadn't been to see Giovanni. He came into the city for Christmas but she hadn't actually seen him. So she decided to go. I tried to stop her but you know Nina . . ."

"He came to Cortona and only told Nina?" He felt miserable.

"She said she wanted to be there, at Giovanni's house, to be with him when the sun rose. The moon was rising as she left. She said it wasn't far and she could see the way."

"I hope so." Despite his excitement, his curiosity was also great. "What did she tell you about Benno?"

"Nothing much," Angelica replied. This wasn't entirely true for Nina had confessed some of her feelings although not all. "She told me about you and Benno with the quarter-staves. I didn't know about it."

"It was what I was asking her to forgive me for, last night."

She nodded. She was still leaning on her elbow but had rolled the coverlet up around her shoulders.

"I'm sorry I did it. Although it may turn out for the best. Who knows? How does Nina feel? Does she really forgive me? Or does she hate me?"

"She doesn't hate you."

"And you, do you hate me or love me?"

Angelica didn't reply.

"So you hate me," he said. At that moment he believed it. Understanding this, she held out her hand, pale in the moonlight. "I don't hate you either," she whispered.

He took her hand and sat quietly, staring at her. They could hardly see one another, yet they didn't take their eyes from one another's face.

"I love you," he said, his voice hoarse.

Again she didn't reply; but he felt her fingers tremble.

After a while, she said, "You shouldn't be here, Nino."

"I have to talk to you, Angelica," he said, swallowing hard. "When will we have such a chance again? There's so much I want to say to you and so much I want to know about you. I think about you all the time but I don't really know you. Tell me about your life at Montanare when you were a little girl and then when you were growing up. Did you have friends and are they still your friends? Please tell me about your life before the moment three months ago when you came into my life and changed it."

She knew she should insist, but it was pleasant to have him here with her, sitting on the edge of the bed, close to her in the dark, his voice thrilling her with his words of love, words she knew she should refuse to hear but which she nevertheless couldn't resist. So she told him about her life at the convent and about her mother, whom his father had praised. "She's a Norman," she said. "If she were a man she would be a warrior, like them. It frustrates her, being a woman, and makes her sad."

"If she were a man would your life be different?"

Angelica nodded. "I think it would."

A cock crowed and Nino went to the window and looked out. It was still dark in the east; there was at least an hour or two before dawn. He returned to the bed and sat down, this time closer to Angelica, who had fallen back with her head on the pillow, her hair spread out around her.

As he stared at her, trying to make out her features in the darkness, love and desire rose in him so strongly that he trembled. She noticed and, thinking he was shivering from the cold, she said, "I'm sorry you can't be in this warm bed. I'm so comfortable and you so uncomfortable. Is there another cover you could use?"

"The cold doesn't make me tremble," he said. "It's something else."

She was silent. "It's you. Having you so near. If I reached out my hand I could touch you. I could kiss you." He remembered that, above all, and to her most of all, he should be courteous. "May I kiss you, Angelica?" he asked. His voice sounded harsh to him and he tried to clear his throat.

She didn't know what to say. She didn't know what to think. All she knew was she wanted him to kiss her but also that she shouldn't want it. She should make him go away, which she knew he would do if she told him to, but she could not. If he doesn't kiss me, she said to herself, that will decide it. Yet if he does, what will happen? She too trembled, from fear and desire intermixed.

He leaned toward her, taking her face in his hands and holding it as he stared down at her. He placed his lips gently on hers, without moving, without making a sound. For a long time he sat thus, with his hands in her hair and his lips touching hers, until he felt her body begin to shake. Then, withdrawing his lips from hers for only an instant, he threw off his shirt and slid into the bed, one arm beneath her shoulders, the other across her body. She was naked beneath the covers and he could feel the little cross between her breasts.

"Please go," she whispered. But even as she said the words, she knew it was the nuns who spoke. She didn't want him to leave her, ever.

Nino woke the next morning to the sound of a spoon stirring the contents of an iron pot that hung from a hook in the kitchen fireplace. The room was full of smoke. Beppe was trying to fan the fire while Mafalda grumbled at him. The two of them had come to the city from Torreone to help with Christmas dinner and now were waiting to go home with their master. Carla was stirring the pot and whistling to herself. She was ordinarily the mistress of this kitchen and Mafalda's seniority made her uncomfortable.

Nino yawned and stretched. He felt tired but happy. He washed and dressed in a corner and then, his eyes twinkling, kissed both Carla and Mafalda. "May I ask, my ladies, if my father is at home?"

"He is not at home, sir," cried Beppe. "He has gone to make visits. He will return at midday."

"Be sure to tell me when he returns, good Beppe," said Nino, who felt at peace with the world and everyone in it. "May I also inquire whether my sister has returned?" He realized he should not have asked this as he was not supposed to know Nina had left the house. No one seemed to notice.

"If you mean my lady Mariana, she has not," said Mafalda in a brusque tone. "According to her friend, she left very early to visit Giovanni. I do not think she had anything to eat."

"And her friend?" He had finally arrived at the only subject that interested him.

"She has gone, too. She appeared to be in a great hurry and would not eat anything either although I pressed her." Mafalda did not approve of persons who refused her offers of food.

Nino had hoped Angelica would still be asleep in the little room and he had been thinking about some excuse to wake her. "Did she say where she was going?" he asked. Mafalda shook her head.

"I'll go for a walk," he said, accepting the crust of bread Mafalda handed him as he threw his cloak over his shoulders and opened the door. The sun was warm and there was no sign of the snow. The piazza was crowded, for there was another market to make up for the one lost to the snow on Christmas Eve.

Nino had never felt so happy. He wandered through the crowd, enjoying every sight as if he had never seen it before. He bought an apple and munched it as he sauntered along, then a piece of hot sausage. By the time he had crossed the piazza, he had made a good breakfast. He found himself in the street where Angelica's aunt lived, where he had not especially planned to be, and suddenly drew up short. Three horses were tied to rings on the front of the house, two of them laden with bundles and packages.

His happiness dissolved in an instant. Her aunt kept no horses and he recognized one of these as her father's big bay stallion. It was pawing the ground and snorting.

Nino waited in a doorway. He was reluctant to go closer for fear of meeting Signor Bordoni, whom he didn't want to see this morning.

In a few minutes Angelica appeared, dressed in riding clothes and carrying still another large bundle. Her face was drawn, her lips set in a thin line. Her father followed her down the steps, grunting at his daughter when he saw she was unable to mount because of her heavy burden. He helped her because he was in a hurry and they started off together, Bordoni leading the third horse.

Nino shrank into his doorway but there was no need, for Angelica, facing straight ahead, saw nothing nor did her father, who was having trouble controlling his two animals. They passed through the piazza, picking their way around the crowds and disappearing down the street toward Porta Santa Maria.

Nino never moved. He didn't know why, but he couldn't call out to her. And yet she was leaving in such a way that . . . He could not bear to think about it.

He pulled himself together, walked rapidly up the street, and knocked on the door of the house. Angelica's aunt kept no servant and she herself appeared at the door.

Nino introduced himself. "I know who you are," said she, "for I dined at your house yesterday. What do you want?"

"I hoped you might tell me where your niece is going."

"Why, home, of course. Where else, with her father?"

"And do you know when they will return?"

"Return? I do not think they will return."

"You mean never?"

"She may return with her husband. She will not return alone."

Nino blinked. "Has she a husband, then?"

"She has no husband, but she will. Not that they tell me!" He didn't want to ask any more, for she was obviously unfriendly. He was all the more surprised, therefore, when she called him back as he was turning to leave.

"My niece was happy in your family," she said. "I would like to thank you for your kindness to her."

Tears came to his eyes and for a moment he wanted to reveal his feelings. But he could not trust her. He bowed. "My mother and her mother were friends. We could do no other."

When he reached home, Beppe told him his father had returned. He went to the little study. His father was sitting behind his desk, idly turning over pages of his account books.

It was the day after Christmas. There must not be any business, Nino thought. Has he no other pleasure but this? Are those books the story of his life? He knocked softly on the door jam. "I'm not disturbing you?" he asked. His tone was urgent.

"No. Come in. Come." His father closed the book.

Nino sat on the stool, feeling uncomfortable. He wanted his father to accept him as a man with a man's needs and desires. The stool made him feel like a boy again.

He knew he must tell his father the truth; he needed his help and wanted his advice. He described what had occurred. Ser Gian listened without speaking.

"I believe Angelica loves me, Father," he said finally. He paused. "Last night . . ."

"Last night? What about last night?"

"I was with her. In Nina's room."

"Yes?"

"We were alone. Nina had gone to see Giovanni. We were together."

Ser Gian stared at his son, a frown on his face. "Was that wise?"

"I don't know if it was wise, but . . ."

"You were lovers, then? It was not the first time for her?"

"I believe it was, father. I'm sure of it." Nino felt that his father was discussing a business transaction. He didn't seem to think of Angelica as a person, as the woman he loved.

"In my house! Angelica's aunt permitted her to stay here last night. I imagine she thought the girl would be safe with us?" Ser Gian continued to frown.

"Yes, father. She was safe. She is safe."

"Perhaps so, perhaps not. Others might disagree with you." Ser Gian was silent. Finally he asked: "And now what?"

Nino swallowed, but he looked his father in the eyes. "I asked her to be my wife," he said. "I want her for my wife. I will never love anyone else and I think she feels the same."

"You say you asked her. Did she accept you?"

"She called me 'husband' when I asked her to."

"How is that?"

"She was crying," said Nino, remembering their parting words. "We had been asleep and I awoke because I felt her crying. I said: 'You don't know what happiness we will share.' Oh, Father, she's so unhappy! Her life is not . . . good. I wanted her to feel happy about us. I said: 'You're my wife and I'm your husband. Call me husband,' I told her. And she did."

"And then?"

"She told me to go. I went to sleep in the kitchen. When I woke up and went to her house, she was leaving with her father. She's gone. Her aunt told me she won't return."

His father looked grim. He didn't say anything for a long time. He looked at his son. "They don't want you for a husband. At least her father won't. I'm not sure about her mother. You, the younger son of a money lender," he said bitterly. "He's conscious of his so-called nobility. On the other hand he owes me a lot of money. I could wipe out the debt." He sighed.

"I love her with all my heart, Father. I'll do anything to win her." Nino's voice trembled. He felt miserable, a little boy asking his father for help. His father hadn't refused, but Nino was afraid he would begin to view the whole matter practically, that is, in terms of the money.

"Her father may have other plans, other commitments," said Ser Gian after a while. "There may be a promise."

"Is there one? You don't know it. And Angelica loves me. Her will counts for something."

"It may count for very little with that man." Ser Gian was musing over the alternatives. "I would have to give you land in Cortona, which would mean depriving Lorenzo. He might accept that, but it would not make him happy. You understand that, Nino? You would need it, too, for you would have to support them, the parents, I mean, as well as yourself and your wife. You understand this?"

Nino nodded, but he didn't look up.

"At least up to a point. If there were children, a family . . ."

"There will be children, Father. She is born to have children." Nino saw his father smile, which made him feel a little better. "Really, Father," he said wistfully, "it is up to Angelica."

Ser Gian looked surprised. The smile left his face. He began to speak, but Nino interrupted.

"You know the new laws, Father. The Papal Bull. It says a man and a woman beyond the age of consent — and both older than fifteen, obviously — may declare themselves married if consummation has occurred."

Ser Gian stared at his son. "That's the law," he replied. "Or so it's said. I don't know many fathers who accept that law. I'm not sure I would accept it if Nina, for instance . . ."

"The law is the law, Father," said Nino confidently.

His father sighed. He opened his hands in a gesture of resignation. "Both must declare?"

"Both, yes. They only have to say, in those circumstances, that they desire to be man and wife, and they're then married. A priest may shrive them or not, it doesn't matter, they're still married. It's a question of their will, what they want. That is the law, Father. Everyone knows it."

It was true, many young people knew about this new law that promised to free them, at least in part, from the tradition of arranged marriages that often forced youths and girls as young as ten or less to marry persons they did not even know and certainly did not love, but Ser Gian was right in thinking the law was far from being universally accepted.

"She must say it then, as well as you," said his father, musing. "Publicly, as I understand?"

Nino nodded. What had seemed easy this morning, as he lay with Angelica in his arms, was beginning to seem so difficult.

"You would force her to say this in the church before the whole town? She is a beautiful young woman whom many admire. You would have her say that . . ." Ser Gian did not have to finish.

Nino shook his head glumly.

"Perhaps if the declaration were made before her father and myself," mused his father. "That might suffice." He paused. "Do you think she will?"

"Declare herself before her father, even in private?" Nino bit his lip. He remembered Angelica's words. But he couldn't believe she had meant them. Knowing the way to happiness, she must take it. Yet he wasn't at all confident. He looked at his father, silently imploring.

"Bordoni would then have to accept you as her husband? By law, yes," said Ser Gian. "And by law I would have to accept her as my daughter. Have no fear, Nino," he added quickly. "If you win her I shall bless you both. She's impetuous, like her mother, but I have nothing else against her."

"She's everything a man could desire in a woman," Nino murmured, his voice choked with feeling. But he realized how foolish the words sounded. He squared his shoulders and stared straight ahead.

"The customary behavior, Nino, would be for you to go to Bordoni and ask for his daughter's hand. Have you considered it?"

"I thought about it, but . . ."

"You fear he wouldn't accept you? I think you're right." He paused again. "There's something to be said for the old law that gave fathers the right to bargain for their children. You're very young. Could he take you seriously? He would have to take me seriously. After all, there's the money. It won't make him love me but it may make him reasonable. Do you want me to try?"

Love burst from Nino's heart for this man who had always done everything he could to make him happy. He nodded earnestly, relieved. His father couldn't fail; after all, he possessed what Angelica's father most wanted. It was only a question of negotiating until an agreement was reached. Why would her father refuse?

"I will do my best," said Ser Gian. He reached for one of the big books on the shelf behind him. "There is a property not far from Bordoni's," he said half to himself. "Perhaps it would interest him . . ." He looked up. "I have much figuring to do. Leave me to do it. By tonight I will know whether it's possible, from my side. And I will have to talk to Lorenzo." He was poring over the book. "Bordoni's side is another matter," he muttered as he turned the pages.

Nino rose and silently left the room.

Ser Gian spent most of the afternoon and evening organizing a proposal he thought Signor Bordoni might accept, then visited his elder son to see if it would be acceptable to him. The arrangement would substantially reduce Lorenzo's estate in favor of his younger brother, but he didn't hesitate to approve. His father embraced him and returned to a night of fitful sleep. Rising early, he set off by himself for Bordoni's fattoria, riding through Montalla and Pergo, villages he had known in his youth, and arriving at Montanare before noon. After asking directions, he reached Villa Bordoni as they apparently preferred to have it called just as the patrone was returning from his hunting, with the bloody carcass of a boar jouncing on the rear of his horse.

"Salve, Torreoni," was Bordoni's greeting. "Come for your money, eh? But the time isn't up . . ."

"Not at all," said Ser Gian smoothly. He dismounted and waited while Bordoni untied the dead animal and unsaddled the live one.

"Well then," said Bordoni, wiping his hands on his tunic. "You didn't come just to inquire about my health?" He didn't ask his visitor to enter the villa nor did he offer him any refreshment. This isn't going to be easy, Ser Gian thought grimly.

Indeed, it was more than difficult, it was impossible. Bordoni refused even to consider the prospect of having Nino as his son-in-law despite the benefits Ser Gian was able to offer, which included canceling the debt, a proposal it pained him to make. Bordoni did ask whether his daughter had given Nino any reason to believe his suit might be successful, and Ser Gian lied, saying that as far as he knew, there had been none.

"That's what I would have thought," said Bordoni gruffly. "She's a good girl."

"I have every reason to think she is. We enjoyed having her as our guest. None of the family was anything but impressed by her beauty and her character. I can understand why my son has fallen in love with her."

Bordoni was somewhat mollified by these remarks. "I'm sorry," he said, "that you have come all this way for nothing. In other circumstances . . ." He didn't complete the sentence. The interview was obviously ended and Ser Gian mounted and rode away.

With a heavy heart he walked his horse up the long, steep road to Cortona. It was now late in the afternoon and he had had almost nothing to eat, but he couldn't bring himself to return with this news to Nino without first discussing the matter with his old friend. Probably nothing could be done, but Messer Uguccio had been a wise counselor in the past; he might be so again.

Ser Gian found him in his great room as was usual, except that now the desk had been moved into a corner to make way for the Christmas Ball.

Casali saw immediately that his friend was troubled. "Tell me," he said. Ser Gian did so; he omitted, however, any mention of Bernardo, son of Giovanni. When, earlier, he had conveyed Nina's refusal of the Conte's suit, he had explained only that his daughter was opposed to marriage in general and especially to Conte Pietro.

The Podestà listened silently; then, after several moments, he pursed his lips. "Well," he said. " Well." Ser Gian waited.

"Speaking as a politician, that is to say a man who must deal with reality, and without sentiment, something I try to avoid, I can say that I see here an interesting situation. Imagine a board on which there are four pieces. Leaving sentiment aside, they can be moved in several directions."

Ser Gian nodded; he was uncomfortable.

"Now, introducing sentiment, we find that two of the pieces desire the wrong two other pieces. Nino desires the Bordoni girl but he can't have her; the Conte desires Nina but he can't have her." Messer Uguccio glanced at his friend. 'That's correct so far, isn't it?"

Ser Gian nodded again.

"Now, removing sentiment again just for the moment, we can see how it may be possible to rectify the — misalignments. Let's move the pieces so that Nino obtains Bordoni's daughter, while the Conte obtains Nina." Almost slyly, he looked again at Ser Gian.

"Your picture isn't quite accurate," he said. "As far as I know — from what he tells me — Nino not only desires Angelica, but she also desires him. And from what you told me, the Conte desires Nina but she most emphatically does not desire him. Thus to move the pieces as you have suggested would be to force one of them to do what he or she doesn't want to do. Three might be satisfied but the fourth would be miserable.'

Messer Uguccio nodded in turn. "Quite right. But let's examine the situation of this fourth piece: Nina, the miserable piece in the game. She is only — what? sixteen? — and hardly knows the man who wants to marry her. He has been depicted as a bad man and he has other defects in her view as well, not least his advanced age. Now let's ask, what if she's wrong about him? In my opinion he has begun to change from the ferocious enemy he used to be; given the chance, he could become a friend. He has also offered to be generous. I would be happy to review the marriage contract to ensure that it deals with Nina as she deserves. And then there may be an advantage, too, of the age difference. He is likely to die while she is still a relatively young woman, at which time she will become a wealthy and still very marriageable widow." He paused. "Unless there is something you haven't told me, Gian, I fail to see why this isn't a rearrangement of the pieces that might satisfy not just three but all four."

Ser Gian licked his lips. He almost hated this old man who could think of living people as mere pieces in a game. Yet he admired him, too. And if he were to tell him now about Nina's real objection to marrying the Conte — her love for a pauper, her promise given to a man who might never return to Cortona, to say nothing of returning in such a manner as to make him a suitable match — God, he thought, what shall I do? What shall I tell this old friend? What shall I tell my son?

Yet he had made his decision well before the conversation ended; when he left, he only muttered something shout talking to Nina again. He had made it for reasons that weren't clear even to him. Messer Casali couldn't see it, but he had placed him in the position of choosing either to sacrifice his son's happiness to his daughter's, or his daughter's happiness to his son's.

He had made his decision but he could never tell anyone he had made it or what it had been. And, like everyone, he had no idea — he could have no idea — what the consequences would be. Every decision carries a price, this he did know; what would the ultimate price of this decision be, and who would have to pay it?

He walked slowly home. Tomorrow he would tell Nino. Not everything, of course; there were things it would be better for him not to know. Am I a coward? he asked himself; yes and no, he decided.

Standing on the steps, he waited a long minute before entering his house. He surveyed the piazza, quiet now in the early darkness of winter; in spring and summer it would be thronged. He thought back to the night when he had led his family down the hill to safety for some and to the loss he could never forget. And he thought of Giovanni and of how he had assumed the leadership of the family when he himself had had, for a few hours, to give it up. And of Benno, too, and of how the boy . . .

Suddenly he knew the other reason why he had made his decision. "Aldo's son," he said, staring with unseeing eyes into the past.

14

The Raid That Failed

Signor Ugo Bordoni owned a property, now much reduced in size from what it had been, of perhaps two hundred acres in Montanare, southeast of Cortona on the road to Pierle. Part of the land was flat, lying in the long valley ending not far from the Bordoni farm at the escarpment of the ridge of the Appennines that divided Tuscany from Umbria. This flat land was rich; here, Bordoni grew wheat, white beans, and vines from which he produced a very average wine. He refused to prune the vines close, instead seeking a maximum yield from fewer stocks; as a result his grapes matured early, with relatively little sugar. Better wine was made by some of his neighbors, but this required more care than he was willing to give and more capital than he possessed. The rest of his land — the major part — consisted of steeply sloping hillsides on the north and south sides of the valley. The south side produced little, for it was shaded most of the year by the mountains. The southward-facing north slope, in full sun, produced excellent olives and better grapes, from which the family's own wine was made, and of which the padrone drank a great deal. There were also two woodlots in which wild boar and other game were hunted and whose chestnuts and oaks provided fuel and timber for building.

The house was near the Cortona-Pierle road, a fortified farm house in the old style, with a high exterior wall, crenelations at the top, surrounding an interior courtyard; a tower three stories high that had served more than once as a keep during the last century; and a rambling dwelling occupying the entire sun side of the courtyard. Here the family lived, in a building having two stories, the lower one, as was customary, providing storage and space for animals large and small. Many of these had the freedom to move around the courtyard at will, or to seek shelter in bad weather. There were half a dozen horses and as many cows, a herd of pigs in a filthy pen, numerous ducks, geese, pheasants, pigeons, and chickens, and an entire warren of rabbits huddled in a dark corner. The opposite side of the wall had slanting roofs built against it, resting on poles fixed in the muddy earth; under this makeshift shelter, wagons and other tools and instruments were stored. Against the outside of the courtyard wall, hovels were constructed as houses for the peasants. In case of an attack they came inside the wall but the fact that their ordinary place was outside permitted the Bordoni family a small amount of privacy.

The upper story of the house ran for some sixty feet along the north side of the courtyard; two stairs ascended to small landings, one at each end. There were half a dozen rooms, all in a row, which opened onto one another; there was no space for a hall, which would have been unheard of anyway in such a house. The line of connecting doors ran along the front; this meant each room opened backward, like a cave, away from the sun and light, but it also meant an additional small amount of privacy could be found behind curtains hung around or in front of a bed. There was a fireplace in each room, all of which smoked, but there was plenty of wood and the family was usually warm. On the coldest days, when the tramontana wind swept down from the peaks, no amount of wood could warm these drafty rooms with their doorways empty of doors and their windows that allowed the wind to whistle through and around the ill-fitting wooden shutters. On such days it was best to spend the time outdoors, working to keep warm, and then to huddle at night under such covers as could be found.

The Bordoni family had lived in this house for more than a century, adding to it from time to time and allowing other parts to fall to ruin. More in the way of destruction than construction had occurred in recent years, so the house had an overall air of desolation and decay. But the site, next to a small stream in the center of a pleasant valley, was excellent and the general lines of the entire edifice were good if mostly unplanned. The large number of animals filled the place with a continuous and unresolvable stench, but this was something you could grow used to; besides, the animals provided a significant amount of heat in winter. The animals also offered to the human inhabitants the only interludes in their otherwise mostly dreary existence. As Angelica well knew, the animals could be funny and touching and always interesting to someone who liked to watch the way they adjusted to the challenges of communal life. The animals were usually friends with one another, in their way. The humans were not.

The war between Bordoni and his wife had been going on for a very long time. It had begun shortly after their marriage, which had been arranged by their fathers. It had continued off and on after Angelica's birth, for he had been disappointed that she was a girl and had never gotten over the feeling he had been cheated by the gods, or his wife, or someone, out of what was naturally his due. There had been several other children, but all had died before they were five of strange and fearful fevers. The small graves were tended by the signora; the signore never visited them. Thus Angelica had been the only child for a long time and, in that warring household, the center and focus of dispute. In the last year, since the decision had been made by Signor Ugo alone without the concurrence of his spouse to wed her to the lord of Pierle, Angelica's fate, as well as her person, had been the subject of bitter daily battles between husband and wife.

Despite her greater intelligence, Signora Bordoni lost most of these battles because she had never learned how to deal with her husband's dogged stubbornness. When the arguments would grow most heated, he would become silent and refuse to speak to her, whatever she said. This would drive her wild with anger and frustration. If he would only stand and fight like a man! He would turn his back and leave the room, and leave the house and the courtyard if necessary to get away from her, and she would be left behind to swallow her own bile and taste its bitterness.

These perennial losses had begun to have a cumulative effect. Angelica's mother, who had once been a charming and beautiful woman, had become, as she herself knew, a shrieking hag whose rantings were ignored by everyone except her daughter. Angelica, who understood her mother better than anyone else and who continued to love her when everyone else ceased to do so, paid careful attention to what she said, for the girl knew how wise the woman was about many things and she sought to learn what she could from her before, as seemed inevitable to the girl, her mother went insane.

It was two days after she reached home before Angelica could speak to her mother, as she wished to do, about what had happened to her in Cortona. For such a conversation she required complete privacy, with the assurance that neither her father nor any of the servants would hear a word she said. Such privacy was not easy to find in that household, especially in winter, but she managed to arrange an excursion to the little village of Montanare with her mother, ostensibly to borrow some thread. As soon as they were out of earshot, Angelica began her story.

She told her mother everything. The woman said nothing throughout the long account, only looking from time to time at her daughter with expressions on her face that varied with the content of the disclosures. When the story was finished, the two walked in silence for a way, the mother taking her daughter's arm and holding it close as they proceeded along the rough and narrow path.

Finally Angelica broke the silence. "You have said nothing, Mother. Do you judge me so harshly you haven't a single word for me?"

Her mother pressed her arm. "I'm very far from judging you," she said. "I will never do so, whatever you do, for you are the only person in the world I love, and without you my life would be entirely meaningless."

Angelica began to cry.

"Don't cry, tesoro. There's no time for tears. And there are others on this path. I don't want anyone to see my beautiful daughter in tears, as if the world could shock and hurt her as it does ordinary folk."

"It has hurt me," said Angelica, regaining her composure. "Or I have hurt myself."

"Yes, you have hurt yourself. What you said to him was true. You should not have learned what happiness could be. You love him very much then?"

"Oh, mamma, I can't tell you how I love him." And again she began to sob; again she regained her composure.

"Well, then, take him: he will come for you or his father will — I'm sure of it. They're good people, rich, powerful, influential. If he doesn't come, forget him — he won't be worth loving. But if he does, follow him wherever he goes."

That's what my mother would have done, thought Angelica. It's what the old Normans would have done; it was the way they lived. Then she remembered that in fact her mother had not done it, for she too had married the man her father had chosen for her.

"It's not as simple as that, mamma," she said.

Her mother glanced at her. They were approaching the village and there were peasants and animals in the path, which had widened to a road. They had to pick their way. "No," she said, "it's not as simple as that. What do you intend to do?"

"I'm going to keep the promise my father made."

"Oh God," said Signora Bordoni. "God forgive her and me, and the man who is my husband!" Her mouth began to work and Angelica feared she would start shouting, here in the

231

village street. But her mother knew if she was to be any help to her only daughter and friend, she would have to stay sane.

"And if he comes for you, you won't go with him? I'll help you if that's what you want. I can create a diversion, have a fit," she said, smiling wanly at her daughter. "You could get away. You would never have to come back. Go, choose happiness!"

"You speak dramatically, mother," replied Angelica. "But the shape of my life was decided long ago. You know it as well as I."

"With God's help you can change your fate, Angelica."

"I can't pray to God to give me happiness, me alone, Mother. I can't desert my father, and I can't desert you."

Her mother stared at her. "Yet you would desert this young man you love and who loves you."

"You will make me cry again, Mother. Please understand; my mind is made up. It seems to me I have only one choice, one path to follow, and I'm determined to follow it. The more you say about . . . him, the harder it will be for me to do what I have to do."

They had reached the center of the village and they took the time to complete the mission that would justify their excursion. The town seamstress, who supplied them with the thread they needed, smiled at Angelica. She always liked to see her. She was so pretty and usually so cheerful. Today she seemed downcast. As a result the old woman was more cordial than was customary with her.

When they were in the country again, Signora Bordoni returned to the subject. "Tell me what you need, daughter, and I'll do it."

"What I most need," said Angelica, her eyes on the rough ground before her, "is to be a maid again. For I'm no longer what his lordship will expect me to be."

"That can be done, or rather, something can be done," said her mother. "Men can be fooled, although I suppose he's old enough so it won't be easy. You won't be his first woman even though you must convince him he's your first man. But I know someone who can help you. She helped to bring you into the world; she can aid you in this matter, too. And she can be trusted."

Angelica nodded. "That's not all," she said. "I feel very strange. It happened only once but perhaps it was at just the worst time of the month. It was only three days ago but already I think I may be pregnant with his child."

"Oh God, oh God," said her mother, half under her breath. She wanted to let go, begin to rail, scream, and clench her fists and beat on the cold walls that surrounded her in their vise-like prison. With a supreme effort she kept control of herself. There would be time for madness. Now her daughter needed her; no one else could help her, no one else could save her.

"In that case," she said, her voice steady, "the wedding must be very soon. The preparations can be finished in three weeks. I have already done most of what's needed. Your bridal chest can wait for the last touches. Your dowry will be our farm, which will pass to your husband on our deaths and revert to you, as your dower right, if he dies before you. Which I hope he does," she added through clenched teeth. She crossed herself either because she knew it was the Devil who spoke or to seal the bargain.

"What's more," she said after a pause, "the men will be pleased by this haste. They will assume you've been disappointed by city life and are now desirous of taking up your real and proper existence. The baby will come a little early but by that time everyone will have forgotten dates, especially if it's a boy. His lordship wants a son." Her voice trailed off. The effort of speaking in this matter of fact way was almost too great.

"It is a boy," said Angelica, her voice so low her mother could hardly hear her. Signora Bordoni ignored this although she smiled faintly. "So. We have three weeks. Let's try to make them a happy time. We'll work together as never before. And then . . ." Her face crinkled and she began to cry.

Angelica stopped and took her mother into her arms. "Don't cry," she said. "All will be well." She remembered Nino had spoken these very words, and she too was close to tears. The two women stood in the path, clinging to one another for a long time. Then they kissed away each other's tears and continued their walk. They were not surprised to find that Signor Ugo was very glad to hear the news.

That night, as Angelica lay in her cold bed, she thought of what her mother had said about running away with Nino if he should come for her. Would he come? She hoped he would not, for that heartbreak would be easier than the other. The hardest thing was, she couldn't tell her mother why she had decided to do what she would do. For she knew, if she didn't marry the lord of Pierle, her mother's life would be forfeit. Poor, abandoned, deeply in debt, her father would punish the mother for the daughter's fault. Sooner or later he would destroy, if not actually murder, the foe against whom he had battled all their married life. Angelica was willing to give up happiness to save her mother, but this she swore to herself her mother must never know.

But her mother did know it. Yet she too had her secret. She knew she would never be able to persuade Angelica that she would gladly give up her life so her daughter might taste the happiness she herself had never enjoyed.

The next morning mother and daughter went to visit the midwife, who was called Nonna Anna by all the women she had aided as if she were the real grandmother of all "her" children. Now very old, she was nevertheless still straight-backed and strong despite her small stature. Sitting quietly on a stool in her tiny house not far from the Bordoni fattoria, she listened while the Signora and Angelica together told her story.

She nodded at each revelation. She had heard every story and had never judged any woman harshly; she had simply done what they needed. When Angelica's was completed she sat for a while, her piercing black eyes searching the young woman's face.

"So," she said, "is it really sixteen years since I helped bring you into the world, madonnina?" Angelica blushed; the term usually denoted a girl who was no better than she should be.

But it was accompanied by a smile, and the old woman went on.

"The question is, what's the true situation? You're either incinta or not; it makes a difference. If you're not, you have more choices; if you are, then very few."

The two women waited.

Nonna Anna began by asking Angelica a series of questions; the import of many neither she nor her mother understood. Apparently they were part of the midwife's secret formula for determining the state of a woman's insides. When she was finished she asked the girl to lie down and gently lifted her clothes, looking carefully and feeling with her knowing fingers.

She nodded to Angelica, who sat up, rearranging her garments. Nonna Anna looked at her mother. "It's not certain; nothing is certain, Signora. But I would say yes. Yes, she is with child. It's only a few days ago you say? That's not long; it's impossible to be sure. But I . . ." She shrugged as though to say, If anyone knows, I do.

"So, madonnina. You have three choices. One is to call off the marriage." Angelica started to protest but the old woman held up her hand. "Another is to abort. This early, that shouldn't be difficult. The third is *fartruccare*; that is, for me to teach you to seem to be what you're not. That would be difficult but not impossible."

She waited. It was as though she had all the time in the world; only other people were ever in a hurry.

Angelica looked at her mother, eyes glistening. "I don't want to abort it, mamma. It's his as well as mine." She lowered her gaze. "The marriage can't be delayed if I'm incinta; and it can't be called off if we have no time to . . . make other arrangements. That leaves the third. You can do it for me?" she asked.

Nonna Anna nodded. "Come here, cara," she said, and Angelica moved toward her hesitantly, assuming the process would begin immediately; she dreaded every moment of it. The old woman motioned for her to kneel whereupon she held her face in her hands, caressing her hair, wiping her tears. "Don't fret," she said softly. "Do you know how many young women have been in your shoes? It's something that happens; and now we have to fix it, that's all. We'll do it. You'll be a beautiful sposa, smiling and happy as if nothing had happened." She paused. "You must work with me. Will you do it? We have three weeks? Basta. Tomorrow morning we'll begin your . . . exercises." The pause before the last word almost made Angelica laugh.

Angelica woke in the middle of the night to a stab of memories. The nuns had insisted it was always the woman's fault. They were right. I led him to do what he did; truly, it was my fault and I deserve my punishment. They said all men will take advantage; a girl must never let down her guard. I allowed him to stay when I should have made him go; I even asked him to come under the cover. After that there was no stopping him.

Or me. Yes, I wanted him to have me, my virginity. I loved him and his love for me; therefore I gave away my most precious possession, or so the sisters said. I gave it to you, my love; it is the only gift I will ever be able to give you.

Seldom had she found it difficult to make men do what she wanted; men were foolish creatures in a way, who would do anything for a pretty face. Yes you, Nino, you were a foolish creature, but I loved you and I will never love anyone else, even though now I can never have you.

Instead I will have the Conte as husband and lover. Can I also make him do what I want because I'm beautiful and he's old? I have to try. I have to smile. I have to learn how to seem happy, to be happy. At least we'll have enough money and father will too, and I won't have to give back the jewels he loaned me for the Christmas festivities. "Madonnina," she called me. I'm worse than that. But I can't turn back now. Madonna, forgive me, please forgive me and do not withhold your loving eyes from me.

And may my child, his child, enjoy health and long life!

Nino was sitting in his window, forlornly staring out over the valley toward the setting sun. Suddenly he saw movement on the Montanina road. He called Robert, who peered with him in the gathering dusk. There seemed to be many horsemen bound for Torreone and the castellino. They looked at one another.

"There is nothing to do but wait," said Robert. "If they are . . ." He didn't finish the sentence. "Anyway, the doors are locked." He shrugged but he did not take his eyes from the road.

It was not enemies, however; it was Nino's father and brother, Messer Uguccio Casali, and a troop of armed men. Nino went to the gate and opened it. The troop remained outside; the others entered. Nina was with them.

There were no smiles; Nina looked as if she had been crying. Nino pretended not to notice. He conducted his guests courteously into his home.

Ser Gian was the first to speak. "The news is bad. There are many rumors. Doubtless the tale has grown in the retelling. Messer Uguccio has kindly come with us to see you. It is said he must prosecute you, or order the Sindaco to do so. Please tell him exactly what happened."

Nino told his story, withholding only an account of what had occurred in Nina's room the night after the ball. Probably his father had already told that part of the story to the Podestà, he thought, and if not, so much the better for Angelica. He described his despair when his father had returned from his failed attempt to win her hand by negotiation and then told how he, Robert, and Beppe had ridden the next day to Casa Bordoni and tried to take the girl away with them. They had not wanted to use force, Nino explained, and when she had refused to go with him, there was nothing they could do but leave.

"Bordoni thought he drove us away," he said. "But he didn't, it was just that she didn't want to go. Or was afraid." Messer Uguccio said nothing after Nino finished. He sighed.

He looked at Ser Gian and Lorenzo. Finally he asked them what they thought he should do.

"It's not as bad as I thought!" cried Lorenzo loyally. "There was no harm done, no one was hurt. And the girl didn't come away with him."

"It would have been better if she had," said Messer Uguccio gruffly. "Nino could have ridden away with her and returned in six months. However . . ." He paused and then turned to his friend.

"Do you think I must arrest him, then? Or is there a way he can escape?"

Nino's father looked down. He hated to be the one to condemn his son, but be saw no way out. "I believe the Consiglio will vote for an indictment," he said.

"Perhaps so," mused the Podestà. "And will he be convicted? An indictment is not the worst thing that can happen. It sets limits. Whatever the decision of the court, that is an end of the affair. Perhaps . . ."

"Perhaps?" Ser Gian was worried.

"It is the end if the other side does not stubbornly desire revenge." The Podestà turned to Nino. He doesn't look angry, he thought, just cold. "You say no one was hurt. Are you sure of that? And you did touch the girl?"

Nino shook his head. "She was in the window, upstairs. I called to her, but she said . . . She refused to come." He didn't want to tell them what she had said. "We were careful not to hurt Signor Bordoni. He cursed me but I did not strike him." Nino looked at Robert. "We didn't even draw our swords," he said.

"That's right," said Robert.

Nino stared at the old Podestà. "Forgive me, sir," he said bitterly. "I've been foolish. I'll do whatever you suggest."

Messer Uguccio almost smiled. "What I suggest — let it not be repeated outside this room — but I would go back to Montanare with my soldiers and I would break the gates and take the girl on my horse and leave with her. I don't like Bordoni any better than his master, the Conte — though where he found that title I do not know. Certainly the Emperor never gave it to him. However, I can't do that, nor can you. There is law at Cortona now; it's not as it was when I was a lad like you. There is law and we are all subject to it, even if Conte Pietro acts as if he isn't." He paused. "So you will do as I say. And I say I distrust the Consiglio in your case. Which is really your father's case. Am I wrong, Ser Gian?"

There was an angry look on his father's face. "I don't think you're wrong," he said.

"Underneath the surface, great changes are occurring in Cortona," the Podestà mused. "On the surface it looks the same as always. But the nobles don't like what's happening. They don't want to give up a single bit of their power. They've had to yield much of it, and now that they can't vote unless they give up their titles and move within the walls, they've had to yield even more. I'm old; they don't desire to confront me. Your father is . . . how shall I put it? The leader of the new generation. He himself cannot be touched. But they could reach him through you."

He paused again. "Do you understand this, Nino?"

Nino nodded. He had known Messer Uguccio almost all his life. He had always been a friend of the family. He was being no less a friend now. "I think I must go away," he said. "As long as I'm here they can continue to attack my family . . . my father, Lorenzo."

Nina covered her face with her hands.

"I think you're right," said the old man, relieved that Nino had come to the decision on his own. "I don't want to drive you from your home. But in your place I would go. The Consiglio cannot be trusted. Sometimes the votes surprise me — I can't understand them. Small men enjoy making examples of big ones, too. Your father is a big man and they would like to make an example of him. So. You'll go away. For how long? Not forever. A year, two at the most . . ."

The Podestà stood up. "Well," he said. "This is the first time I've been in your castellino since you restored it. I like it! We'll keep it safe for you." He held out his hand and Nino

239

knelt and kissed it. The old man started toward the door. "I wouldn't wait," he said, "now that the decision is made." He looked at Ser Gian. "I'll leave some of the men here to ride back with you. I don't want you on the road alone." And he disappeared.

No one spoke for a long time. They drank the ale Mafalda brought, but they had nothing to say to one another.

"There have been threats, Nino," said Lorenzo finally. "It's said, sooner or later they will come for you, in the night, when the guards are asleep. They'll set fire to the house and kill you when you come out. You and Robert, the 'foreigner.'"

"They call me that!"

"You speak with an accent. In the country they care about such things. You aren't one of them. Neither are we but we were born here."

Nino nodded. "Where do you think I should go, Father?"

Ser Gian had been staring straight ahead, apparently paying no attention. Now he shook himself. "To France," he said. "Go to Paris or Chermont, where your property is. They will take you in — won't they, Robert? Don't be downcast. The world is larger than Cortona. You will find this to be true when you are away from it." He looked at Robert. "You will go with my son?"

"My country shall be his, my lord," said Robert. "We will go to Chermont and rest from the journey. Then to Paris. There are worse places, caro mio!"

Ser Gian stood up. "You will laugh at this one day, Nino, but for the moment it's serious. Now there's much to do." He went to the door. "Mafalda! Come and help your master. And Beppe too. Where are you, Beppe?"

In fact Beppe was almost under his feet, for he had been listening. "Take me with you, sir!" he cried. "I'll be of help to you, sir. I'll even learn French." He ducked as Robert tried to box his ears.

"I will take you, Beppe," Nino said.

They worked until his father had to leave, Ser Gian and Lorenzo returning to the city just as the gate was closing. Nina stayed with her brother; her father said it wasn't safe, but she insisted, and Nino was happy to be able to spend his last evening with her.

They ate supper, then Robert went to bed. Nino and Nina sat together by the fire. "Do you remember when you left for the convent? I refused to see you go. I thought the world had come to an end."

"Giovanni gave me his dog. It made me feel less homesick and I was happy to take it with me to the friars."

"But not in church" Nina laughed. Then she wiped her eyes. "It's no better now."

"It's worse now. Then I really wanted to go although I didn't want to leave you, but I was going only five miles away from home and coming back at Easter. When will I come back to Cortona, Nina? When will I see this house again?" He looked around him.

Nina gritted her teeth. "I will kill Bordoni and the Conte, too," she said fiercely. She was laughing and crying at the same time. "Then you can come home. And marry Angelica if you want."

Nino smiled. "If I can't marry you." Soon his face fell and he stared into the fire. "I don't understand what happened," he said after a while. "I don't know why she didn't come with me. Whatever the reason, it was a good one. Therefore, please forgive her, sister."

Nina shook her head.

"Anyway," Nino said, "I'll write to you and tell you about Paris, and you write to me about Cortona? I will miss everyone and everything. Tell me all the news. Perhaps in a year or two, as Messer Uguccio says, it will be safe . . ." He hesitated. He did not believe it would be that soon.

Nina didn't believe it either but she did not say so.

During his first summer in Paris, Nino did not go to Troyes for the Hot Fair even though it was only a two-day ride for a man on a good horse. His father had warned him he might fall into the hands of their enemies. It was hot in Paris that August and the long dull afternoons were stifling. A dry wind churned up the dust in the streets but did not manage to disperse the clouds of flies that buzzed over the piles of refuse stinking in the heat. Nino longed to mount his horse and ride to Troyes — or anywhere — but he had promised, so he sat and sweated.

Knowing his father and brother were so close made him more homesick than ever. Unable to respond to Robert's chatter, he would sit for hours dreaming of Torreone and a past that now seemed very far away. He thought of the wheat ripening and being harvested on the hillside, of the grapes growing black and more full of juice every day, of the olives beginning to turn from bright green to gray to black. Mostly he thought of Angelica, his mind picturing over and over again their short time together. He had been happy once. Would he ever be happy again?

Robert tried to interest him in the frantic life around them. Robert himself enjoyed it and made many new friends. Some were women and he tried to lure Nino into a relationship that would help him to forget. The Italian was attractive to the young French women. But they soon realized he had no real pleasure from them, so they abandoned him. He was left to brood in the loneliness that, exhausting as it was, he preferred to society.

At the end of August, when the fair was over, a Torreoni messenger rode to Paris bearing letters. There was a terse letter from Ser Gian, with financial news. It included a draft on a merchant of Provins on whom Nino could draw for funds as needed; it also reported, without comment, that Caterina and her son were well. And there was a letter from Nina, which he saved for last although he dreaded what it might say.

Robert was sitting with Nino when he opened it and saw his friend's face go pale. The letter was long, and Nino read it slowly and, having finished it, read it again. Then he sat staring into space, the letter dangling from his lifeless fingers.

Robert touched his arm, but Nino didn't move. "Do you want to tell me?" he asked after a while. Nino started. He looked up, his eyes dark and impenetrable.

"She's married," he said, his voice grating. "She married that old man soon after I left. Very soon. She was in a great hurry." Robert cleared his throat. He said nothing.

"Why did she do it?"

Robert shook his head. He was about to make one of his cynical remarks but then he realized he could not. Even he could not believe Angelica had been just another woman. Instead he said, his voice soft: "She must have had her reasons."

"What reasons could there be for such betrayal?" Nino passed his hand over his eyes. All the time he had believed he would see Angelica again, that they would be able to have each other, man and wife.

"I don't think I can live," he said after a while.

"If not, two others will not live either. I, Robert de Beaumont, and my lady, your sister."

Nino nodded but he had not really heard the words. Only later did he realize how discourteous he had been by seeming to take his friend's loyalty and love for granted. After another long pause, he said, "What shall I do now, Robert?"

"Wait. Happiness will come again."

Nino shook his head. He held the letter in his hand, staring at it. He continued to muse over it, reading it again from time to time. Then he folded it, placed it inside his shirt, and stood up. He was pale, but on his face there was a look of determination. He did not mention the letter again.

In the fall of that year, Father Rafaelo came down the hill from his little house near Porta Montanina to visit Ser Gian Torreoni. He felt like an old man now, and his legs hurt him when he climbed up and down the hill, so he remained in his house most of the time; he depended on a boy living nearby to bring him provisions.

He told Ser Gian it was a long time since he had seen him and he wanted to know how he and his family were getting on.

"Well enough, not too badly," Ser Gian said. Cortonesi never declared that things were really well for fear they might get worse. But Ser Gian was puzzled. Father Rafaelo had seldom visited or exhibited any interest in the welfare of the family.

"Since I have come so far," he said when he rose to leave, "may I inquire whether your daughter is at home? It is some time since I have seen her."

Again Ser Gian was puzzled; as far as he knew Nina visited the old priest regularly. He sent for her and when she appeared Father Rafaelo asked her if she would lend him her shoulder on the long climb up to his house. Nina saw him through his low door and helped him sit on the little stool that, apart from a small table and a sleeping mat, was the only article of furniture. She was about to leave when he said to her: "I have received a letter that I do not understand. Perhaps you can help me."

His trembling fingers rummaged through a scant pile; finally he found what he wanted. He held the piece of stained parchment in his hand.

"A soldier, an Aretine who had been wounded in the wars up north, came to the city a day or two ago. He was on his way home, but he stopped . . ."

"This isn't on the way to Arezzo," Nina said quickly. "This is out of his way."

The old priest nodded. "I thought that, too. At any rate, he wished to see me, for he said he carried a letter from a comrade. He did not tell me his comrade's name, although I asked him. But when I read the letter it did not seem to be for me at all. I could make nothing of it. Perhaps it is because of my eyes . . ."

He paused. "Perhaps you may be able to read it more easily than I," he said after a while.

The letter was in Latin. "To Amica, Greetings," it began.

I am in Lombardy in the service of the Archbishop. I am well. My hopes are green. Spring has come and summer and now autumn.

There are many changes but there has been no change in Amicus.

Nina fell to her knees before the old priest. She grasped his hand and kissed it, tears running down her face. He patted her head and caressed her face. "My child," he said, "my child."

About the Author

Charles Van Doren grew up in New York and Connecticut. He has taught English at Columbia University and the University of Connecticut. His books include *A History of Knowledge*, *The Joy of Reading*, and, with Mortimer Adler, *How to Read a Book: The Classic Guide to Intelligent Reading*.

He lives in Connecticut.

Robin (Richard) O'Connor
undoingdepression.com
860-435-0588